'Pre-dating and pre-empting a
and the originator of the most .
Macpherson is the Newgrange
stand-up comedy'

'The comedians' comedian'

IRISH TIMES

'Ian was one of the first stand ups I ever saw live, and I longed
for gags like his'

HARRY HILL

'One of the most creative and intelligent comedians I've ever
seen'

THE GUARDIAN

'For a funny Celt, catch tonight's last episode of the current
Book at Bedtime – BBC Radio 4. The memoirs of Fiachra
MacFiach, read with perfect gravity by Ian Macpherson,
reveal a sort of Irish Pooter'

THE FINANCIAL TIMES

'Comedy's answer to James Joyce'

ARTHUR SMITH, BBC RADIO 4

'*DisComBoBuLatE* – with host Ian Macpherson – delivered
a brilliant, thought-provoking and highly entertaining mix of
literature and comedy at the Edinburgh International Book
Festival. It was one of the popular hits of the festival and also
one of my own personal highlights'

NICK BARLEY, DIRECTOR,
EDINBURGH INTERNATIONAL BOOK FESTIVAL

'Fiachra MacFiach, Genius, bursts from the womb clutching a slim volume, his mission to storm the citadel of poetry. *Deep Probings* will destroy you: it is fiercely, resentfully and damagingly funny'

LUCY ELLMANN

'Travis Bickle meets Holden Caulfield and William McGonagall down Ireland's mean streets. Read this and you'll never sleep with a poet again'

ALAN BISSETT

'The *Spinal Tap* of Irish literature'

BRIAN BOYD, IRISH TIMES

'Macpherson's book has more typographical errors than *Flannigans Wake*, and they provide the reader with welcome comic relief'

ALASDAIR GRAY

The Autobiography
of
Ireland's Greatest Living Genius

Fiachra MacFiach

Edited by Ian Macpherson

To the estimable Henry.

Ian Macpherson

Oct 2011

Gnarled Tree Press

First published in 2011 by Gnarled Tree Press,
an imprint of Cloudberry Books

www.irishgenius.me

Book One: Deep Probings first published by Thirsty Books in 1999

ISBN 978 0 95690 560 4

British Library Catalogue-in-Publication Data
A catalogue record for this book is available from the British Library.

Typeset by Hewer Text UK Ltd, Edinburgh
Printed and bound by Bell & Bain Ltd, Glasgow

For Magi and Rosie the Mammy

Foreword

Some years ago I was trying to retrieve an odd sock which had apparently found its way to the top of a tall wardrobe in my bedroom. I looked around the room but could find nothing to stand on. At which point my eye was drawn to a brief, almost filmic scene outside the bedroom window. I watched transfixed as, in almost total darkness, a black-clad figure deposited a large cardboard box on a nearby skip. It – the figure – then strode off. End of scene.

Intrigued, I put the sock on hold and ventured out. No sign of the black-clad figure, but the skip was full to bursting with broken chairs, a rungless stepladder, rubble. Nothing to help with the sock. Until, that is, I examined the box. It was solid, the right height, and turned out to be exactly what I needed. I took it inside, placed it in front of the wardrobe, and recovered the sock. I then left the box to its own devices.

When I moved six months later I took the box. There would, I reasoned, be other wardrobes. Other wayward socks. My next port of call, however, came kitted with no wardrobe. Only a tall chest of drawers. The box was, therefore, redundant.

I decided to get rid of it, so I put it out by the bin. But my octogenarian maiden aunts from Dublin, who were staying at the time, got it into their wizened little heads that I was up to something. They weigh in at under five feet, so they assumed I was trying to put the top of my chest of drawers out of bounds to aunts of restricted growth. I could see the way they were thinking.

What could possibly be up there? Naughty lady magazines, obviously. We know Een better than he knows himself.

I wasn't so foolish, of course. Operating on the principle that the last place you look is the obvious one, I had left the magazines face up on the coffee table. So the aunts never found them.

I'd assumed, of course, they were searching them out to grass me up to my mother. Not so. Turns out they were merely looking for work. But the box at any rate, courtesy of my aunts, was back. And there it stayed until, some months later, a group of local kids rapped on the front door on bonfire night.

'Penny for the guy,' they chorused, pushing a rusty pram into my ankles.

'I'll do better than that,' I said. 'I'll give you ten times that amount. And all you have to do is take this box here and toss it on the bonfire of your choice.'

Deal done, I closed the door a happy and, as I thought, box-free man. The children had been paid well above the going rate, and I had no doubt that the responsibility of disposing of the box would stand them in good stead in later life.

The following morning I sauntered out. I say sauntered. Truth is, I started sauntering, tripped over a discarded pram and went flying. As I began my descent I had a good look at the box for the first time. For there it lay where the lazy little sods had slung it. Beaten, battered, posted twice round the world to every university archive with a section devoted to dead poets and, superimposed in bold capitals over the many addresses – RETURN TO SENDER.

I was, when I finally landed, incensed. And, though not normally a violent man, I gave it a damned good kicking. Result? The box burst. Paper everywhere. I was about to leave it to the local council – or the elements – on a first come first served basis, when a lone page flittered past my line of vision. Happy chance? I'm a confirmed printophile. If it's written down I'll read it. So I stopped what I was doing and began perusing as it fluttered gently earthward.

Happy chance indeed. I had unearthed a treasure trove, hit the mother lode, call it what you will. I've painstakingly edited the contents – articles, journals, letters, and a battered old tape, recorded, by the sound of it, inside a crisp packet – into the manuscript which follows.

But enough! Let genius speak!

Ian Macpherson
Dublin, 2011

Ah woe! Alas! Pain, pain ever, forever!

BOOK ONE
Deep Probings

I

It is not for me to draw parallels between my own life and that of Christ. But ponder this: I entered public life in millennial times. I wrote my masterpiece in a two-hour burst after a twenty-nine-year gestation period. And true, Christ was crucified while I was merely held on remand, but I'm willing to bet he experienced similar difficulties getting the Bible published. This is the trouble with genius. When the film rights are eventually sold it can often be up to two thousand years too late for the author to cash in.

But I wonder if Christ suffered, as I did, in his formative years. I imagine him sullenly holding a handful of nails while his earthly father put the finishing touches to a kitchen cupboard, reflecting, not without justification, that his mind was on higher things. Whereas, at a certain age, we MacFiachs were expected to become tillers of soil and hewers of wood before school, after school and, later on, where school used to be.

Now the artist, not unlike the Saviour, must have time to inhabit an elevated plane of consciousness; to dwell on matters sublime. My father either didn't understand this or chose to ignore it and we were encouraged to dirty our hands at an early age in the ultimately futile battle against nature. Digging. Milking. More digging.

My father would begin with broad hints about the field above or the lambing season being particularly busy. If that didn't work, your Wellington boots would be placed beside all the other Wellington boots in time for the next dawn exodus. If you chose to ignore this hint the boots would stand as a constant reminder throughout the day. They would be admired by all for their cleanliness and paraded in front of visitors in a heavily ironical way.

With my brothers this form of primitive psychological warfare worked, but I was made of sterner stuff. It may not have been obvious to my parents – being simple peasant folk – that I was touched by genius, but the following scene must have given them some sort of clue. I had spent several days ignoring the boots, the hints, the nudges, the winks, and happily exerted myself instead on my noble calling.

On the third day of this routine my mother was bent over the kitchen sink scouring her interminable pots when my father returned from work followed, in descending order of seniority, by Ferdia, Fintan, Fergal, Feardorcha, Fachtna, Fiachna, Finnias, Francis, Fergus, Finian, Fadharta, Fursa, FX, Flann, Finn and Fats. I had sixteen brothers but nothing, as I recall, in the way of a sister. All were about to remove their soil-encrusted boots after a hard day in the fields and place them beside my immaculate pair as a prelude to their muscle-bound banter when they spied me spread out on the floor with pencil and paper.

Silence fell, broken only by the scouring, the squelch of boots, the pipe suck.

The drumming of my fingers on the page.

I, Fiachra MacFiach, was about to produce my first word.

My siblings stood round in a circle and I could feel them thinking, yes, he *is* different.

They were transfixed, rooted to the spot, mesmerised by the poetry of this unforgettable scene. I could describe the tension of the moment; how the neighbours drifted in and cheered me on; how my father lost a modest sum when the word wasn't 'Father'. But this is not a cheap and sentimental novel. I don't propose to milk the tension for dramatic effect. I was the centre of attention. I was intellectually advanced beyond my years. Enough. I merely record that I took that first historic leap onto the page with a bold if illegible squiggle. The word I was struggling towards, I recollect, was 'Spawn', the main topic of conversation afterwards: why I had chosen to write it with my foot. But who knows, for who can comprehend the mind of genius?

This turn of events confused my father for a while. The boots stayed where they were, but he seemed less sure of his ground. Perhaps I *was* different, he seemed to be thinking. That evening, at any rate, he whipped out his melodeon and began playing a jig, perhaps in celebration of my emerging otherness.

It was, I suppose, a small price to pay.

II

If my own ingenuity kept my boots clean up to a point, it was luck which played a bigger part in allowing me to develop at my own pace. I have mentioned several of my brothers, omitting only the last-born. In much the same way that nowadays every Irish household produces a well-known novelist, in those days the youngest child was destined for the priesthood. So it was with little 'Father'; and from an early age he was afforded the preferential treatment of the chosen one.

That this state of affairs was monstrously unfair is beyond question and illustrates the unequal standing of art and religion in the Ireland of those dark times. I, the artist, was expected to soil my hands like a common labourer, while Little Father was treated with fawning servility at all times.

I suffered his outrageous assumption of superiority with saint-like stoicism, helped no doubt by not having a jaundiced bone in my body. Had I been the jealous type I might have been infuriated by his self-satisfied expression, the work-shy softness of his skin, the deference accorded him as a child of the cloth while I, his superior in all matters, was treated like the common herd.

Yes! If I had been in any way capable of envy, I say, my poetic soul would have blackened with rage and I would have pummelled the doe-eyed little scut to an early grave. As it was, I bore this monstrous, this shameful, this crying-out-to-heaven injustice with remarkable and commendable fortitude. True, I was accused on more than one occasion of violence, but this was mostly the result of youthful high spirits and usually consisted of nothing more than sitting on his head or, on one memorable occasion, trying to give him a bath in the kettle.

I was severely punished for the latter; forced to confess to the little blighter and given three Hail Mary's, an Our Father and, worse, full absolution in a 'magnanimous' gesture of reconciliation. The next time I gave him the kettle bath treatment, I resolved, I'd put his head in first.

The fact that Little Father was destined for the priesthood meant that his nappies, his romper suits and his first surplice were all of finest clerical black. He finally graduated to full evening dress with tri-cornered hat at the age of two and would glide around the house tut-tutting at my artistic endeavours or blessing my mother as he passed the sink. And I have to admit it: in the eternal struggle between Art and Religion he seemed to have secured an easy victory for the men in black. He would have suited the job well. He had the soft hands from an early age. He only had to work on the sanctimonious look. That he never got the chance to develop beyond the hands owes much to the MacFiach dynasty's eating habits.

Mealtimes were unchanging in their uniformity. Because of the number of children involved, a large tureen of our staple diet, the ubiquitous Kerr's Pink potato, was placed at the head of the table and the contents passed along. It was the responsibility of each child to look after the next in line. Ferdia to Fintan to Fergal to Feardorcha and so on. The pot having been placed on the table, potatoes were fired expertly from hand to smaller hand. Is it any wonder that eight of my brothers played the execrable game of rugby for Ireland, their proudest moment being 'the glorious missed try of '73'? The ball, as they are apt to recount, passed between all eight of them. It was subsequently tossed, just under the post, to the present writer, who wasn't, I am more than happy to report, there.

So it was with the potatoes. Down the line they came, each child feeding his younger sibling with a skilful sideways pass. Until, that is, they came to me. I must, at this point, broach the delicate subject of my shortcomings: the need to fulfil my exalted destiny; to exclude trivia. This is not, strictly speaking, a flaw – it is, in certain respects, an admirable trait – but it can lead to unfortunate consequences. And so it proved on this occasion.

I recall remarking to one of my brothers that I hadn't seen Little Father for some time.

'Father,' he said pointedly, 'is dead.' And, although I hadn't actually asked, 'Malnutrition,' he added, equally pointedly. This would perhaps explain why my mother was attacking her household chores with less than her usual brio. And why dinner was infuriatingly late for some time to come.

It might be felt by some of my more impressionable acolytes that Father's end was in some way hastened by a misguided attack of sibling rivalry on my part. Nothing could be further from the truth. My poet's soul was otherwise engaged. I had simply failed to notice the little feller.

A verse I wrote some time later captures the poignant mood:

> *It's hours past dawn*
> *But the curtains are drawn*
> *You're still in your bed*
> *They tell me you're dead*
> *You were so I'm told*
> *Just three short years old*
> *But God! I got riled*
> *When you called me 'my child'.*

(from the Irish)

III

This sequence of events could hardly be seen as auspicious. Happily, however, I was vindicated by the parish priest – also called Father – who insisted that it was God's will. He went further. He came over to where I was sitting and patted me on the head.

'What God is telling us,' he simpered, 'is that this child here is destined to be the priest.'

I was too young at the time to understand the implications of this outrageous synthesis or I would have debated the matter there and then. As it was, the debate came later. In the meantime I enjoyed all the privileges of the priest to be. My boots were removed from the line. I was treated with due deference. My parents called me 'Father'. I was given a large tub of moisturising cream for my hands.

I was a poet with the perquisites of a priest but none, as yet, of the responsibilities. That day would come, of course, but in the meantime I set about taking advantage of my newfound status.

I could describe in minute detail the months that I lorded it over the household as 'Father'. I was granted, for a while, the luxury of doing as I pleased; but the artist was born to suffer and I thank the parish priest for giving me the opportunity to return to a life of misery.

One day, when I had developed the smug expression, unctuous manner, sanctimonious turn of phrase and delicate hands of the cleric in embryo, I was summoned to see him. My career had been mapped out, he averred. I would serve him as an altar boy, moving on to the position of head altar boy and from there leaping forward from novice to curate to priest, parish priest, bishop, archbishop, cardinal and, 'the Lord save us, perhaps the Pope himself!'

'Pope Fiachra the First,' he chortled, rubbing his flaccid hands together with relish. 'Let's make it happen.'

I studied him carefully to see if he was perhaps jesting. He wasn't. It was, granted, an interesting career plan, but the artist can have no truck with corporate structures. I pointed this out to him in the vocabulary I had available to me at the time.

'Nonsense, my child,' he said, and had the temerity to suggest that the ability to rhyme was a passing phase and that I'd grow out of it as I matured.

'On the contrary, my child,' I replied.

As I developed my theme he sat meekly phrasing his reply, his pale hands intertwined in an attitude of humility, his lips moving in sibilant near-silence as he worked on his forthcoming speech. I spoke to him of the preoccupations of the poet: frogspawn; galoshes; the difficulty of writing in a language where nothing rhymes with orange.

'A nice point, my child,' he began, 'but consider this. God has called you. End of story.'

'Perhaps I could have that in writing, my child,' I replied, not untetchily.

'And what leads you to suppose that God, the God of Wrath and Hell Fire, the All-Knowing God, the God of Rage, of Ire, the Great God Almighty, has time for personal correspondence, my child?' said Father.

I must say that I was beginning to find his debating tactics negative in the extreme. God had called me. He didn't wish to discuss the matter. Father was pursuing a narrowly Jesuitical line of argument. I, ergo, would have to borrow from a different spiritual model. So deciding, I gave him the full force of my left galosh on his shin in the fond expectation that he would go away enlightened.

He might indeed have done so in a different setting had I not ignored the pertinent fact that it was his home. He contented himself with hobbling after me as *I* went away.

'Priest killer,' he cried. 'I know where you live.'

If the latter was meant as a threat it wasn't needed. By the time I arrived home my parents had got the message: I was no longer to be the priest. All bets were off. My father started dropping hints. Heavy hints, sometimes with an undercurrent of menace.

He also knew where I lived.

IV

The showdown, when it came, left me with no option but to accede to my father's heinous demands. I was inserting an early attempt at aphoristic wit into my journal when I noticed him standing over me.

'The field above,' he said, 'is ready for the plough.'

I glowered at him.

'There's still some daylight left.'

In the parlance of popular culture this was a bad western. I stared him out.

'I believe there's a spade in the cow shed,' he snarled.

I raised my pen majestically.

'This, sir, is my spade! I'll dig with it.'

Foolish words. Metaphorical language is sadly wasted when discussing manual labour with the peasant class. He yanked me up to the field by the collar of my jacket and I ran through a full set of nibs before his mood softened back to dour.

'Have it your way,' I fumed. 'Where's the cow shed?'

It goes without saying that the true artist must have time to chew the cud of his thoughts. To this end he should drink only sufficient alcohol to merit the prefix 'tortured'. He should lie low during the breeding season. Above all, he should avoid manual labour. And yet. And yet. A spot of honest toil is not without its compensations.

I began to place selected poems by my fellow versifiers in the cracks of dry stone walls and work towards them. I later realised that it was quicker to walk straight over to them and the spade became merely a handy instrument to lean on as I read. In this way the hedges soon became littered with verse. Lo a Yeats. Yon a Joseph 'Mary' Plunkett. A fine poet and openly transsexual before there was money in it. At a time, indeed, when a job in the civil service might depend on withholding such facts.

My father used to watch me from the house as I leaned over the spade reading. He affected to think of me as a waster and a fool and yet secretly he was very proud of me. Many years later I was incarcerated at Her Majesty's pleasure and my father's wallet was found to contain, on his deathbed, a faded transcript of the court case.

This exalted state of leaning on my spade reading might have continued indefinitely had I not been jolted out of it by the machinations of one of my less fortunate brothers. When I refer to Fadharta the Simple as less fortunate I am merely referring to the yawning gap in our respective intellects. On a scale of nought to ten we are separated by the latter, but although Fadharta was simple he was sly with it.

I was first alerted to his devious nature by an incident which shocked me to the marrow. It is well known that Irish fields are filled with stones. Always. This is known as the Second Sorrowful Mystery of Agriculture. The First Sorrowful Mystery deals with the fact that the Irish small farmer is always in possession of a three-day growth. Never two. Never four. Three. This has never been adequately explained, but I have solved, inadvertently, the mystery of the stones.

I was leaning on my shovel reading, as I recall, a witty dissection of machismo in the civil service by Joseph 'Mary' Plunkett when out of the left curve of my eyes I spotted Fadharta removing stones from his field by *putting them in mine*. So stunned was I by this flagrant breach of the unwritten code of the countryside that I almost fell off my spade. Here was my giant, foolish brother taking advantage of my genial nature – another character weakness, I'm afraid – to present his own field in a more favourable light.

I was apoplectic. Granted the farm had its fill of walls and each wall had its fill of stones. Some of the walls in the more exposed corners of the farm were even protected from the buffetings of nature by other walls. There was, I admit, nowhere else for a stone to go. But Fadharta's solution to the age old question, albeit the brainchild of a simpleton, was provocative in the extreme.

He was dealing with a mind, however, at the sharp end of the spectrum. I waited for him to pack up and leave for the day. I moved his stones back. I added a few stones of my own to let him know I meant business. There the matter rested until the following morning. I went and stood in my own field as was my wont and cast wry sidelong glances at Fadharta over *The Boy's Own Book of Polish Verse*.

His moist and protruding lower lip flapped disconcertingly as he scratched his head in puzzlement, but his deviousness finally won out over his simplicity and by midday the stones were back in my field.

This state of siege and counter siege continued for three

months. Fadharta took to moving the stones back last thing at night which caused me to undo his work before cockcrow. Not that I should have bothered for as soon as Fadharta had worked out this pattern of events the stones were always back in my field by morning. My father was delighted with our level of activity.

'The lad can work when he wants to,' I overheard him saying.

The fact that twelve weeks of strike and counter strike had left the fields in question exactly as they were seemed to bother him not at all, which may explain why he experienced some difficulty eking a living from the rude earth.

The problem was resolved to my satisfaction by a simple ruse which proved beyond Fadharta's powers of understanding. I removed the stones from my field at midnight, as was my regular practice. I then went back at 2 a.m., as wasn't, and cleared his field back into my own. When I returned in the morning, sure enough, the simple fool was standing happily in his field, victorious in his own small mind, surrounded to the tips of his Wellingtons by both our stones. I returned with some relief to my reading and both fields remained fallow till the following year.

V

After this daily simulation of honest toil and the good homely sustenance provided by my mother between her bouts of washing up, I enacted a nightly scene which baffled the poor simple folk I lived with but which furnished me with further raw material for my art. I decided to experience the speech rhythms of the natives in order to transmute the base metal of their speech into the assayed gold of my life's work.

Normal procedure is to ascend to the attic and press your best ear to the floor, taking copious notes as you go. This possibility failed to present itself to me as we had no attic, so I climbed up into the rafters nightly and took notes from there. I admit to being a mite self-conscious as I was in full view of the assembled throng, which was afforded, in its turn, a full and comprehensive study of the artist at work.

One night was probably much like another but I recall a particularly idyllic scene. Mother was taking a well-earned break from her washing up and cutting a new suit for the author from her dress. Father sat not playing the melodeon, turf smoke curling wistfully upwards from his pipe. I remember the conversation very clearly as one of the neighbours had dropped by and observed me scribbling furiously up above.

'Is that fellow a bit odd?' he said, referring to myself.

'He is aye,' said my father.

'He is surely,' said my mother.

My brothers all murmured agreement.

'Was he by any chance dropped on his head as a child?' asked the neighbour.

'He was aye,' replied father, 'but it didn't work, for he was exactly the same afterwards.'

An idyllic scene, I grant you, full of a way of life that is long since gone. I can see them still, frozen in time like a yellowing photograph, their eyes turned upwards to the embryonic genius in the rafters. In many ways a typical family of that era. Father; mother; seventeen brothers, although Fats' parentage was questioned by some of the more scrupulous neighbours, and not without good reason. My mother couldn't remember a thing about him before his forty-second birthday. He sat alone at mealtimes eating Creole dishes of his own making and had a back catalogue of hits from the fifties.

He was also black.

VI

This is not a linear narrative. I am far too intelligent for that. In one respect, however, I bow to tradition. I refer to the obligatory 'We made our own entertainment in those days' reference without which the Irish memoir, however revolutionary in structure, seems somehow curiously naked.

We made our own entertainment in those days. This consisted of my father playing the melodeon. Only when legislation was introduced in 1963 to ensure that every household supplied itself with a television set was this pernicious activity effectively stamped out.

VII

The early years of my schooling were overseen by a succession of kindly spinsters, most of whom took early retirement for one reason or another.

I remember one lady in particular; Elspeth Funge (Miss), as the newspaper which reported her suicide called her. We knew her simply as Miss Funge or Miss, and I'm afraid our relationship was problematic from the start. Miss Funge dealt with us in the patronising way that is common to all primary schoolteachers. There are those who collaborate with this tendency and I have personally known cases of children who have affected a speech defect in order to gain preferential treatment. For example, Joey the Lisp Adair was rewarded with a regular supply of apples in this way, which supplemented the earnings from his extortion racket outside the school gate.

No fetching lisp nonsense for MacFiach, however. One of my many character flaws is my iron-willed, unyielding integrity. I make no apologies for it. Looked at from another angle, indeed, it isn't a flaw at all but an illustration of high moral character. At any rate it coloured my relationship with the said Funge who was quite unable to deal with constructive criticism. I well remember our first fracas.

'Now, Fiachra,' she simpered in her affectedly unctuous way, 'if I have three apples and I give you one apple how many apples do I have left?'

I was tempted to point out that this was an unlikely scenario and that Joey the Lisp Adair would probably end up with all three one way or another. But I didn't. I merely pointed out that if she couldn't work out that simple conundrum for herself she might be advised to consider a change of career. Harsh words perhaps, but justified, I feel, in the circumstances. My intellectual development appeared to have been entrusted to a half-wit.

Further proof followed within hours of the above. She informed us that she was not one for newfangled notions but would concentrate her attentions on the three Rs. And these were? These, if you please, were reading, writing and arithmetic.

My hand shot up at a speed not seen since the heyday of the Hitler Youth; before self-doubt crept in.

'What is it, Fiachra?' she said, unaware that her days as our font of knowledge were numbered.

'Reading, writing and arithmetic,' I said. 'That's one R, one W and an A. Phonetically, I am willing to allow, an extra R might be admissible, but arithmetic? I think not.'

I completed my terse if pointed speech with the observation that her grasp of the fundamentals was sufficiently questionable to warrant a vote of confidence. Not in so many words – I wasn't quite as articulate as that at eight – but she got the message. Her facade of superiority crumbled and she left the profession, and subsequently the world, shortly afterwards.

VIII

Mr Scully, some years later, was a good deal more robust. I decided to give him a pseudonym for the purposes of this memoir and chose a name at random from the Magherafelt telephone directory (1982 edition). The name I chose was also Scully, but a different Scully. And I have the address and telephone number to prove it.

A lay teacher at the local Christian Brothers' secondary school, it can't be said that Scully took an instant dislike to me. As I was sitting for some time behind a lumbering buffoon named Brendan Gilhooley, he didn't know I was there. This was certainly satisfactory from my point of view as it allowed me to concentrate on a poem which I was frantically scribbling into my journal against the impending bell.

I blush to recall the work now. I was still in thrall to the tyranny of rhyme and my biographers may detect the influence of Housman (A.E.) in a poem about a cad from Kinnegad who goes to the bad, becomes the victim of a jihad, changes his name to Vlad and moves to Leningrad. It may be pointed out with some justification that there was no Muslim community in Kinnegad at that time, and my later liberation into blank verse might have been speeded up if I had incorporated a margin note which said, simply, 'Bradford?' But looking back at my journal now (Vol. XI) I see that I was more concerned with the last line.

> *He was, Mavourneen, but a child.*

I crossed that out. Child didn't rhyme with egad. Nor was it a para-rhyme, even if you recited the poem in impenetrable Glaswegian. I tried again.

> *He was, Mavourneen, but a boy.*

Egad/Boy? Worse than useless. I was stuck at this point when the bell rang and it was lost forever, gone to that limbo of the poetic world where unfinished masterpieces pine for completion but trail off instead with a *dot dot dot*.

I may have been upset by the inflexibility of time, but when Mr Scully decided on a whim to set us a home exercise I sprang to my feet.

'With respect, sir,' I said, 'the bell has gone. We are now officially outside your jurisdiction.'

For a squat man he moved fast, and with all the natural grace of his simian antecedents. Nor did he pause to explain where he stood on the matter. He simply lifted me from my seat by the nearest available ear and fired me at the partition, his tiny raisin eyes filled with pleasure and hate.

As if they had been waiting for just such an occurrence a large group of Christian Brothers appeared at the door – Brothers McKay, McKee, McKinney, McKeown, McCrankey, McCrum, McCroom, McConkey and McCropolis if I remember correctly – and chastised their lay partner with mild reproach.

'Corporal, Mr Scully. Not capital. Corporal.'

IX

Over the succeeding days, weeks and years Mr Scully tested the boundaries between those noble forms of punishment. Unacceptable? Perhaps, but the creative artist must suffer for his muse and this, I suppose, was as good a way as any. I was unwilling to say anything about it at home for obvious reasons, but my father soon got wind of what was happening.

One morning he donned his best galoshes, marched into the teachers' room and came away, as he himself put it, with some excellent tips.

Is it any wonder, though, that my creative output all but dried up? I spurred myself on by thinking of all those great men in the trenches who pursued their art in six feet of water, rats gnawing their nethers, with only the light from an exploding shell to proofread what they'd written. But they were only dealing with the Hun. Mr Scully was a much more formidable opponent.

Take the following example. During one of the periodic lulls – Mr Scully busy arranging his underpants over his belt – I was browsing through a recently published slim volume by budding versifier Seamus Heaney. I must say in passing that I admired Heaney at the time for mirroring my own poetic thought if in a more commercialised way, and I was reflecting on the fact that the greeting card industry might be his natural home when a shadow fell across the page. I need hardly add that it came attached to my learned friend.

In moments of stress the mind is known to work on several items of interest at once. In the millisecond it took to divert my gaze from page to face I grappled with the following:

The sad realisation that I was about to die unpublished.
The observation that crash helmets should be made compul-
sory in Irish schools.
The thought that in moments of stress the mind is known to
work on several items of interest at once.

I placed my hands over my ears in the hope that my tormentor
would experience some difficulty in finding them, but imagine my relief on discovering that he had no apparent interest
in the left or, failing that, the right. He was standing over the
oaf Gilhooley and holding up a magazine dedicated to the
celebration of the female form. In a fair world, it must be said,
he would have beaten Gilhooley to a pulp. Instead he merely
confiscated the magazine and advised the slavering wretch to:

a) Venerate his mother, and
b) Give all other women a very wide berth.

This advice took the form of a long and rambling dissertation, so I returned to my book. I felt immensely heartened
that the author was making a name for himself as the mass
appeal of his light verse would undoubtedly lead to greater
exposure for his weightier compatriots; to wit myself and, for
all I knew, others. I was basking in the reflected glow of this
thought when the book was ripped from my grasp.

'Well, what have we here?' said the remarkably jocular
Scully. He held it up.

'A poetry book, bize. Well, excuse *me.* Excusez-*moi.* I think
we all know which side *this* boyo ties his shoelaces.'

He smirked and winked at his infantile audience, which
responded with ribald mirth, then waved the Gilhooley
manuscript in my face in an effort to humiliate me further. He
suggested that I might like to be referred to in future as Sissy
MacFiach and I'm afraid the name stuck for a time, much to
the consternation of my Aunt Sissy.

X

I don't propose to dwell on my schooldays longer than is strictly necessary. I was beaten, ridiculed and, worst of all, forced to play Gaelic games. Now I wish to state, categorically if necessary, that I have nothing against sport in theory, but actually participating is a different matter entirely. It might be said, in fairness, that some sports are worse than others. Rugby, for instance, is a fussy game which interferes with one's ability to write.

During a cricket match, on the other hand, I almost finished a 6,000-word essay – on Joseph 'Mary' Plunkett's eccentric habit of playing mixed-sex golf with himself – whilst fielding at third man. I would certainly have completed it too if a member of the opposition hadn't wittily (sic) unplugged my typewriter.

But Gaelic games! It has been said with some accuracy that war is a substitute for hurling. This is perhaps to denigrate the former unjustly. And yet I was expected to don a pair of ridiculous shorts once a week and feign pugnacity. My usual solution was to engage the opposition goalkeeper in intellectual discourse with, I have to say, mixed results. The goalkeeper as a breed is noted for stolidity and large hands but not, as a rule, for philosophical agility. On the positive side, however, he doesn't run off when you're getting to the crux of the matter.

And to give goalkeeper Gilhooley his due he was a good listener. He remained crouched in an attitude of mindless concentration as I argued that Gerard 'Manley' Hopkins' middle name was a misguided, not to say misspelled, sop to the cult of machismo. I was interrupted twice in the first five minutes though not, in fairness, by the rapt Gilhooley. No. On both occasions the ball flew up field in my general direction and, as Mr Scully was officiating I thought it best to show willing.

Twice I took a wild swing at where I imagined the ball might be. Twice it flew past the hapless Gilhooley and between the posts. The effect was immediate and deeply depressing. I became the unwilling victim of a sustained exercise in male bonding, Mr Scully eyed me with a new respect which I found chilling, and Gilhooley advised me to move away with a neat line in post-war slang.

The long-term effect was no less unsettling. As the opposing team struggled to reassert itself Mr Scully trundled round the field shouting 'Where's MacFiach? Where's MacFiach? MacFiach to the rescue.'

I informed him, curtly, that I was giving the other boys a chance, but this had the opposite of the desired effect. Respect turned to adulation. Not only gifted, but humble with it.

We lost that game, I'm told, but my unfortunate contribution had been duly noted with the result that I was chosen, to my absolute horror, to represent the school in the year's big fixture. Not having any choice in the matter I resigned myself to my fate and once again positioned myself within lecturing distance of the opposition goalkeeper.

'Rainer "Maria" Rilke,' I began. 'Genius or charlatan?'

XI

It is not for me to pursue the almost uncanny parallels between the lives of Christ and myself, but I often try to imagine his sullen adolescence: raising his eyes to heaven, for instance, as his mother recounted yet again the divine circumstances of his birth – probably in front of his peers. Adolescence is fraught with danger for the highly gifted and I certainly hope I never have to live through the experience again.

My own adolescence arrived late, due perhaps to the preponderance of cold winters, and I emerged from the experience at the age of twenty-seven with my dignity – and clothing – in some disarray. The period in-between was perilous. I have mentioned the urge to procreate as one of the great enemies of the artist, but the adolescent knows nothing of this. Nor cares. Nor, I repeat sadly, cares.

I have always preferred my hormones dormant, but creating the right environment for this is difficult at any age and when age matches shirt collar size it is well nigh impossible. I recall firing a snowball at a female child when I was six for the sheer pleasure of inflicting pain. The same scenario at the age of twelve apparently denoted love. Such is the frightening fall from innocence.

Sleeping on bare boards has always been a great help to me when faced with a certain sentimentality in my verse, but it was to prove no help in matters hormonal. As a male and an artist I pined for, but rejected, the lure of the female. In particular I pined for and rejected the lure of Bridie, perhaps the loveliest of the seventeen Gallagher sisters, her slightly crossed eyes and unfortunate ears notwithstanding.

We were already linked amorously in the public mind through no act of my own. The parish priest had the tedious notion of joining both our families in stage wedlock for a production of the world's first Catholic musical, *Seventeen Brides For Seventeen Brothers*.

It closed, mercifully, after a three-night run at Oughterard parish hall, but nuptials, whether of stage or life, were not for me. I constantly reminded myself that I was an artist. I was here to observe the world, not to join in. And yet, unfortunately, I was the blameless object of rampant female desire. Women found me irresistible.

I tried wearing spectacles with gaffer tape round the centre. I also developed a nice line in acne and a boil on the left side of my nose which set my spectacles at a pleasing angle. I even went to the extremes of carrying a violin case on my infrequent trips outside. All to no avail. I had made a fundamental mistake. I had thrown the snowball of love and Bridie had received it, like Cupid's dart, smack between the eyes.

The snowball linked us indefinably in some way, and while the other adolescents who lounged around the crossroads would tease me as I passed, Bridie was different. True, she called me Sissy and spat at me like all the rest, but as she told me later, she was just trying to attract my attention.

XII

That I finally succumbed to Bridie's relentless pursuit was due in no small part to the oaf Gilhooley's adoption of the crooner's so-called art: the composition and subsequent wailing of the most appalling dirges in the Country and Western idiom.

I made the dreadful mistake of remarking to same that I too could earn a fortune if I was prepared to prostitute myself.

'Take your own field,' I said, my mouth running away with me in my youthful braggadocio. 'Why, even the world's biggest fool could see the commercial possibilities of a song which mentioned every place name in Ireland.'

There. I had said it. He ran off in a state of high excitement. I thought no more about it. Gilhooley, I reasoned, was the type who would never go back to obscurity because he would never leave it in the first place.

Wrong, wrong, wrong.

Gilhooley wrote the song. He credited me, to my perfectly understandable horror, as co-author. My protests were treated as yet another example of my humility. Is it any wonder that my spots, my broken spectacles, the generous boil on my nose and, yes, even the violin case, went for naught? I had collaborated in the composition of a song of such monstrous awfulness that its appeal to the general public was unbounded. I had become, in spite of my best efforts to the contrary, an attractive proposition.

Now there are those who would say 'What's wrong with that?' Precisely this: I have a duty to my reputation as an artist of integrity. I am reminded of the haunting case of Eric Boone. Mr Boone, I'm told, has spent the past thirty years on the wilder fringes of classical experimentation. His *Duet For Nose Flute And Mongoose* is highly thought of, if difficult to perform. And yet in the public mind he is merely the nephew of the man who sang *Love Letters In The Sand*. Full stop.

I was in danger of a similar fate. My masterpiece lay some way in the future, but that was going to be of interest to American academics and, if all went to plan, few others; its wilful incomprehensibility, its multi-layered impenetrability keeping the common herd at bay. Not so my unwitting collaboration with the appalling Gilhooley. Permit me to illustrate my point by printing the first of its innumerable verses.

WHERE THIRTY-TWO COUNTIES MEET
I was born in Letterkenny
I come from Castlebar
I hail from a satellite village near Roscrea
Sure I love the girls from Wicklow Town
And the boys from Donegal
As they watch the sun go down on Galway Bay

I'm a Gannon from the Shannon
I'm a Macken from Macroom
And me name is Sean McGinley from Lough Dan
I'm a divil from the Divis flats
A tinker up from Tuam
I'm a cute hoor with a pig farm near Strabane

I'm a Belfast Dublin Kerryman
I'm a Leitrim Longford Derryman
I'm from Letterfrack and wherever I may roam
You can meet me here
You can meet me there
You can meet me at the Mammy's up in North Kildare
If I'm in it
For a minute
That's th'oul home.

And there it was. Thanks to my perceived contribution to this excrescence, the name Sissy was quietly dropped. People reserved their spittle for more deserving cases. If I had composed a great symphony, painted an Impressionist masterpiece or written a slim volume of towering genius as, indeed, I was later to do, the vilification, not to mention the spitting, would have continued unabated. What does this say about the teeming masses? The question, I need hardly point out, is rhetorical; the answer implied in the exasperated, nay world-weary, tone of voice.

XIII

I began walking out with Bridie shortly afterwards. Bridie liked the song. Inference? We were totally unsuited to one another. I was an artist and an intellectual, she a simple country girl whose idea of a good time was a hoedown and a packet of Kerry Creams.

After the initial thrill of my supposed song-writing prowess – she credited me with sixteen of the thirty-two counties in question – I failed to satisfy her limitless appetite for dross. The fact that she later married an estate agent and went to live in the Foxrock area of Dublin illustrates how low she set her sights, but I was an adolescent then and knew nothing. I poured my heart out to the poor girl. My hopes. My dreams. My pact with Posterity. I spoke to her of dissonance, assonance, para-rhyme. She spoke of white dresses, engagement rings, the relative merits of the quick-fold buggy and the Dreadnought pram.

Our total incompatibility must have been obvious to her but she persisted. I have always had this problem with women. They seem to be attracted to the unattainable. I have dedicated my life to art; they sense that. It drives them, frankly, wild with unrequited longing. I recall one particular case where a woman of my acquaintance, on my suggesting that she put me out of her thoughts forever, snorted that I was the last person to be in her thoughts, that I was a dour, humourless bore, an insufferable prig and a royal pain – not necessarily her exact words – in the fundament. She rounded her speech off by firing a four-person cafetière at my head, but I took no notice: I, Fiachra MacFiach, read the subtext.

So it was with Bridie. She became aware that I operated on a higher plane and dropped gentle hints that I might try to lower my sights.

'Wouldn't it be nice to have a good time,' she'd say and, when I'd ask her to define her terms, she'd say, 'Ah, you know.'

I tried to pacify her with Kerry Creams but it was heavily intimated that the same biscuit was part of a broader package – and sitting on a damp wall listening to a disquisition on Joseph 'Mary' Plunkett's ambivalent relationship with his half-sister Mary 'Joseph' was not, in her view, part of it.

That I endured the relationship says much for my forbearance, but my youthful inability to keep my mouth shut came into play again with further disastrous results. The nincompoop Gilhooley had taken to following me about like a faithful whelp in the hope that I might supply him with further inspiration for his doggerel. I pointed out that he had covered the country pretty comprehensively and that I could be of no further use to him.

Still he persisted, and not without reason as I was soon to find out. In a state of some frustration I remarked, concerning Bridie, that while I dreamed of Art and the immortal verities, she dreamed of the bright lights of Magherafelt. Gilhooley clapped me on the back with admiration and delight.

'*She Dreamed Of The Bright Lights Of Magherafelt,*' he enthused. 'Waltz time surely.' And off he went in search of his dreaded banjolele.

XIV

My eventual split with Bridie was negotiated through a third party. I was summoned to meet her father, a simple rustic type with simple rustic values. I had never previously encountered him but based my all too accurate delineation of his character on the fact that he was a farmer. And to be brutally honest about it I had no desire whatsoever to meet him. Let's face it. A man who spends a goodly part of the morning hours staring at cows' nethers is hardly likely to sparkle on the conversational front after lunch. And yet the pressure from all sides was intense. I was bundled into my best suit. My mother followed me about the place trying to flatten my hair with saliva. My father remarked that Bridie was the pick of the Gallaghers but that I should hold out for six heifers anyway.

'Better still,' he said, 'why not hold out for cash and start a new life in Manchester?'

It was almost a relief to arrive chez Gallagher, but I couldn't help feeling that there was a hidden agenda. And so, in the most unforeseen way possible, it proved. I remember vividly standing alone in the living room while the seventeen sisters giggled in the hall. Eventually Gallagher Senior appeared. He strode towards me and, proof perhaps that he was as ill-equipped to deal with the situation as I, he attempted to examine my teeth and hooves. After this initial misunderstanding we got down to the serious business of bartering.

That I remained unaware for some time of the objective of the bartering may be divined from the conversation which ensued.

'You've been walking out with my daughter,' he said.

I put it to him that I was well aware of this. The man was obviously an idiot.

'Damn your insolence, sir,' he cried. 'What are your intentions?'

Ah. So he was capable of asking a sensible question after all. Perhaps I had misjudged him.

'My sole intention, sir,' I said, warming happily to my theme, 'is to write a slim volume of such majestic beauty that the very heavens will open to receive it, and subsequently to bask in the everlasting glow of Posterity's approval.'

He was dumbfounded. It was, admittedly, ambitious but, damnit, I had the talent. All I required was time, and, as I heavily intimated, less interference from meddlesome bores.

'I demand to know your prospects,' he said.

I stared him full in the face.

'I am an artist, sir. A genius in embryo. Those are my prospects. Perhaps I could turn the question back on *you*. What are *your* prospects?'

'I work for a living, you insolent young pup. What do *you* do?'

'I repeat that I am an artist, sir. I write.'

'Do you tell me so? And have you actually written anything yet?'

'Not,' I replied grandly, 'as such.'

'I know the type.' He followed me, not without menace, round the chaise-longue. 'So how do you propose to provide for my daughter?'

It was my turn to be struck dumb.

'How,' I gasped, 'do I propose,' I continued, 'to provide for your daughter?'

I repeated his words exactly in an effort to locate my bearings. The question was, let's face it, way out there in the stratosphere, beyond fantasy land. I decided to humour the man.

'In a word, sir,' I said, 'I don't. Does that answer your question?'

He looked at me for a moment. Then he started to laugh. A manic sort of laugh, tinged with lunacy. The seventeen daughters giggled on in the hall. The mother, no doubt, was locked away in the attic, cackling merrily at some private joke. I had stumbled on, almost married into, a madhouse. I still have nightmares about being detained there forever; and when I get to the bit about being an estate agent from Foxrock I always wake up screaming.

XV

In other circumstances – if, for instance, her family had been sane – I might have been able to offer Bridie a life of penury. But it was no doubt better this way. The artist is stateless, creedless, and almost inevitably does his own typing. I resolved to have nothing more to do with the pleasures of the flesh. Not that I'd had anything to do with them yet anyway. I had been too busy talking about my plans.

But what was it Burns said about the best laid plans ganging aft aglae? A great artist, Burns, but an appalling typist. What he meant, I assume, was that they often go astray and, such is the universality of his art – at least in Scotland – he could have been talking about me. No sooner had I escaped the lunatic clutches of Bridie and her fellow Bedlamites than I set off for home. My hormones, ignoring the direct route, decided to take a detour past the Widow Bernelle's.

It might be fitting, at this juncture, to bring up the vexed question of my sexuality. This, of course, is an intensely private matter involving only myself, and yet I sense the unauthorised biographer lurking in the wings, dripping ink. Better, perhaps, to come clean.

The Widow Bernelle was a sexually precocious woman in her late sixties. She had moved to the area some forty years previously and the fact that she wasn't a local was held against her in all the usual ways. She would have been burned as a witch but was saved by damp matches. A planned exorcism of her house was cancelled because the parish priest, a vain man, liked his hair the colour it was, thank you very much. She was also denied the feminine pleasures of small talk.

Widow Bernelle was swinging on her gate as I passed, a glass of what might have been cold tea in her free hand, a Consulate dangling lasciviously from her lower lip.

'Well, hello there, lover boy,' she said, her voice husky from impending cancer.

I stood transfixed by her rasping laugh.

'Miss Bernelle,' I stuttered.

She came over and appropriated my trembling hand.

'Less of the Miss,' she purred, easing me towards the house. 'Call me Widow.'

I'm not sure what a widow's pension amounted to in those days but she may have been having trouble with her electricity bills. At any rate the living room was bathed only in candlelight. A fire crackled merrily in the grate. A jeroboam of champagne rested on a bed of ice. As Widow Bernelle sat down I heard the soft rustle of silk stockings. She patted the vacant place on the sofa beside her. I sat on what may have been a wooden footstool and watched intently as she popped the cork and poured the bubbling liquid into pink-hued, tall-stemmed, frosted glasses.

A couple of mouthfuls of this heady brew had the remarkable effect of loosening me up and I regaled the widow with bons mots, witty asides and a thorough dissection of the world of poetry and my exalted place therein. She seemed to experience some difficulty in following my thesis, however, if her constant interjections were anything to go by.

'You can get iambic with my pentameters any old time you like,' she said at one point, and, 'Show me your dithyrambs and I'll show you mine.'

Not, I felt, a woman with a firm grasp of the fundamentals, but I ploughed on.

With a crook of her finger, and a delicate rustle of re-arranged thighs, she motioned me over. I declined politely but was immediately struck with remorse. Although a magnificent beauty, she was, as I say, in her late sixties and may have been a trifle deaf. I compensated by raising my voice to what in normal circumstances would be regarded as shouting.

Some time later two more bottles of champagne and the oppressive heat from the fire had taken their toll. I slumped on my stool in a state of no small inebriation. The overheated widow was forced to reduce her outer garments while my lively and stimulating discourse ground to a drowsy halt. Not thinking that I would notice, Widow Bernelle blew the flickering flames out one by one. I had been right about her finances. She even had to ration her candles.

She moved to where I was sitting and began to fondle my top button.

'You must be far too hot in this overcoat,' she murmured. 'I'm far too hot myself and I'm wearing, why, next to nothing.' She giggled throatily. 'You know what, lover boy? I blame those naughty little dithyrambs.'

I tried to explain that it couldn't possibly have been the dithyrambs, but she seemed more interested in button-fondling at this stage. Having prised open the top one she proceeded to lose interest in it and diverted her attention to fondling the next one down. She was right: it *was* hot. But the thought of sitting there with only vest, shirt and jacket covering my top half made me feel that some sort of response was in order. There were four remaining buttons on the coat. What then? Not knowing what the correct procedure was in such circumstances I began to feel distinctly uneasy.

The situation was resolved to our mutual satisfaction, I'm delighted to say, with a solitary button remaining. She had been fondling for some time and was on the verge of prising when she purred, 'I think it's about time we got – how shall we say? – metrical. A quick couplet or two never harmed anyone. Hmm?'

I leapt to my feet.

'You're absolutely right,' I responded, whipping out my journal and setting to work. She watched in dumbstruck awe as I filled page upon page, guided only by the light of the fire's dying embers.

I staggered out of the house some hours later, rejoicing in the fact that I had come prepared for this most pivotal of occasions. I like to describe an intensity of passion as I go along – a sort of work in progress – even if this means that I miss out somewhat on personal involvement. At sunrise I opened the journal, expecting that the writing would be jerky but legible; writing in the dark is hardly conducive to excellence in the calligrapher's art. But I needn't have worried. The page was blank.

I had omitted to take the top off the pen.

XVI

It is often said that of all the enemies of artistic promise, politics is surely the most insidious. Who knows what heights Churchill might have achieved if he had refrained from meddling in Germany's plans for world domination. I could so easily have fallen into the same trap myself. That I failed to get sucked into the black hole of making the world a better place was due in no small part to my iron resolve.

Take the following. I was fourteen years old and just recovering nicely from my most recent school-induced injury. We had been set the home exercise of drawing a map of Ireland for the great Hibernophile Scully, before the bell had rung this time, so there was no escape.

Once home I set about humouring the fellow before getting down to my real work, but the coastline of Ireland is composed of the most infuriating mix of inlets, peninsulas, headlands, bays and islands, capes, promontories and juttings, seaboards, banks, leas, zigs, zags and squiggles. I had no intention of wasting the whole evening on these absurdities so I made a few minor adjustments. I drew the West Coast when the tide was out and, having spent more than my allotted time getting from Donegal to Dundalk by HB pencil, decided to omit the six counties of the northern state altogether. They were, after all, technically British. In retrospect it took as long drawing the county boundaries. It was refreshing, on the other hand, to get away from the sea.

As we stood in line the following morning to show our handiwork, Mr Scully sat on his desk swinging his chubby legs and glancing at each map with yawning indifference. This meant they were traced to perfection. Mine, I thought, was more a work of inspired imagination than a slavish copy. Apart from the absence of most of Ulster, the map featured another glaring innovation. My starting and finishing points were the tip of Mizen Head, but the latter had ended up several degrees north of the former. That this failed to elicit comment pays tribute to the galvanising effect of my technical omission.

That Scully remained silent when he first encountered my cartographic skills hardly surprised me, frankly. A work of art doesn't yield all its multi-layered secrets at once.

But there are pauses and pauses.

This, I discovered, was one of the latter.

He had merely gone to a place beyond rage. When he returned some time later he was like a man newborn. He set about me with an enthusiasm and vigour remarkable in one of his advancing years.

There was an almost balletic grace about his movements as his squat, long-armed frame swung, literally, into action. I suspect that this is the case with the human animal when- ever it involves itself in something it loves doing. And Mr Scully oozed pleasure from every pink pore. Never, before or since, have I witnessed a living creature so at one with the universe, so totally in control of its own destiny, so illustrative of the dictum that teaching is not a job, it's a vocation. It might be pointed out that my remarkable objectivity in the face of impending doom is almost clinical. To an extent, yes, I would have to agree. But the mind is capable of grappling with several different concepts at any given moment and I was simultaneously able to cope with the following:

The sad realisation that I was about to die unpublished.
The observation that small firearms should be supplied to all
pupils of Irish schools to help lessen the odds.

I was about to further reflect that in moments of stress the mind is known to work on several items of interest at once when Mr Scully's brogues hit the floor with a pine-splintering crash. I have never seen Nijinsky dance but perhaps, after all, I don't need to. I stood transfixed, the rabbit to his headlights as he bore down on me, every sinew primed for maximum impact. All thought vanished from my head. I was alive only to the moment. The putrid smell of stale beer and Woodbine. The bead of sweat, with its own private rage, that suicide-bombed the floor. The imminent crunch of bone on bone.

At this point the headmaster popped his head round the door and was about to intercede on my behalf when Mr Scully showed him the offending, and about-to-be-bloodstained, map. He shook his head sadly.

'Ah no,' he sighed. 'Ah no now. That's going a bit *too* far.'

He gave me a pitying look as I bounced off the partition. Mr Scully then proceeded with his merry task in the purest state of primal, unfettered joy.

Violence, I suppose, just seems to suit some people.

XVII

That the above worked to my advantage some years later, in the form of a free trip to Derry, was due in no small part to the fact that my eldest brother Ferdia was appraised of the situation. A rather morose individual, he blamed everything on 'the Brits'. Bad harvest? The Brits. Extra day to plough through in February? The Brits. I could go on, and Ferdia frequently did. Ferdia had left home to die for Ireland but returned twice a week with his dirty socks. The map incident coincided with one of his visits.

I had grown into a fine young man by this stage, and had developed a pleasingly severe aspect which suggested that I was sole custodian of some deep truth; which, of course, I was. I was still some years away from the first flowering of my genius but felt that the time was ripe to chew the artistic fat with my peers. It was time to walk abroad.

I donned my best tweed jacket, my scarf and recently acquired fedora, and took possession of my ageing father's walking stick. This would undoubtedly confine him to the house for the duration of my absence, I mused, but the true artist has little room for sentiment. Besides, I had a long walk ahead of me.

Suddenly Ferdia burst through the door, stubbed his toe on the step and blamed the Brits for putting it there in the first place. He then ordered me out of the house at gunpoint. When he was in this sort of mood it was best to humour him so I did what I was told. My parents, I have to say, did nothing. They had been advised that Ferdia's temper tantrums would disappear as soon as he had achieved his aim of a united Ireland, and in those days you didn't question the medical profession.

Ferdia had obviously heard about the map. Once outside he informed me that he was going to drive me to the above-mentioned city where I would spend some time with friends of his. Time to grasp, he insisted, 'the reality of the situation'. There was no point appealing to his better nature – he didn't have one. Nor did he have a car. I contented myself with pointing this out. He looked at me with a new respect.

'Good point,' he said. 'Wait here.'

He disappeared down the road with some traffic bollards and a detour sign. Ten minutes later he was back.

'Hop in,' he shouted.

I flung father's stick into a ditch and with a screech of tyres we raced towards Derry, a balaclava pulled low over my brother's face against the midsummer sun. Almost immediately we passed a woman with a distressed-looking toddler. We could, Ferdia supposed, have given her a lift – there was, after all, a baby seat in the back – but as he said himself, 'You never know what you're getting involved with these days'.

As a child Ferdia would regularly lecture me on what he was pleased to call 'the reality of the situation'. He took to frogmarching me on visits to like-minded folk and, as I knew most of them from school, I often wondered if the blindfold was strictly necessary. He also had an infuriating habit of saying 'When are you going to write something for us?' As far as I knew he wasn't married and I found his use of the royal plural, I have to say, a bit of an affectation.

If the offer of a lift was more than a happy accident, what happened next was proof that I was born blessed. As we approached the city gates I was becoming somewhat apprehensive. What if I had to sit listening to his tedious friends for hour after hour and was left with no time for the business in hand? I needn't have worried. Ferdia had been muttering for some time about the inconsideration of people not filling their tanks and it became necessary for him to drop into a bank near the centre for petrol money.

I was pondering my options when a cacophony of police cars descended on the bank, sirens wailing, the officers' moustaches glistening with purpose. The balaclava and gun had turned what was intended as a simple withdrawal into quite an occasion, and I wasn't to see Ferdia again for several years.

XVIII

Derry is a vibrant city, in many ways living up to its title as the Belfast of the North. I surveyed it with an almost painterly eye. Its streets. Its portals. Hallowed, for the most part. I wandered about the same streets and, indeed, portals, happily released from the tyranny of dogma. I met a man busking with a lambeg drum and cheerfully placed a small coin in his bowler, although I had to fall in step and take his hat off first. I could afford to be generous. I was about to move among my peers, with particular reference to Heaney, and was reminded, as I strolled merrily along, of the advice given to me some years after his death by poet, playwright and bon viveur W.B. Yeats.

'I wish only to be a poet,' I gushed, my ouija board trembling with anticipation.

'In that case,' he ejaculated, 'be from Northern Ireland.'

An excellent piece of advice and one that I have tried to observe to the letter.

I further reflected on the subject matter of my forthcoming tête-à-tête with Heaney and began to trawl through my early experience for insights into my genius which might be of interest in casual conversation. I recalled in particular three images from my early life which established beyond all doubt that I,

Fiachra MacFiach, was destined for greatness. I propose to dwell on each image in brief but loving detail.

> *a) My mother stood with her back to me, her arms thresh-ing about in the sink. Like many women in those days she supplemented the meagre family income by taking in wash-ing-up. A fascinating insight into these times can be found in 'Irish Mothers and Other Household Objects', a Catholic Truth Society pamphlet. I also recall that her faded tweed dress had a small gap at the back in the exact shape of my romper suit.*

> *b) As her arms appeared, disappeared and reappeared bearing plates, cups, saucers and the other paraphernalia of the eating process with metronomic regularity my father appeared at the open half door, his back stooped slightly from years of honest labour, the galoshes which protected his Wellington boots flecked with frog-spawn, a thin trail of turf smoke rising from his ever present pipe.*

> *c) The local constable grunted past on his bible-black, crow-black, midnight-black, head-stuffed-in-a-bin-liner-whatever-the-time-black bike, his giant constable's-uniform-blue buttocks heaving with pleasure.*

This trinity of the mind was to stay with me well into adult-hood and provide the creative wellspring of my greatest masterwork. But enough of this reverie. There was work to be done. I decided to get down to the business in hand and approached a member of the general public.

'I wish to be directed to Heaney's,' I declaimed, but the addressee appeared not to understand the question. Undoubtedly foreign, I thought, so I decided to rephrase the question.

'Heaney's,' I said, enunciating loudly and with deliberation. 'How much street I go?'

Not only did the poor woman appear baffled this time, but she seemed, for no apparent reason, rather upset. I removed my hand from her lapel and she scurried off.

I was scanning the passing throng for an Irish face when a newspaper hawker said 'First left, pal. Third shop from the corner.' I thanked the fellow, purchased a newspaper as a gesture of goodwill and tossed it, and its germs, into the nearest available bin.

As I hurried towards my destination, I pondered what the hawker had said. Third shop on the left. Shop? This suggested that Heaney had an alternative source of income, a wise move in the circumstances. I had read his second book. I was therefore pondering the possibility that the emporium in question might well be the city's main outlet for greetings cards, when I arrived at the distinctly unhallowed portals.

I scrutinised the sign above the door.

'S. HEANEY – FISHMONGER,' it said. 'WET FISH A SPECIALITY.'

I almost felt sorry for the man.

Apologising mentally to my highly sensitive nose I went inside and, yes, the fish was indeed wet. I informed the woman behind the counter that I wished to speak to the man himself and she in her turn informed me that he was outside gutting some cuttlefish and would be back forthwith.

When he finally came in I saw, with astonishment, that he had obviously passed the three score and ten mark some years previously. I've heard of publicity photos being retouched and the like, but the public image of Heaney is, I feel bound to say, flattering in the extreme. The public persona is, I also have to say, a mite friendlier.

Heaney in the flesh was glum and taciturn, if not downright hostile.

'I am a great admirer of your work,' I began.

He appeared to take no consolation from this but asked me what I wanted.

'Indeed,' I continued, 'I was so taken with your first slim volume that I rushed straight out and bought a pair of Wellington boots.'

He seemed faintly irritated. A queue had begun forming behind me, no doubt all wanting him to sign a book or help them out with some puzzling symbolic passage. He asked me again what I wanted. What *fish* I wanted, if you please.

This is a wily ruse. The artist pretends to be more interested in some mundane activity than in the exalted plane of his muse. It's a defence mechanism and one I propose to use myself when hounded by American academics. So with Heaney. All this talk of fish was merely his way of deflecting criticism, but my fellow interrogators were less persistent than I. They caved in under the weight of his pseudo scorn and pseudo job, contenting themselves with packets of cod roe and the like, expertly weighed and packed by the criminally overstretched female assistant.

There are defences and defences, I'm afraid, and Heaney had obviously been stung too often. He persisted with the ridiculous conceit that he was merely a simple monger of fish.

Finally I exploded in the face of his false modesty.

'For God's sake, man,' I bellowed, 'I haven't come all this way to discuss fish. I am here to talk about poetry!'

'But I have no interest in poetry,' he objected.

'Then why do you write the damned stuff?' I countered furiously.

'I don't,' he muttered, nervously dressing a crayfish, 'write poetry.'

'Oh, all right then,' I said. 'Light verse. Call it what you will.'

By this stage the queue stretched out the door. Who knows what they must have thought of the imbecile. The final straw came when his busybody of an assistant butted in.

'Will I call the police, Stanislaus?' she said.

This was the crowning insult. Stanislaus? Not only was he

hiding behind fish, but a pseudonym? This elevated artistic modesty to ridiculous heights. I vowed to have nothing more to do with the insufferable doggerel-smith, bought a half-pound of whiting – reduced for a quick sale – and stormed majestically off.

XIX

For some days after I arrived home I mused on the implications of the Heaney[1] incident. His cuttlefish-gutting day job may have been a misguided bid for bourgeois respectability. More likely it was a safety net against the almost certain poverty of the true artist. On the other hand, Heaney appeared to have cast off the shackles of his parents – they were nowhere in evidence at any rate – and it seemed to me that the time had come for me to do likewise. I had come to see mine simply as material for my art but it's difficult to mythologise one's parents when they're pottering about the same house.

The circumstances of my leaving were fortunate in the extreme. Throughout adolescence my father would often place a warning hand on my shoulder.

'Whatever you do, son,' he would say, 'don't go near your mother's chest.'

He was referring, as I later found out, to the metal box which occupied pride of place under the marital bed. My parents, you see, always knew I would be the one to go to university. With peasant cunning they understood instinctively that I was the chosen one – I had certainly reminded them often enough – and so had actually saved up to send me away. Hence the chest.

University is, it need hardly be said, a wonderful place to attend if you want to do something else, and I would often fantasise about the works of genius I could germinate by the simple expedient of avoiding lectures. But which university to grace with my presence? I closed my eyes and stuck a pin in my bloodstained map of Ireland.

Limerick.

I decided on the best of three, five, eleven, seventeen, thirty one. At this point the pin had landed on Limerick nineteen times, the place where Belfast should have been four times and Monasterevin once. As I knew for a fact that there wasn't a university anywhere near Monasterevin, I chose Dublin. I notified the university of my decision. I then wrote to my mother's distant relations, the Dublin Clooneys, informed them that I would be spending three years in their locality and would be pleased to stay with them for the duration. Confirmation, when it came, could not have arrived at a better time.

I was alone in the house, both parents being simultaneously absent: one of the few remaining pleasures for the older generation is attending funerals and at the time of which I speak my parents had a couple slotted in. Mother had left sufficient victuals for three days, along with directions to the stove. I married victuals and stove and prepared for the luxury of uninterrupted work.

Hours passed. Days. Weeks? The true artist has no concept of time. And so it was on this particular occasion. The Muse was upon me. But however long I had been immersed in my art I was jolted brutally back to the world of affairs by a loud banging on the door. The Muse fled. The banging continued. I decided, after due deliberation, to open it and proceeded to do so with barely concealed rage. Outside stood a large crowd of locals. Sweet Jesus, I thought. Mummers come to entertain the inhabitants with peasant doggerel, off-season carols, or handkerchief-flapping dance.

But no. They were merely passers-by who felt duty bound to inform me, if you please, that the house was on fire. And so, on further inspection, it proved.

It says much for my powers of total concentration that a pair of gently smouldering eyebrows – a fair to middling warning to a lesser poet – had failed to rouse me from my work. I was marvelling on this fact, and sharing my wonder with the rough-hewn mob, when some unlettered lout suggested I contact the fire brigade. This, I'm bound to say, is typical of the peasant class. Faced with the possibility of exploring the mind of genius, they find some excuse to return the subject to the mundane, the everyday.

But things were about to take an unexpected turn. Even as the roof ignited, the postman arrived with a letter from my uncle.

You'll be the parasitic pseudo-poet who killed his brother, it began.

A fine example of mordant Dublin wit, no doubt, but humour is a luxury of the idle class and I was a busy man. I pocketed the letter unread and moved gingerly away from the first falling beam.

It is not for me to speculate as to how the fire started. Ferdia blamed 'the Brits' and it certainly bears all the hallmarks of a politically motivated act, the consequences of which could have been tragic in the extreme. Fortunately, however, I was leaving anyway so the inconvenience was minimal.

As soon as it was safe to do so I went inside to collect what remained of my belongings and I must say I was sorely tempted to sue the fire brigade. In dousing the flames they had completely soaked my work in progress. A blank notebook, I grant you, but they weren't to know that. On a happier note I went to the remains of my parents' bedroom to claim my inheritance. My mother's chest being impervious to fire I pocketed the not inconsiderable sum it contained, bade farewell to my youth and headed south.

XX

I am, to my almost certain knowledge, the only undisputed genius of the MacFiach line. Great Uncle Alistair found fame of sorts as drag artiste Sweet Alis MacFiach while my distant cousins Joel and Ethan Clooney received an Academy Award nomination for Best Short Film by Identical Twins. But, even if we count the latter as one unit, the term genius seems curiously inappropriate in this case. Cinema is, after all, a minor art form, closer to basket weaving or balloon sculpture than to my own lofty pursuit.

It was arranged on my arrival in Dublin that I would stay in the twins' room – Joel and Ethan being away at film school – and that I would pay my way by tutoring cousin Rosemary when not engaged in my own studies. My uncle's wife – my aunt – had gone to live in a women-only commune in Dunfanaghy and my uncle, when not away on business, would sit around the house drinking heavily and weeping.

Cousin Rosemary, the youngest of the Clooneys, was by common consent exceptionally beautiful although I must say that I find baldness in a woman, whether by accident or design, singularly unattractive. It was perhaps understandable, then, that Clooney père saw fit to lecture me on matters of propriety regarding his only daughter. He took me to one side and informed me, a steadying hand on my shoulder, that Rosemary was 'getting to that age'. Not knowing what age that age was I decided to humour him in his cups, and said that I was delighted to hear it.

He wept into his glass for a seemingly endless moment before embarking on a maudlin homily. The odd phrase and word hit home. 'Like her mother'. 'Salacious'. He tried this one several times till he got it right. The other word that stood out was 'fornication' and his concluding burst – 'If anyone so much as lays a finger of lust on my daughter he's a dead man. I have the contacts.' – was delivered with fire, passion and clarity. He concluded by saying that Rosemary was particularly weak at algebra.

I resolved to begin her lessons with 'Transsexual Subtextuality in the Poetic Output of J "M" Plunkett'. But first there was the small matter of settling in. Joel and Ethan's room was a shrine to cinema. They had often stayed at my parents' house as children and I well remembered them getting me to stand watching them, in all weathers, in the field at the back of the cow shed while they checked camera angles and lighting. Such dedication to their admittedly populist art was reflected in the books, posters and film scripts that lined the walls of my study-to-be.

I cast a cursory glance at their various projects. This was not mere idle curiosity on my part. I had overheard them speaking, on one occasion, about their desire to find a subject that would encapsulate the complexity of modern Ireland. I had coughed politely in order to draw attention to myself and they had both appraised me for some time, falling silent in the process. In the hope that I had thus inadvertently planted a seed I rifled through their effects.

I discovered in passing that my eccentric cousins weren't the only family members involved in this most ephemeral of art forms. A two-reel bio-pic from the silent era charts the historic occasion on which Joseph 'Mary' Plunkett represented his country at tennis. Plunkett, apparently, was the mixed doubles team. Great Uncle Alis won two Oscars for the part – the first time Best Actor and Actress had gone to the same person – but this, of course, still doesn't make him a genius.

I was about to give up on my search when, aha! A folder marked 'Work in Progress' containing several likenesses of myself captured over the years, interspersed with requests for funding for a 'serious' film based on a 'genius'. Vindication! The seed had, indeed, been planted. I put the folder to one side and surveyed the rest of the room. Posters, books and boxes of cinematic trinkets dominated the small space. Impossible for a poet to work with such distractions, it goes without saying, but such was the depth of their collection of mindless trivia, with the obvious exception of the folder, that it took me several days to bin the lot.

XXI

My university career, by this time, was over. It had been shortened somewhat by my failure to register for any course, a fact which had upset the bureaucrats. I had decided on history as my main subject – as a way of contextualising myself – and in the opening lecture revisionist historian Professor H. Doody developed his thesis, I believe, that the Great Famine coincided with an almighty surplus of chocolate biscuits.

As I had more important matters on my mind I decided to give it a miss. What if the muse should strike while the professor was busy pontificating? If my experience of that pompous breed is anything to go by it would have been well nigh impossible to shut him up.

No. I decided to head straight for the library which was, to my intense annoyance, full of nervous students busily taking notes. The fact that examinations were only nine months off no doubt explains this, and there wasn't a seat to be had in the place. I stood to attention for some time, weighed down by the tools of my trade. Notebooks. Poetic texts. Scarf. A

young woman eventually vacated her place. Others were waiting alongside but I was the hungry one. I got the seat.

The woman in question had left some of her possessions
on the adjoining desk. Books. Purse. Flask. Reading glasses.
A couple of bags. Lunch box. As a helpful gesture I bundled
these on the floor in a neat pile and set to work. Some minutes
later she returned, muttering furiously to herself, collected
her belongings and skedaddled without so much as a thank
you. I remember reflecting at the time that to mislay a biro
suggests a careless nature. But books? Purse? Flask? Glasses,
bags and lunch box? And talking to herself? This suggested a
mind on the borders of sanity, so I wilfully ignored her in case
she decided to embarrass herself further.

I had only just set about my work when it became apparent
that I needed to visit the lavatory. I left my book open, scarf
draped casually across my chair. Inference? I'll be back. And
so it must surely have been obvious to any rational human
being, but Ireland was going through one of its periodic two
hundred-year cycles of religious hysteria and was overrun by
nuns; most of whom, I regret to say, were in the library at the
time.

My books, on my return, had been placed on a nearby
trolley. My scarf was folded neatly on the floor. And in my
place? Yes. A nun. Now I am not a violent man, but her vow
of silence limited the option of rational debate. My aforementioned belief that war simply suffers from a bad press came to
the fore.

The Irish legal system, however, is weighed heavily in favour
of the Church: as far as I know it's still illegal to hit a nun. The
next best solution, I decided, was psychological warfare, so I
stood behind the chair and read over her shoulder. This form
of mental torture is renowned for its effectiveness and, need-
less to say, some hours later she vacated the seat and the library
was left to darkness, as the poet Gray so judiciously put it, and
to me. And, it must be said, the janitor. Followed, well before

midnight, by a couple of burly, moustachioed security guards and, the following morning, by the Machiavellian intrigues of the college bureaucrats.

My truncated academic career confirmed me in the belief that third-level education is the civil service of the mind. Some days later I applied for a fellowship at the same university and my failure to get the post reinforced my theory that the true artist is always an outsider.

I lost no time in expounding my views to cousin Rosemary during our next session. Not wishing to appear boastful I referred to myself in this context only in passing, but confined my thesis to the outsider status thrust upon Joseph 'Mary' Plunkett in spite of his excellent marks in the civil service entrance exam. Cousin Rosemary sat rapt with attention, drinking in my every word. All too soon, however, the lesson came to an end and she closed her algebra book with a pleasing demureness. Mathematics is not a girl's subject, granted, but she was a bright student and would, under my guidance, do well.

XXII

In many ways, as I say, an idyllic time.

The master-pupil relationship with Rosemary ripened into something deeper. Lecturer-audience. The sole blot on our intimate sessions was the constant interruption of her increasingly inebriated father. The pattern, if disruptive, was at least predictable. He would insinuate his head round the door, stagger in and motion me to one side. There would follow a supposedly confidential man-to-man with a hand placed heavily on my shoulder to help him remain upright.

Rosemary, he would begin, was getting to that age. I replied, on each occasion, that I was delighted to hear it. He would then weep into his glass for a while before embarking on his bombastic, and seemingly eternal, set speech. The odd word and phrase hit home – but 'salacious' presented a regular problem, interrupting his thesis which was, essentially, to warn off all would-be suitors on pain of imminent death. A brief reference to algebra would conclude the proceedings and off he would slope to nurse his secret sorrow.

I describe the above because a later confrontation suggested my personal involvement in his drink-induced vision. We had positioned ourselves to one side as was the regular practice. His hand was on my shoulder. He had forsaken his habitual tumbler of whiskey for the decanter, and was more inebriated than usual. On this occasion I couldn't understand a word he said but I was, after all, his guest. We were speaking man-to-man. I knew the ground rules.

He slurred his opening gambit.

'I am delighted to hear it,' I replied when silence reigned.

He wept into his decanter for a while. I stood there wondering what to do if the muse should strike. Then he was off again. A pause.

'I'm sure she's the image of her mother,' I replied, 'but not being on intimate terms with my aunt I hardly feel qualified to comment.' There followed a disjointed ramble which appeared to include variations on the letter 'S'. This, too, eventually ground to a halt.

'Salacity is indeed a state best avoided,' I averred.

He then placed his decanter on the nearest available surface, released his grip on my shoulder, raised himself up to his full height and inserted his thumbs into his waistcoat, a model of sudden sobriety.

'I am delighted to hear you say it,' he said. 'But I put it to you that it is not this child who is guilty of salacity, you young blackguard! It is you! I put it to you that it is not this child who is the hunter, you adolescent miscreant! It is you! I further put it to you, you libidinous voluptuary, that you have defiled this child with your lecherous eyes and come-hither manner. Know this: I abhor your impudicity. I repudiate your carnal concupiscence. I heartily forbid your concrescence. And as for your lustful concubinage, you low cur: nip it in the bud. Forthwith. Because also know this: I have the contacts.'

So saying he strode to the door and slammed it dramatically in his wake. I was outraged. This drunkard, this dipsomaniac, this sot, had dared to accuse *me* of leading other than a blameless life. I stood trembling with wrath. The door opened. He reappeared, clutching a fresh decanter.

'By the way,' he slurred, leaning against the jamb, 'she's particularly weak on algebra.'

XXIII

Despite these regular interruptions, however, our daily lesson ran smoothly, and as I often made it my habit to take the afternoon air it seemed inevitable that Rosemary should join me on one of my walks. A mistake as it turned out, and yet the experience began agreeably enough. Bearing in mind the statistic that in ninety-seven per cent of traffic accidents in sunlight there's a bald pedestrian nearby, I stayed well away from the road, and cousin Rosemary matched me stride for manly stride in her twelve-league army boots.

All went well as we set off from the house. All was fine as we turned the corner down to the seashore where Brian Boru had famously pitched his tent in 1014. Locals are still bitterly divided as to whether he had a valid permit and I was about to observe that we Irish are still steeped in old battles when I noticed that cousin Rosemary had become distinctly agitated. We were passing the main gate of the local convent school at the time and there she parked her boots, a defiant look in her wild adolescent eye.

I was about to develop my thesis tangentially when a member of the religious order approached the gate and this led, it pains me to report, to the wildest torrent of vilification I have ever encountered between one human being and a nun. I have since located most of the expressions in a dictionary of north Dublin street cries and am only dissuaded from quoting her impassioned speech word for word by the expectation that this memoir will eventually become a standard text in secondary schools in the English-speaking world.

Cousin Rosemary's basic thrust was that the sister in question was a *****, a *******, and a **** – ******.

'You abused me as a child you ****,' she elaborated. 'You are a ****ing ****, a ****ing ******, and a ****ing ****ing ****ing ****ing ****.'

The sister in question, who appeared to be black if her face was anything to go by, stood less than two feet away, and a conversational tone, to my mind, seemed more appropriate.

But cousin Rosemary ranted on regardless. A crowd began to form comprising both lay and religious. The Mother Superior appeared. A Caucasian lady of indeterminate age, she shook her head sadly.

'Don't be silly, Rosemary,' she said. 'Sister N'gola has spent the last forty years with the missions in darkest Africa. You really are the most appalling fibber.'

Cousin Rosemary trembled with rage.

'I'm going to have a child by an intelligent man before my sixteenth birthday you ****,' she snarled. 'So **** you.'

Mother Superior pressed her fingers together in an attitude of prayer.

Rosemary thrust her arm through mine and held me as tight as a car clamp.

'Come on, lover,' she spat. She strode off down the street and I followed helplessly in her wake. As we reached the corner she turned and gave Mother Superior an aggressive salute.

'Rome sucks, *****.'

I didn't catch the reply.

I tried to put the above scene out of my mind by returning to the subject of Irish history. I even broadened it out to include a dissertation on my place in it but my thoughts were elsewhere. I tried to think of some way of extricating my arm from that of my libidinous cousin. *I* was an intelligent man. Rosemary was obviously aware of this. She had also referred to me as 'Lover'. This posited a potentially explosive and time-consuming scenario. But I noted that the further we got from the convent school the less the pressure on my arm, and after half a mile or so I was back in control of my own destiny. I kept a wary eye out for any other convents, just in case, but the moment had passed. Peace of a sort descended. My monologue proceeded undisturbed.

We walked along the promenade for a while, and shortly cousin Rosemary decided to return to the parental home – no doubt to make notes of what I'd been saying. I was not unrelieved. I had spotted a couple of distant figures in black waddling towards us, bibles aloft.

The day and I were hot. The sky and sea were blue. I decided to purge myself of my recent trauma by immersing myself in the cleansing waters of the salty main. I walked along the strand for some time until I had left the world of people behind. I removed my clothes and laid them neatly on the sand. I placed my work in progress beside it. I toyed with the idea of bringing the precious document into the water with me but felt that this would unduly restrict my movements. I wished to merge totally with the life force. To become one with the universe. To float free of the mortal state. Besides, I would only be gone for thirty seconds.

I ran to the edge of the sea and, with a whoop of joy tempered somewhat by my natural reserve, tested the water with my toe. I pondered my options. It was certainly colder than I had expected. I was beginning to feel curiously undressed and the gulls' cries seemed, in my present state, to have turned to mocking laughter.

It proved, on closer inspection, that it was indeed mocking laughter which assailed my ears; not of gulls, however, but of small boys. I caught a brief glimpse of them as they disappeared into the sand dunes with my clothes. They seemed highly amused by their action but it's rare for the victim of ridicule to laugh heartily at his own humiliation unless there are television cameras present. I was about to give chase when I noticed that my work in progress remained where I had put it.

They had taken my clothes but left my notebook! This was beyond humiliation. I was mortified. The notes were mainly random – aphorisms, bons mots and the like – but there were also fragments of verse. Did they not like them? I imagined them flicking through the pages and being unimpressed. I was devastated. These insecure thoughts, typical of all great artists, lasted but a second before my rational mind took over. They were, after all, mere children, so giving chase would be futile. I could never have hoped to explain my working methods. I might, on the other hand, have got my clothes back.

XXIV

This left me with the problem of returning chez Clooney, a distance of some two miles through a hostile bourgeois landscape, in a state of total undress. I could have waited till darkness and clambered over back gardens, but the sight of a naked man negotiating garden walls in the dead of night is open to misinterpretation, even in these liberal times. I decided, instead, to brazen it out. If I walked along as if fully-dressed, I reasoned, the chances were that the broad mass of people would accept that I was, indeed, in that happy state.

How wrong I was. I had intended my arrival back at the Clooney residence to be discreet. It turned out to be anything but. I was seen down the drive by a crowd of well-wishers and pubescent girls on bicycles, and was about to tip-toe round the back when the front door opened and Mother Superior ushered me serenely in. She gave me a beatific smile and averted her gaze at her leisure. I followed her inside and closed the door with relief.

Père Clooney was waiting for me in the living room and I have to admit that, on the surface, things looked pretty bad. I was expected to give cousin Rosemary her daily grind at five thirty and it was now well past six. But my uncle had other things on his mind. He was also remarkably sober.

'Come in, m'boy,' he said. 'Brandy? Cigar?'

I demurred. I was about to suggest that I run upstairs and find some clothes but he seemed agitated. Best, perhaps, to indulge the fellow.

'On second thoughts,' I said, 'perhaps just a snifter.'

I helped myself to a Havana and we smoked and drank for some hours in silence. Cousin Rosemary sat demurely on the sofa, eyes downcast. Mother Superior smiled beatifically beside her.

In many ways I was glad she was there. A mature woman about the house, even one with a fixed beatific smile, exerts a civilising influence and Clooney responded accordingly. He exuded geniality where before had been tetchiness, harmony where before had been conflict. I found myself warming to the man.

'The thing is, m'boy,' he said eventually, 'Dublin . . .'

'Ah yes,' I said, beginning to feel, by now, the mellowing effects of the brandy, 'Dublin. City of Joyce, Beckett, Johnson, Mooney and O'Brien.'

I crossed my legs discreetly from a standing position.

'Yes, yes,' my uncle replied testily; ruffled slightly, perhaps, by my superior knowledge. 'Never mind about that now. The thing is, m'boy . . . It's not really you, is it? You being an artist and all that. Solitude. That's what you need. Somewhere quiet to jot down the odd limerick. Eh?' I could see that he would never understand the soul of a genius but he had struck a chord. 'One of those uninhabited islands off the West Coast now,' he continued, 'that'd be just the ticket. Away from all those distractions, d'ye see. My . . . how's her algebra, by the way?'

I ignored the question, rhetorical I fancy, and looked at the man with a new respect. I sighed wistfully and poured yet another large brandy.

Mother Superior coughed beatifically. My uncle looked startled and weighed in afresh.

'The thing is,' he said, 'I have the tidy sum of five hundred pounds here – Irish money – that says Yes! Your dreams *can* come true!'

I was flabbergasted. Here was a man who had every reason to believe that my intentions towards his daughter were not entirely honourable and yet his main concern was to subsidise the arts. I looked at the notes in wonderment.

'Five hundred pounds!' I said.

Mother Superior shifted beatifically in her seat.

'Offer him six.'

My God! Religion and Art in happy union at last! Huzza!

My uncle grappled with the new figure.

'Six hundred pounds!' I said.

Mother Superior's smile broadened and set.

'Did he say six? He meant seven fifty. Didn't you, Mr Clooney?'

My uncle grappled with the new figure.

I laughed, involuntarily, with delight. Mother Superior stood beatifically up and dressed me with her eyes.

'Nine hundred,' she said, 'and that's his final offer.' She extended her hand. 'Let's shake on it.'

My uncle produced his wallet with trembling hands and peeled off the required number of notes. He looked not unemotional as he placed them in Mother Superior's free palm. Without extricating her hand from mine she flicked her commission from the top and passed me my six hundred-pound cut.

'It's more than worth it, Mr MacFiach,' she beamed. 'You are, after all, a most intelligent man.'

Rosemary blushed demurely from the sofa. My uncle downed a celebratory tumbler in one.

'Nine hundred,' he slurred. 'Jesus Christ! I was quoted eight fifty by a hit man.'

I failed to see what that had to do with supporting the arts but was pleased to accept his generous gift and found myself, some forty minutes later, deposited fully dressed on the Galway road with sufficient victuals for a light lunch, a large sum of money in my back pocket and the screech of my uncle's tyres in my ears as he executed a U-turn and roared off home.

XXV

I began my journey west in a state of no small inebriation. In mitigation I merely point out that I am an artist and while it has never been adequately proven that sobriety harms the creative faculty, it's hardly worth the risk of finding out. My uncle had very kindly supplied me with a road map which suggested, mistakenly, that the main route to the western sea-board was one-way. It also seemed an excessively long journey so, at the next petrol station, I bought a smaller map.

But time was of no consequence. I was a free spirit, unbur-dened by the cares of the world, and was about to pursue my art in splendid isolation. In spite of my noticeably handsome features and easy charm I had managed to ward off the atten-tions of the women of Ireland with almost laughable ease. I was shortly to embark on a relationship, however, which would test my steely resolve to snapping point and almost cause me to betray my great gift.

I was passing a field at the time. Oh, it was much like any other field. Flat. Stone-encrusted. Enclosed by dry-stone walls and a metal gate over which peered an ass. Her long, mourn-ful face followed me as I shuffled wearily along, my light lunch long since eaten. One of her forebears had borne Christ in triumph into Jerusalem, but I was thinking only of easing my weary feet, as we could hardly expect the same type of recep-tion in Athlone.

I opened the gate and motioned her out. Nothing. I doubt if the Bible goes into detail about this bit, but an ass is not noted for its obliging nature and this particular one had a generous helping of the relevant gene. I was on disagreeably intimate terms with her rump before I gave up and marched off in disgust. As soon as I was gone she trotted happily out of the field and followed me down the road.

It is often said that the ass is the most loyal of animals, if a mite unwieldy as a house pet, and this particular model was no exception. We exchanged what may have been a bond-ing look. All the more unfortunate, then, that several miles down the road I spied a second ass both younger and fitter and managed, after a good deal of effort on my part, to engi-neer a straight swap.

This may sound like an easy enough task but the first ass didn't want to go into the field and the second ass didn't want to come out. After much jockeying for position and the best part of a bag of carrots, I found myself standing in the road with both asses in the field, staring at me over the gate as they munched carrots. Half an hour later I had both asses where I wanted them, but *I* was eating the carrot. It was nearly night-fall before I had the situation finally resolved. I read some days later that the new owner of my old ass had his entire stock destroyed because of a contagious wasting disease traced to the same poor beast. Lucky swap.

I was right about Athlone. No flower-strewn paths or shady palm trees. Just the odd honk from an irate motorist as we negotiated the town's labyrinthine traffic-light system. And so on out to the west with its rugged terrain and match-ing people. I decided to give the ass a name. Assumpta. It is perhaps only when we leave Ireland that we fully comprehend what a ridiculous name Assumpta is, but Assumpta wasn't to know that. Besides, Assumpta the Ass was pleasingly allit-erative. It had the ring of a children's best-seller about it, although I was damned if I was going to lower myself to that level of hack work.

Assumpta proved a stout friend and a wonderful listener. The odd braying noise merely acted as a pleasing counter-point to my discourse. It was as if she was saying 'Do you tell me so?' or 'Pray continue, fellow. You interest me strangely.' As with all the best travelling companions my subject matter was wide ranging, my treatment of it witty and informative in the extreme. I spoke at length, for instance, on the subject of book titles. *Eminent Neanderthals. Urdu The Hard Way.* And that paean to conscientious objection *They Died with Their Slippers On*. None of which, by the way, I had read.

No. I confine my reading to the poetic arts. I live and breathe great poetry and it was while remarking that one of the benefits of a Catholic education is that it introduces us to doggerel we would not otherwise have read that I was struck by an excellent idea. The bards of old would ply their trade from house to house, enlightening the inhabitants in return for full bed and board. The Rhyming Priest springs to mind as an excellent example of this genre, although his subject matter was somewhat limited.

> *It's much to be prayed for that one day the Pope'll*
> *Convert the poor people of Constantinople.*

Fine as far as it goes, and rhythmically sound, but take, then, the following:

> *I hope that the Pope, that good friend of the Celt,*
> *Will convert the poor heathens of Magherafelt.*

Or, indeed:

> *I pray that the might of the Vatican See*
> *Will convert the vast hordes of the heathen Chinee.*

Vast hordes I like. Vast hordes is good, but the Rhyming Priest was in many ways a victim of his own success. He hit upon a winning theme and milked it to death; his own in this particular case. His decision to crack Belfast was ecumenically sound but he ended up on a Shankill Road bonfire after taking bad advice.

My decision to follow in his exalted footsteps was not taken lightly. I am not by nature an exhibitionist, but my speech accepting the Nobel Prize for Literature would demand certain performance skills. Projection. Clarity. The ability to feign humility. It was no bad thing to start practising on the peasants of Connaught. Having established that Assumpta would remain out of sight until I had a foot inside the house I rapped boldly on the first door I came to.

'I am an Artist,' I declaimed. 'I demand sustenance in return for which I will entertain you with verses to delight the mind.'

I discovered, in the course of such visits, that ninety per cent of Irish homesteads possess at least one shotgun, usually loaded; but I am an artist, not a market researcher. I merely pass the information on.

XXVI

My luck seemed set to change as I negotiated the winding, pitiless mud tracks of Connemara, after a chance meeting with an itinerant musician of my acquaintance. I refer to Blind Cearbhúil O'Dowda, an uilleann piper who hails from the stony vicinity of my parents' old home. His pipes could often be heard over the intervening bog if the wind was from the north. Or, for that matter, from the south, east or west; and my father professed himself an admirer.

'That Cearbhúil has a lovely tone,' he said once. Cearbhúil, at the time, was in Australia. My father's critical appraisal coincided with some of the local children winding a tomcat through Mother's mangle. An understandable mistake. I, too, often thought I heard my father squeezing a tune from the dreaded melodeon when, in fact, it was merely his mother dying of consumption. But Blind Cearbhúil, and his mournful pipes, were a special case. As soon as I heard that high-pitched wailing tone I knew exactly who it was. Two musicians like that, my admiring father used to say, and the country would sink under the weight of misery.

I reached the brow of the intervening hill and there, in the distance, a fire blazed, joyful in the act of burning. Two figurines sat round it: Cearbhúil and a female companion who, on closer inspection, turned out to be that mythological hardy annual, the snaggle-toothed old crone. A dying breed, sadly, in these days of improved dentistry and skin cream. A not unattractive blend of methylated spirits and horse manure wafted up from her person and she beckoned me to sit.

We passed a pleasant time swapping verses and stories, the more depressing segments highlighted by Blind Cearbhúil's melancholy wail and Assumpta's attendant brays. This fine old tradition was given a thorough workout through the evening hours and we were being entertained by one of Blind Cearbhúil's interminable airs when Assumpta became suddenly restless. Blind Cearbhúil stopped pumping his bellows, a remarkably considerate gesture to a dumb but suffering animal. The music trailed off some time later.

'There's a crowd of people coming,' he said nervously.

Hmm, I thought. A classic case of stage fright. Fine with a couple of friends round the camp fire, but give him a real audience and he disintegrates. MacFiach, on the other hand, rises. The crowd may have been attracted by the lure of the pipes and the fire, but they were heading, without knowing it, towards more elevated fare. This was a golden opportunity to test my latent verse-speaking skills.

They were still a good way off, which gave me plenty of time to prepare. I set to work sifting. A hint of Plunkett, naturally. A soupçon of Yeats – as an accessible build-up to my own greater complexities, I hasten to add. Heaney? Certainly not. I was still bridling from his ridiculous subterfuge and the growing suspicion that he might even have short-changed me on the fish. My programme was still a tad light. Blind Cearbhúil had lost his nerve. I would, by the look of things, have to go it alone.

I decided, therefore, to compose a piece especially for the occasion and, opening a notebook and untopping a pen, waited for the muse to strike. Time being at a premium, I was concentrating intently and not without desperation when Cearbhúil stood up.

'No doubt about it,' he said, 'they're definitely coming this way.'

He commenced gathering his belongings together in some haste, as did his lady friend. Very well then. I would face the challenge solo.

The necessity of carrying the evening on my own stimulated my endeavours. The sky was clear. The fire was bright. If I could seize the moment the symbolic resonances would be profound. This, people would say in years to come, is the spot. I, they would continue, was here. I began to have great plans. In this very place, I decided, I would start the MacFiach Summer School. Readings. Seminars. Doctoral theses from obscure midwestern universities analysed and dissected in the bars which would spring up around the event.

From this it was but a short leap to MacFiach night. Robert Burns was in great demand, while he lived, on Burns night, and the same would apply to MacFiach on MacFiach night, which would be held annually on December the twenty fifth; his birthday. I was thinking of the increased sales of my work generated by this event – with a spin-off industry in mugs and key rings – when I was rudely interrupted by Cearbhúil.

'Are you coming?' he screamed at me.

I most certainly was not. There was too much at stake. But at least he'd jolted me out of my reverie and back to the business at hand. I continued to trawl the subconscious depths of my teeming genius. What may have been seconds or millennia passed. Then! Hallelujah! The Muse! I pounced on the page, scribbling furiously and emitting sounds which seemed to well up from the pit of my stomach and demand to be heard. I had been consumed by a great vision which might have run to volume upon volume had I been granted the gift of solitude. Three words, however, were all I was allowed before Cearbhúil, that damned interfering busybody of a blind piper, shook me violently.

'Are you mad or what?' he yelled.

'Not yet,' I replied with venom, 'but when I am, you infuriating pedant, you'll be the first to suffer.'

Harsh words, but fully justified in the circumstances. The unthinking fool had killed a masterpiece at birth.

He and his fancy woman looked suitably startled, then fled like mice before the scythe when our prospective audience marched into view. I was destined to face them, on this historic occasion, alone. I stood to greet them, sans masterpiece, and heard one of them shout, as they were still some distance off, 'We'll have no dirty oul tinkers here.' It's *'thinker'* I sighed inwardly. *Th. Th.*

I was painfully aware, of course, that the word 'tinker' exists in its own right, meaning itinerant, gipsy or even, in certain dictionaries, tramp. This linguistic clarification took but seconds and was followed, crisply, by three concurrent thoughts:

That it might take longer to explain this to my approaching guests.
That the baying sounds and wielding of cudgels suggested a possible antipathy to intellectuals.
That three thoughts can coexist happily during moments of impending death.

With seconds to go I leaped on board Assumpta and she stumbled resolutely off into the surrounding darkness. As a final gesture I tossed my aborted masterpiece in their wake. It was, in its present form, of no further use to me.

XXVII

On the basis of this brief account of my trip I fully expect a commission for the obligatory travel book. The route from Dublin to the West may not have the romance of, say, Newtownmountkennedy to Cadiz, but unlike certain parties I have a fine eye for detail of place and, more than that, my relationship with Assumpta had developed, over the long days of my wanderings, into something uncommonly deep and spiritual.

My journal entries around this time display signs of maudlin sentimentality which have never, heaven forfend, seeped into my verse. I poured my heart out to that dear ass in a way that I have found possible with no other man, woman or beast of the field.

She was much more intellectually curious than Bridie, with an ability to walk past nuns without erupting which contrasted pleasingly with cousin Rosemary. No. Assumpta loved, honoured and, on a more regular basis than the modern female of the human species, obeyed. The ideal mate, in many ways – if only she could have typed.

And here I must stifle a sigh. For we arrived, eventually, at the broad Atlantical ocean. Opposite us, my new island home, where I might yet write my masterpiece. Behind us . . . what?

I began to see that the island represented the artistic impulse, while Assumpta, sadly, stood for domesticity, a nine-to-five job and constant worry about the price of oats and hay. And yet oh! the agony of loss. The people brushing past on the narrow quay. The captain barking orders. The moon lighting up the mournful expression on Assumpta's long face. True, she looked mournful even when dancing one of her periodic jigs, but behind the plaintive expression on this occasion was a new and unbearable grief, a black sadness at the heartbreaking inevitability of it all. The inexorability of fate. Her instinctive understanding that I was destined to follow my muse.

'Go,' she seemed to sob. 'Go. Leave. Get on that accursed boat. I . . . understand.'

The engine chugged into life. The captain barked a final command. I left Assumpta on the quayside and climbed aboard the boat that would take me out of her life, forever. Assumpta stood, silent and impassive, and watched me as I left, her languorous face and melting eyes cutting me to the quick. The boat chugged round the headland and out of sight but I kept watching as her feet, body, neck and finally her long and melancholy and still languorous face slowly disappeared until all that remained were the pointed tips of her majestic, ever-attentive ears.

> *Methought I heard her mournful bray*
> *But 'twas only the wind in the rigging.*
> — Old Song.

XXVIII

I recently offered my journals to the classics department at the University of Alabama in return for an honorary doctorate but was curtly informed that if I wanted an honorary doctorate I could pay the $100 administrative fee like everyone else. They offered a Doctorate of Divinity at a knockdown $50 'while stocks last', but not wishing to enter Northern Irish politics as a psychopathic Presbyterian I failed to see the point.

The journal is, therefore, still in my possession, and the section dealing with my island adventure affords a penetrating insight into the creative mind.

THE ISLAND JOURNAL OF FIACHRA MACFIACH

ONE
Arrived, at last, on island. Accommodation spartan – small attic room above MacAdoo's public house; rent in advance. By pressing ear to floor can experience speech rhythms of fine old Gaelic community. Decide to learn Gaelic. To immerse myself in the culture of my antecedents. Tonight, however, rest. Boat over a tug: squat; black.

TWO
Spent morning unpacking. Paper. Pen. *Complete Plunkett* (J 'M') Several anthologies (Verse). Spare scarf. Wad of notes.

THREE
Grappled with muse. Medium: verse. Subject: tug. First line:
   A squat, black tug ...
   Muse fled. Writer's block. Spent hours on line
   A squat tug, its colour black ...
   There was a tug, a squat, black tug ...
   Both lack resonance.

FOUR
Asked MacAdoo for name of good Gaelic teacher. Recommended himself. Demanded money. Gave him week in advance. Phrase learned today: Buíochas le Dia tá alán airgead agam: Thanks be to God I have a lot of money. Repeated phrase for MacAdoo. Doubled rent.

FIVE
Rejected
 A squat, black tug ...
 Line now reads
 O squat, black tug ...
 Other plans for day scuppered.

SIX
Spent morning with ear pressed to floor.
Experienced racing from Haydock Park.

SEVEN
Frustrating day leafing through *Collected Plunkett*
(J 'M'). Verses about tugs – nil. Later same p.m.
wandered abroad. Mud road led to other mud
road. Other mud road led to boat slip. Squat,
black tug bobbing on water. Looked distinctly
unpoetic.

EIGHT
Second lesson. Phrases learned: Bhfuel tabhair dom
é más ea: Well, give it to me so. First conversation
in Gaelic.
 Myself: Buíochas le Dia tá alán airgead agam.
 MacAdoo: Bhfuel tabhair dom é más ea.
 Excellent progress.

NINE
Ear to floor. Experienced old Audie Murphy western.
'Routine oater' – I. Times.
 Scoured anthologies. Favourite topics for verse:
spring; death; mothers. Least favourite: tugs.

TEN
Third lesson. Phrase learned: Go bhfóire Dia orainn,

táim skint. God's curse on it I have no money.
Repeated phrase for MacAdoo. Given notice to quit.

ELEVEN
Spent morning packing. Paper. Pen. *Complete
Plunkett* (J 'M'). Several anthologies (Verse). Spare
scarf. Loose change. Pressed ear to floor for last
time. Experienced early Norman Wisdom comedy.
'Strictly for the fans' – I. Times.

TWELVE
Met MacAdoo on tug. Going on extended holiday.
Unexpected windfall.

THIRTEEN
Back on mainland. Decide to abandon tug verse.

FOURTEEN
Inspired by muse.
    Medium: verse.
    Subject: mother dying in Spring.

FIFTEEN
Writer's block.

XXIX

I left Ireland an embittered exile. It was the done thing. No
further explanation should be required for this. Embittered
exile is, after all, an ennobling thing in itself. And yet there
were practical reasons for my decision. I entertained the not

unfanciful notion that Bridie might try to sue me for breach of promise. Besides, my parents' present circumstances ruled out a return to the landscape of my birth. Forced to quit the family farm by the perfidious machinations of the Brits, they had been thrown on the mercy of the state, not having any alternative accommodation or, for that matter, money.

The prospect of sharing a dormitory with them and who knows how many other ne'er-do-wells had a certain romantic appeal but I would hardly get much writing done.

A return to Dublin was also out of the question. Oh, I had no doubt that my relatives would be pleased to see me. The ties of family are hardly loosened by the passage of time. No, I had more professional reasons for my principled decision. I mentioned, some time back, my application for a fellowship at Dublin's Catholic university. Not having heard anything while on my travels, I resolved to revisit my old campus. They might have been desperate but unable to contact me, although I'm sure a brief television news-flash would hardly have upset the few remaining fans of Audie Murphy or, for that matter, the decadent aficionados of *Racing from Haydock Park*.

At any rate, I was working my way back to my alma mater with visions of a lifetime of wine and cheese when fate chose embittered exile over the soft option of academia. I was cutting a swath through the stones of Westmeath when three people ran from the ruins of an ancient castle, remonstrating wildly. As the first two got into their car the third party, a man in a suit, charged after them, frantically waving a newspaper.

'No, no. You're thinking of *Ideal for first-time buyers*. The ad distinctly says *Would suit DIY enthusiast.*'

He flung the paper to the ground in disgust and stormed off. A gust of wind ruffled the pages and, as luck would have it, one of them blew across my face as I marched resolutely along. The following headline hit me at eye-level: 'Nun Awarded Fellowship At Dublin's Catholic University.'

Now I am not a pedantic person. Far from it. I am also a feminist to my fingertips. But consider this; I had applied for a position as a fellow. Now a fellow, unless I am much mistaken, is a man. So 'pedantic'? I think not. And yet . . . this was a sign, surely. Get out, MacFiach. Now. Your work is elsewhere.

XXX

And so it was that some days later I found myself sharing the night boat with those poor unfortunates unable to make a living in their homeland. My journey, it need hardly be added, was geared to an altogether more glorious purpose.

And it is perhaps appropriate that I wrote the bulk of my masterpiece on that night boat to England. It was as if the physical break with my roots had unblocked my genius. I spent the entire journey writing furiously, oblivious to all around me. And, at the end of my epic voyage, there lay Ireland on paper.

I will deal with my working methods elsewhere. Suffice to say here that the first poem was out almost before we had lost sight of land.

'Lines for Seamus Heaney' operates on fourteen different symbolic levels, some of which I myself don't understand, although an American doctoral thesis will no doubt enlighten me, perhaps posthumously, to the awesome nature of my own profundity.

Why 'Lines for Seamus Heaney'? To be honest I pitied the man. I'm not sure a fishmonger lives on after the last person who's eaten his produce. My generous gesture will at least ensure him a footnote in history.

I reprint the work on the strict understanding that it acts merely as an appetiser to the full slim volume.

The gnarled tree explores
The muddy field,
Its lecherous roots probing
The wet, brown clay
Like the gnarled and crackling fingers
Of a tough, old, two-quid whore.

My father's gnarled spade
Impales the ground
With a soft, sensual, sucking sound.
His bent back,
Old and gnarled, shields the spade
Like cupped hands over a butt-lighting match.

A gnarled toad squats, croaks,
Leaps and lands
Beneath my father's downward thrust.
Spade and toad meet
Like the inevitable consequence of something almost tribal.

Frog lies squelched beneath blade.
My father pulls at the gnarled wood of the spade,
The ground sucks
And all is as before.

The gnarled tree.
The probing roots.
The clay-sucking spade.
And deep in the wet, brown clay
The once quick frog.

Still.

Silent.

And probably still gnarled.

XXXI

A lesser poet would have stopped there and disappeared to the night boat bar, but not MacFiach. I merely glanced around to check where I was before giving further vent to my art. I was seated in a passage on my gently swaying suitcase. Opposite me, on their own luggage, sat a catatonic couple, rheumy-eyed and wan. The energy had been sucked out of them by their horrendous offspring, an angelic little monster who forced them to attend to his every whim. I glowered at the brat as he smeared chocolate on his comatose mother. He burst, gratifyingly, into tears. I set about 'Further Lines for Seamus Heaney' and forgot all about the wailing minor in the joy of creation.

The verse in question obviously reads, now, as if it had always existed. But not so. It was wrested from the very depths of my soul and I was midway through the penultimate line when tragedy struck. My biro ran out. I was distraught. What to do? I looked wildly around. Most of the passengers were hidden behind piled-up crates of cheap Australian lager. The couple opposite were indulging in that curious half-sleep that always expects to be woken. Their charge had been bought off with a colouring book. He was working at the time on a circus scene, his child-sized face puckered up in concentration, a black crayon in his podgy little fist. I gathered up my belongings, double checked the aforementioned parents, grabbed the crayon with a lightning raid on his unsuspecting hand and was halfway to the door before the wailing resumed.

It was a wild night on deck but I managed to finish what was perhaps my most moving lyric to date. If the child responsible for supplying me with writing materials is reading this, may I just say 'Congratulations! You have not been born in vain.'

The lyric will become, I fancy, my most requested piece at readings. Four words in and the remainder will assuredly be drowned out by sustained, impromptu and heartfelt applause.

> *My mother's plump hand* . . . (SUSTAINED
>   APPLAUSE)

The written version will proceed as follows:

> *. . . grips the neck*
> *Of the plunger. Water*
> *Swirls and squelches*
> *Slops*
> *Plops and sluices.*
> *The plunger plummets,*
> *Hammers home with a plump slap*
> *And sucks itself stuck.*
>
> *My mother heaves.*
> *Strains.*
> *Throbs.*
> *The plunger taunts. Hard.*
> *Erect.*
> *Clamped.*
> *My mother, stung, grits her gums,*
> *Pulls*
> *And PLUCK! – the plunger unplumps with a*
>   *slurp and a suck.*
>
> *My mother, spent*
> *Sits, sighs and sleeps.*

I watch her wilt and sag,
Her bulges droop
And in her sleep

She softly

Plumps her blubber.

It will no doubt shock my many admirers to learn that this enduring opus was almost consigned to the depths of the Irish Sea. Fortunately, however, as a preparatory exercise I decided to map out a first draft on a separate sheet of paper. I naturally keep a copy of all drafts filed away for my official biographer's use. But, as I say, it was a wild night. No sooner had I written the title and jotted down a couple of disparate images than the sheet of paper was ripped from my hand by a gust of wind and flew overboard. The only other person on deck was a young man of impressionable age. By his size and general demeanour I took him to be an athletics student at a minor American campus.

'Quick,' I cried. 'Grab that!'

Inspired by my obvious passion he leaped across the handrail and disappeared heroically into the night and the pitiless sea.

The paper, I'm afraid, was lost forever.

I managed to forge an almost perfect facsimile for posterity but am bound to report that it lacks the fire of the original. Sadly, the loss of that historic document was far from the only negative aspect of this unfortunate incident. I used the word 'heroic' to describe the young man's exit. This was not strictly true. As he flew over the side he appeared to have second thoughts, not being fully aware of the importance of his gesture. At any rate he took a wild lunge at my windswept scarf, which unravelled from my neck at an alarming speed. He thus went, without nobility, to join the aforementioned document in its watery grave.

As far as the paper is concerned I accept a certain degree

of responsibility, but the impetuous young fool must shoulder full blame for the scarf.

On a happier note, my arrival at the facsimile's final full stop and the boat's arrival in port coincided to the second.

A thrilling end to an historic voyage.

XXXII

The trip to London was less stimulating. I was motioned over to a table by a customs officer having prepared, in advance, a witty riposte to his inevitable 'Have you anything to declare?' My bold reply would mark me out from my fellows as a first-rate mind. It would amount to a declaration of my genius and of nothing else. This witty riposte would be passed on by word of mouth, quoted in one of the more salubrious broadsheets and eventually traced back to its self-deprecating author. I cleared my throat in readiness. The customs officer eyed me balefully as I emitted a hearty chuckle.

'Would you mind opening your bag, sir?' he said.

I replied – I can't recall the exact words – that I wouldn't mind in the least, officer. An appropriate answer, certainly, but hardly the stuff of legend. His fault, I feel, for denying me the appropriate feed line.

The train journey augured well. I had the good fortune of sharing a carriage with an American couple. I had always thought of Americans as happy-go-lucky, fun-loving and outgoing, but this couple were glum in the extreme. Catatonically glum. As the train sat idling in the station, I began to look on their countryfolk in a new and more favourable light. A few more like these and I'd consider living there myself.

The peace was shattered, however, by the arrival of the

chocolate-covered couple, their offspring still in tow. No sooner did he set eyes on me than he began howling in a most offensive manner. I tried losing myself in my work but it proved impossible. The child wailed on and on, and appeared to do so without pausing for breath, much like a human bagpipe.

Such are the times we live in, I'm afraid, that I was powerless to respond, experience having set a pretty bitter precedent. I was, on that occasion, approached by a woman in a supermarket who screamed as follows: 'I cannot abide people who smack their children.'

'How dare you, madam,' I replied, 'they're not my children.' But the response from security guards, management and a local mothers' vigilante group formed in the wake of the court case, meant that I have since treated children, and small people generally, with delicacy.

Which brings me, regrettably, back to the endless wailing.

'Now, now, Justin,' said the father, 'that's the gentleman's crayon.'

I mean, Good God! You don't reason with a three-year-old!

Fortunately they got off at Wolverhampton and apologised with an ease born of obvious practice. I waved them away magnanimously, but the little blighter tried to jump from his mother's arms and claw at the window as they passed outside. The damage, however, had already been done. He had succeeded in totally shattering my concentration, and moments later I tossed his damned crayon in the bin, contenting myself for the remainder of the journey with adding to the prevailing mood of towering gloom.

I should have kept it, of course. It did, after all, write a masterpiece, but my letter to British Rail to this effect some weeks later received the following reply:

Dear Mr MacFiach,
We regret the loss of your half-used child's black crayon on the Holyhead–London service last month. Not having a

*precise day of travel we double checked every train used on
that particular route to no avail. Cleaning staff are trained,
naturally, to spot items of cultural importance in the waste
bins and you may be assured that a few heads have rolled
over this incident.*

Good thing too.

To return to the journey, we arrived at London Euston
without further incident. As we got off, however, the male
half of the American couple broke what I had taken to be a
vow of silence.

'For the last time, Martha,' he growled, 'I thought he was
with *you*.'

Observing my look of distaste – I was with neither of them
– the gentleman saw fit to explain.

'Pardon me, sir,' he said. 'It's our kid. He's gone AWOL
and, boy, are we mad.'

A brief description of the 'kid' in question showed him to
be none other than the scarf-snatcher of ill repute. The totally
unnecessary loss of said scarf had begun to fester by this stage
and I treated his ex-parents to a terse, if minutely detailed,
synopsis of the events leading up to its loss.

By the time I had finished I was seething with anger. I
demanded – and got – monetary compensation. A spare scarf,
admittedly, but it could so easily have been otherwise. They
both wept for the wrong they had done me and I left them
with the pointed observation that if people only considered
the problems of others it might help to put their own in
perspective.

XXXIII

My time in London flew by. I was staying with my brother Francis and his estimable wife Philomena when one day he came into my study and coughed politely. Some two hours later I finished what I was doing and gave him my undivided attention.

'Fiachra,' he said, 'your original plan, I believe, was to stay for a couple of weeks.'

'That,' I replied, 'is substantially correct.'

'Well, that was three years ago.'

I have to say I was flabbergasted. Three years? Why it seemed like only, well, a couple of weeks. I thanked him for keeping me up to date on these matters and suggested that Philomena might like to bring me a cup of tea when she had a moment. I then returned to my work.

Not for the first time I was distracted by loud noises outside.

'He'll have to go,' shouted Philomena at the top of her voice. A good woman in her way but one of the Birkenhead Begleys: in that particular locality voice projection is a necessary tool of survival. But this 'He'll have to go' business. She often said it, always at the top of her voice, and I could never quite figure it out. Apart from myself, Francis, herself and her first child – whose name escapes me – there was no one else there. Curious.

Philomena might often appear to the outsider to be coarse and aggressive but she understood the importance of art. No sooner had I arrived than I gave her the first draft of 'Lines for Seamus Heaney' as a belated wedding present. Yes! The original copy! Admittedly it looked like a verbal bomb site, but I'll bet the Bible looked pretty ropey before it was typed up. So this historic document was intended as a very special offering indeed. That she was aware of the fact was plain from the disbelieving drop of her generous Liverpudlian jaw.

Imagine my horror then when she failed to have it framed, as I humbly suggested, and put in the place of honour over her mantelpiece; where the middle flying duck presently flew. Days passed. No sign. I eventually confronted her with my puzzlement. What was the problem? Where, in a word, was it?

My sister-in-law positively exploded.

'Where is it?' she cried. 'Where is it? It's in the British ruddy Museum is where. You don't expect us to keep a valuable manuscript like that on the premises! Think of the insurance!'

Her speech was peppered with colloquialisms but the gist is in the above. I stood corrected. I had grossly misjudged the woman.

XXXIV

Three years in London! Well, well, well. Time to find a publisher, and I posted some carefully selected samples of my work to Faber and Faber. What followed gave me an insight into the world of publishing which suggested that I might experience difficulties getting my genius recognised. Faber, it appeared, liked my work. Faber didn't.

I had entered the rarefied world of the book publisher, where pap is rewarded with a bloated advance while genius is left to fester with its mentally unstable sister-in-law, penurious. There was nothing for it. Necessity dictated that I approach an agent. Something about the term 'bloated advance' lost its negative implications when Philomena was in full flight.

Not being au fait with the breed known as agent I was unsure of the correct procedure in procuring their services, so I got hold of a book with the misleading title *The Compleat Letter Writer*. Compleat? It was nothing of the sort. The selection was arbitrary in the extreme. Example: 'A woman has given birth to fifteen children by artificial insemination and wishes to thank the rugby club which donated the sperm.' No less than three different approaches to the problem with a generous selection of rugby clubs to choose from.

Encouraged by this seeming inclusivity, I looked up the section 'Genius Wishing to Procure Services of Agent.' Nothing! I was, it would seem, on my own. I returned the book to the library with a curt note in luminous yellow on the frontispiece warning other readers of the yawning gap between title and reality, then got down to business.

I located an old typing manual, *Learn to Tope The Easy Wax,* whose pullout booklet, *Write and Get Laid for It,* gave me all the information I needed.

I chose an agent at random. My introductory letter described the agent class, approvingly, as the midwife of art. It mentioned that advances running into millions seemed to be the norm these days but that I, as a first-time poet, would be happy to settle for slightly less. I toyed with 'considerably less' but didn't want to come across as an easy touch.

Not receiving a reply by return of post I decided to drop by. Put the chap at his ease, so to speak. My bullish ambition has a habit of overwhelming people on paper, but meet me in the flesh and all melts into camaraderie and banter. And so it proved. I stated my business to a menial and, on being told that the agent was busy, stated with some emphasis that I too was busy but had allocated the next half hour for the business in hand. She bowed to my iron will and pressed the intercom.

'There's a Mr MacFiach to see you,' she said.

A pause. She pursed her face and stared sourly in my direction.

'I pointed that out to Mr MacFiach but he seems, well, quite insistent.'

Her employer, too, bowed and, much to her annoyance, I was ushered into his office. It was spacious. It was plush. I had chosen well. As he closed the door on his menial I got straight to the point.

'Well,' I said, 'what do you think?'

He backed away slightly, cowed, perhaps, by my penetrating gaze.

'What can I say?' he said, heading for the comfort zone of his chair.

I followed him over and sat on the desk.

'I have no idea.'

This, it need hardly be said, was an untruth. He could obviously have said that I had written a work of genius and that he had spent the morning alerting the publishing world to the brightest star in the artistic firmament. Modesty in the face of my gift is, however, one of my less attractive flaws. I held my peace.

He seemed agitated, and began surreptitiously fingering the contents of his waste bin. Without doubt a sick man, but that was his problem.

'MacFiach,' he mumbled. 'MacFiach.'

He seemed to be searching for the apposite phrase, so I leaned across the desk to spur him on.

'I presume,' I said, 'you saw what I was trying to do.'

'Trying?' he said, startled by my forthright manner. 'Trying? More than trying, MacFiach. You've succeeded triumphantly. Having said that . . .'

'You don't think it's too dense?'

He waved my question away. 'On the contrary.'

'What?' I said. 'Not dense enough?'

I knew damned well it was dense enough, but I was testing him. Why choose the wrong agent when I could have my pick?

'No, no,' he said, fearful of losing a prospective client of no small prestige. 'Spot on in the density department. Perfectly dense. Not to mention' – he seemed unnecessarily sycophantic at this point but I could take it – 'densely perfect.'

I sprang to my feet.

'I'm delighted to hear you say it. It's just that fourteen different symbolic levels can tend to overwhelm the first-time reader.'

'Fourteen?' he said. 'Twenty at least. Possibly more. Who can tell?'

I chortled wryly and made some witty comment about the artist not fully understanding his own work. He sighed dramatically and lamented the fact that he had a full roster at the moment, that he wished one of his clients would die and that his secretary would see me out. I chose to ignore this. I gave him the hard MacFiach stare. Almost a glare to some ways of thinking but a look that pierces, at any rate, soul to soul.

'And which,' I asked, 'was your favourite piece?'

He looked suitably alarmed at the magnitude of the question but gave an answer, after an interminable pause, which pleased me greatly.

'I can honestly say,' he said, 'that they all stand, at present, absolutely equal in my eye.'

I could work with this man.

'I am delighted by your answer,' I averred, thumping the table that now stood between us. 'But we must sacrifice one to the press. Strictly for publicity purposes. You know the sort of thing. One of those boxed items in the obscure hinterland of Saturday's *Irish Times*. A message to the reading public: "Le nouveau MacFiach est arrivé."' I paused. 'Which one?'

He leaned across the table.

'To be brutally honest, MacFiach,' he said, 'your work is so deep, so resonant, operating as it does on such a multiplicity of levels, that you cannot possibly expect to be published in your own lifetime.' He marched to the door. 'I am humbled by your genius.' He opened the door with a flourish. 'You write for future generations, MacFiach. Make no bones about that.'

For one in his exalted position to recognise the claims of posterity on my work is beyond high praise. I left his office in a state of euphoria, his parting words resounding in my joyful ears as I feigned nonchalance and strutted gaily to the exit.

'Come back in two hundred years, MacFiach,' he thundered. 'We'll clean up.'

XXXV

Armed with this positive response I set about my work with renewed vigour, uninterrupted by the mental instability of my now-pregnant sister-in-law. The pregnancy itself, however, was to have implications of profound consequence.

I had taken to walking the streets of London for the purpose of kick-starting my muse and had just sent an old gentleman sprawling on the footpath. London is a city of some twelve million people and it's nigh on impossible to avoid them all. He had the good grace to apologise for creasing my notebook and went on his way in a state of some confusion. On the ground where he had fallen, among the debris of this mighty city, lay one pair of dentures, a pacemaker and, more to the point, that day's edition of an English broadsheet open, fortuitously, at Other News.

'Heaney Helicopter Tour' it said.

It seemed that the once-bashful bard was to use the proceeds from his fish sales to fly around Britain reciting to the masses.

I closed my notebook and rushed home. It was time for MacFiach to take, as I believe the saying is, to the road. I couldn't afford a helicopter, of course. No fishmonger I. But my brother Francis had a car of some description and this would do to be going on with. As if reading my mind, he was about to unlock it when I arrived back at the house.

'Excellent fellow,' I said, climbing in the back to avoid conversation. But what was this? Ye Gods! Philomena was already in there, fondling her large stomach and moaning softly. A quick jaunt in the country was the last thing she needed and I made the point with some force.

'No, no, Fiachra,' said my brother, 'it's her time.'

'*Her* time,' I said. 'What about *my* time? Look.'

I pointed skywards. A helicopter hovered overhead as if to taunt me.

'That . . . impostor,' I said, 'has got a head start already.'

It was no use. Francis, normally the gentlest of men, ordered me to get out immediately. Acting, as I supposed, on orders from the ungentlest of women. So be it. I, Fiachra MacFiach, am an artist and above such trivia. I pointed out the folly of my emasculated brother's position. Then I vacated the car.

As it drove off I raced to the back of the house and yanked a rusty bike from the overgrown weed patch that passed for a garden. I leaped aboard and started careering down the street, the helicopter still hovering above me, taunting, taunting. I had gone perhaps a mile when I was struck by the sudden realisation that I had no money, no publicity, no venues, no dates – and my poems were back at the house. I also appeared to have a puncture, no lights, and the unsolicited attention of a passing police car. I dismounted and walked home, resolving to be better prepared next time. And wouldn't you know it? Francis, Philomena and the car were back before me. 'False alarm', apparently. I said nothing, but this '*her* time' codology was in danger of scuppering my career.

Without realising it I spent the following two hours scowling at Philomena as she watched her women's programmes.

Francis tried to lighten my dark mood by insisting that the helicopter circling overhead was merely monitoring traffic. I didn't believe him at first but then spent the rest of the evening and most of the night writhing in a state of steadily increasing outrage. Not only did the appalling Heaney have a thriving fishmongering business and a healthy income from the light verse circuit, he was also 'coining it' in his spare time with a job in traffic control.

Naturally enough I wrote to the same man suggesting that he was taking unfair advantage over earth-bound poets. I further suggested that he might care to support my cause with a direct debit. Not that as a genuine artist I was in any way interested in money, but Francis and Philomena seemed unhealthily obsessed with the stuff. Overdrafts. Mortgages. The price of prams. As a result I tried to steer clear of them as much as possible, but a private income would enable me to steer clear of them full stop.

Emboldened by my letter to Heaney I decided to solicit funds from other sources and had just made a list of possible benefactors when Francis approached me for a 'quiet word'. Money, with Philomena pregnant again, was a terrible problem, he explained. They might have to consider renting out the spare room. This was fine by me, I said, but I suggested that Francis have another look at the layout of the flat. As far as I knew there *was* no a spare room. I'd be more than happy, however, to help him look. Francis went away with a chastened look. Shortly afterwards, a loud wailing sound from the living room proved my point. They had obviously bought the property, mistakenly, as a three-bedroom flat.

What with all this talk about money and Philomena's increasing hysteria it became nigh on impossible to work. Things quietened down a little when Francis took a part-time night job to supplement his meagre clerical salary. But Philomena, at this juncture, was nine and a half months pregnant and almost intolerable to live with. On the slightest pretext she was off to the hospital and my witty remark that she must be having an affair with one of the orderlies was received in stony silence. An admission of guilt, perhaps? I resolved to breakfast on my own in future. I also resolved to keep my personal affairs to myself following a rather revealing incident at the same repast.

The post had just been delivered. Bills for Francis, a personal letter from Ireland for myself. Francis, who had earlier bridled at my suggestion that he should get more sleep, stuffed his letters irritably in the toast rack. He watched with apparent fascination as I opened mine. After staring at the missive for some moments, I gasped in disbelief.

'This,' I spluttered, 'is an outrage. This,' I continued, 'is outrageous.'

It is possible from the above outburst to gauge my feelings precisely. My normal fluency had given way to a faltering outburst of variations on a single phrase. My mind's eye swirled with exclamation marks.

'Listen to this!' I cried.

Philomena woke with a start and removed her face from the butter dish.

My dear Fiachra, I read, *how's she cutting?! Well, 'Where Thirty-two Counties Meet' really done the business all right! Plus! 'She Dreamed of the Bright Lights of Magherafelt' is hot off the presses! What a team! Go aisy with your cut! Any more ideas?! Yours Truly, Brendan!*

The imbecile Gilhooley was trying to implicate me in his appalling musak. This could destroy my reputation before I even had one. My position in history was in the balance. I grabbed hold of the enclosed cheque and tore it to pieces, a series of noughts across the front of it swimming before my eyes. Francis shook his head slowly and walked to the door. Philomena burst into tears and sank back into the butter dish.

Both had seen the integrity of the artist at work and responded as each saw fit.

XXXVI

That morning I fired off an irate letter to the dunderheaded warbler advising him as to what he could do with his 'Yours Truly'. It was, perhaps, not coincidental that this outburst of ire was followed by a period of total concentration on my work. I was masterful, filling page on page of my journal with taut and supple prose. That same evening I became pregnant with the muse. Rejoice!

The true artist is born in a state of married bliss. He, or, in a smattering of cases, she, could hold out an edition of his collected works and say 'I'd like to introduce you to my wife.' I tried it once with odd consequences, but the implication is clear: it is impossible to devote one's full attention to family life *and* art. Permit me to illustrate the point.

Francis was rounding off his working day with an evening shift at Ward's Irish House.

Fact.

Philomena was heavy with child.

Fact.

I was pregnant with the Muse.

Fact.

Francis was out. I was in. Philomena was about to give birth.

Fact. Fact. Fact.

You begin to see the broad picture. Because of my brother's inability to control his own affairs, I had been cast in the role of *in loco husbandis*. Philomena decided her time had come.

The normal rules of civility – not her strong suit in the best of circumstances – deserted her in their entirety at this juncture. She burst into my room.

'Get me,' she demanded, 'to the hospital. I'm dilating.'

In artistic terms so was I, but consideration for others is not Philomena's strong suit so I held my tongue.

'Can you drive?' she said.

I was about to explain my feelings about driving under the influence of genius but she cut across my opening word.

'Then call a taxi, please.'

This, at least, is the doctored-for-schools version. Her actual words were muscular and forthright but by this stage I'd had enough.

'The hospital,' I said, 'is within easy walking distance. It's a beautiful night. Let's go.'

And, grabbing hold of my notebook and a couple of spare pens, I marched on ahead.

Philomena followed. She had no choice, as I'm damned wilful when the mood takes me. And the mood was certainly taking me here. We hardly spoke en route. To be brutally frank I felt a bit hard done by. My mind was full of conflicting thoughts and images. My muse. The brusque response of Ward's Irish House to Francis' request for pre-natal paid leave. The fact that I was wrong about the proximity of the hospital. And the weather. It rained all the long, long way.

Now I am not, I think, a difficult man to deal with. My needs are simple, my expectations few. But I hope I am never forced to write another poem in a hospital. Medical staff, be they doctors, nurses or people with mops, seem congenitally incapable of remaining silent or standing still. Hither and thither they rush without any apparent thought for others. I was, as I say, heavily pregnant with the muse and, true, I gave birth to a masterpiece later that night. But I did so in spite of the most appalling intrusions.

My previous experiences of waiting rooms has taught me that they are nothing but breeding grounds for the worst type of bore, so I accepted the nurse's offer of accompanying Philomena to the birth room. She seemed unwilling to engage in banter – we hadn't spoken since leaving the house – and this suited my purposes admirably. I laid my journal and notebook down at the end of the bed and set to work with a will. I was making excellent progress when Philomena began uttering the most extraordinary noises and calling loudly for her mother, who was in Birkenhead at the time. I managed to ignore this for a good while, confining myself to the odd 'Shhh'.

Matters took a turn for the worse, however, when the nurse started to fuss about the room, talking to Philomena in a very loud voice, although Philomena by this time seemed in no fit state for conversation. Then the nurse, a large girl from Galway, turned her attention to me. It might be worth considering an epidural, she said. I must say I found this vying for custom distasteful in the extreme. Besides, I wasn't there to be tampered with so I politely, if a trifle frostily, declined.

Work, at this stage, was achieved under the most extreme duress. Philomena began to direct a stream of abuse at me that was totally uncalled for. She then broadcast a series of personal details for anyone who cared to listen. I was a pompous, insufferable, priggish bore. I was – I can hardly bear to write it down – a fifth-rate scribbler of verse with delusions of mediocrity. I had a mole on my left buttock.

I was absolutely furious.

'Now look here,' I said, intending to put her straight on the verse business, but at this point the nurse came back and cut across my speech.

'Ah sure they're all like that with the ould husband,' she said. 'It's a sure sign the babby's on its way.'

'Damn your impertinence, woman,' I replied testily, 'I am not her husband.'

This, for some reason, struck her as having humorous intent.

'That's a good one all right,' she chortled, her large Galwegian frame rippling with mirth.

As soon as she had left the room I gave Philomena a stern lecture on her obvious lack of training in literary criticism, but she started screaming that it was coming and I was reminded of what I was doing there in the first place.

I took my chair over to the corner of the room and was delighted to discover that she was right. Within minutes I had produced, without fuss or personal abuse directed at a single innocent third party, what may well stand as my finest achievement to date.

I am referring, of course, to 'Yet Further Lines for Seamus Heaney'. I went home shortly afterwards and slept for twelve full hours, exhausted by my miraculous fecundity.

The constable cocks his leg,
Heaves
And mounts his black, hard bike.
Curse-black, hob-nail hard,
Its saddle flat,
Sprung,
And tough as a bog-oak knot.

Generous trousers strain, compress,
Their vast blue acres
Cupping soft,
Pink, drooping mounds.
Blubber-soft. Piglet-pink. Plush.

Saddle sits coiled, poised, sprung.
Mounds descend, drooping, pliant, cupped.
Face hangs immobile.
Eyes like afterthoughts set deep in

Welts of skull-smothering
Flesh
And, rising from the welted mass,
The nose:
A granite-pocked hillock
With caves of wire-taut sproutings.

Something stirs. Below the nose,
Sunk,
A mouth grins, sensual as slit pork.
The bike moves off.
Curse-black.
Hobnail-hard.

And not a saddle in sight.

I reprint it here in full, safe in the knowledge that readers not yet in possession of *Deep Probings* will want to read it twice.

XXXVII

Philomena, I'm afraid, became impossible to live with on her return from the hospital. Not a day passed but she ordered me out of the house on some pretext or other, usually a product of her fevered female imagination. To my eternal credit I never burdened Francis with any of this, even after the unfortunate incident with the pram.

The fact that I bear Philomena no malice concerning this occasion surprises me to this day. Most men, I think, would have cried 'Enough's enough!', but I am long-suffering to a fault. I was also motivated by loyalty to my sibling, who would have been devastated had he arrived home to a curt note in place of his youngest living brother.

The circumstances of the above debacle can be easily related. For whatever reason – maternal incompetence, perhaps? – Philomena's infant cried from one end of the night to the other. I contented myself, selflessly, with sound-proofing my head under the pillow. This, combined with large quantities of cocoa, usually induced sleep, without which I can be quite an irritable person. If, however, this method failed I would commence pounding the wall with my fists. I soon discovered, unfortunately, that this produced the oppo-site of the desired effect, so I made sure that Francis doubled the quantity of cocoa on his weekly shopping list.

During the day the child – a boy, I believe – would habitu-ally sleep off the exertions of the night, while Philomena was usually to be found slumped in front of some appalling televisual representation of life in Australia, often herself asleep. Such was precisely the situation as I was leaving, one afternoon, for the park. I liked to take pen, paper, journal, research notes, flask, light lunch and a spare scarf into the outside world as a break from my more intense poetic activity.

Unable to find an appropriate bag for my various posses-sions I was struck by the fact that the gap between the child's feet and the end of the pram afforded ample room. I resolved therefore to wheel the child into the park with me. I set off in the best of spirits and, in spite of upsetting some workmen who were laying cement along the footpath, and failing to notice an articulated lorry with potentially tragic consequences for my copious notes, we arrived in the park unscathed.

There, ensconced upon a bench, I passed a pleasant couple of hours – days? weeks? – in a state of absolute concentration, broken only by an aggressive-looking gentleman's best friend relieving itself against my left leg, and a group of youths wish-ing to retrieve their cricket ball from the pram.

Twice.

Other than that I could have been in Wordsworth Country, and I tripped home gaily at eventide, a more than happy man.

I had just arrived at the front door when I was met by an hysterical Philomena. Where, she wanted to know, was the baby? I snapped my fingers in irritation. I had often forgotten my flask, my lunch box, or sometimes both, but this time I was without flask, lunch box and my notes. And where were they? Why, in the pram, of course.

It might be argued that this was because the pram was not normally part of my entourage but Philomena, like many women in times of stress, was not capable of rational discussion. She cut right across my explanation in the rudest way possible and phoned the police.

All was well that ended well. My notes were safe. The child was reunited with its mother well before the park closed for the night. Philomena, as relieved as I was, had a final word with the officer at the door.

'I want this man out of my house,' she shrieked. 'Now.' With that she was gone. The officer tittered through his moustache.

'Tough time for the husband, sir. Young baby and all that.'

I failed to see what any of this had to do with Francis, but the simple soul obviously meant well so I concurred. He then insisted on showing me pictures of his own children and went on about them in the sentimental way that marks out people of low intelligence.

Nothing more was said about Philomena's appalling outburst when I went indoors, but a man has his pride and I seriously considered leaving for a full five minutes afterwards. My suitcase sat on top of a wardrobe and I must have stared at it for some time before transferring my attention to the wardrobe mirror instead.

What I saw before me was a man who had been moulded by the merciless anvil of life into a vessel of integrity, spirit and perfection. I squared up to this vision of myself without flinching, nor did my eyes look away but returned my own gaze with studied calm. I imagined myself as the hero of the more challenging class of romantic novel; my steely gaze, firm, jutting jaw and generous, furrowed brow were all attributes of the sort of man women find irresistible, and I resolved to accentuate this image with a pair of cavalry twill trousers and a cravat at the first available opportunity.

Women, or at least the ones I have in mind, are not fools, however, and behind the outward show a hint of gravitas is always welcome. I permitted myself a quiet chuckle. I would certainly not be found wanting in that department. My shock of neo-auburn hair was beguilingly flecked with grey. Behind the calm of my eyes lay the vast deeps of my soul with its dark, murky places, its pools of sunlight and, flashing hither and thither through its fathomless depths, endless varieties of interesting fish.

XXXVIII

I sat at my desk with some satisfaction shortly afterwards and tried to write a piece about the afternoon's perambulator incident from the pram's point of view. That I was unable to do so may have been because the event was too recent. More likely it was to do with my emotional involvement. I put it to one side, but without any sense of failure on my part. Whatever my sister-in-law's tantrums might be, the graph of my professional life was on an upward curve and I followed madly in its wake.

My parents had been rehoused in an old persons' compound within walking distance of Heaney's fish shop. Thanks to a weekly contribution from their state pension, a limited edition of my slim volume *Deep Probings* had been published at my own expense. Like all great works of literature it began its passage through life alone and unlauded. Initially it was read only by the select few, but I had reason to believe that my profile was about to be raised, as witness the following sequence of events.

I am no businessman, but I know enough of the seedy game to understand that a shop will only supply where a demand exists. This, I believe, is known as supply and demand. Prunes, to take but one example. In countries where people don't eat them, shops don't stock them. The onus is then put on the prune farmers of that country to convince the populace that a packet of prunes forms the backbone of the modern shopping list.

As with prunes so, in a more highbrow way, with *Deep Probings*. The world, I reasoned, was in need of its multi-layered resonances. But it was not yet aware of the fact. With this in mind I resolved to visit a selection of bookshops in central London and begin to create exactly that demand.

The first bookshop I entered, as luck would have it, featured a popular book signing by 'one of Ireland's finest authors' (sic). I won't cheapen this memoir by mentioning the fellow's name, but the priest that every Irish household used to produce has been supplanted by the author of bad novels. And this smug young buck was their titular head.

The Bridges of Monaghan County, his latest exercise in word processing, was apparently the story of a passionate, if unconsummated, affair between a pig farmer from Clones and a cello-playing prodigy from Minsk. The 'brilliant spin' on the story was that the pig farmer was the woman, which allowed a certain Hollywood actress, once again, to extend her range of accents in a twelve million-dollar 'option'.

I passed the row of autograph-hunting sheep in outraged silence and made my way to one of the few assistants who wasn't drooling over my yarn-spinning compatriot.

'I wish,' I projected, 'to purchase a copy of *Deep Probings* by artist of the written word Fiachra MacFiach.'

My basso profundo request switched attention away from the preening cretin with the fawning queue.

'*Deep Probings*?' said the fresh-faced young ignoramus masquerading as a book monger. 'Would that be an engineering book?'

'It would not,' I ejaculated. 'It would be, and indeed is, a book of poetry. A poetry book. Filed, no doubt, under Irish but universal in its range and subject matter.'

He looked at me as if he was about to burst into a fit of wails, but that was hardly my fault. The use of the term engineering may have been an unintentional slight but a slight it was nonetheless. A woman of more mature years came over and sought to rectify matters.

'You'll find Irish poetry under H for Heaney,' she said, 'but I'm afraid we don't have any MacFiachs in stock at the moment.'

I expressed the hope that she would see to the matter at once, before turning on my heel and marching back to the exit. She accompanied me as I ran the gauntlet of Mr Pap for The Masses and his fans, held the door with commendable deference and, with a final 'Good day, Mr MacFiach', went back to join the appalling throng. I walked on, I freely admit, in a state of euphoria. If a lowly shop assistant knew me by name, I reasoned, could fame be far behind?

XXXIX

I don't believe in an external deity, choosing to see God in myself and the odd flower, but some days seem to take on a spiritual dimension as if fated to produce sweet epiphanies. This was obviously one such. No sooner had I left the immediate vicinity of the bookshop than I spotted my former pedagogue, Mr Scully, striding along on the opposite side of the road. I was naturally curious as to why this enemy of Empire was making his way through the heart of what remained of it. The most obvious reason suggested itself – he had forsaken the cane for the bomb – but my mind was soon put at rest. With a confidence born of previous visits he disappeared into a sado-masochistic emporium of the erotic arts.

What is it about the past that it colours what may well have been traumatic experiences in a rosy glow? The shop in question sparked the memory of my last day at school. Mr Scully had been in playful mood at the prospect of the long break and was sitting on his desk unravelling some underpant elastic, happy as a kitten with a ball of wool. Sun softened the floorboards and the mood was one of somnambulant ease.

'So tell me, lads,' he said, 'would I have a nickname now by any chance?'

Of course he had a nickname. His nickname was Mad Dog, a sobriquet inherited from his mother. He knew this. He exulted in it. The reason he feigned ignorance? He was simply after the following scenario:

'Your nickname is Mad Dog, sir.'

'Do you tell me so? Ah sure now isn't that a shocking thing entirely. I must be an awful man so.'

'Ah no, sir. Hard but fair.'

'Mad Dog is it? Well, boys oh boys oh boys oh boys oh boys. I must be a right terror and no mistake.'

'Ah no, sir . . .'

And so on until he was finally convinced of the fundamental soundness of his methods.

On this particular occasion the plan backfired. My fault, I'm afraid. The heat of the sun. The softness of the floor. A bluebottle attempting the impossible flight. And I, the sleepy poet, drowsing in the midst of all, my mind working, working, working. As a mental discipline I had set myself the task of naming all the world's great poets, grouping them in interesting ways to make the task more piquant. Poets whose first language was Ancient Greek, for instance. Poets whose middle name was Clarence. I had just reached American Female Poets Who Committed Suicide when I heard my name in the middle distance.

'Well, MacFiach. What's my nickname?'

The tone was not unkind. It was, as I say, the last day of term. A temporary ceasefire. For this reason, perhaps, I failed to jolt immediately from one world to the other. I vaguely remember deciding to answer the real world question swiftly and return without delay to the world of the limitless imagination.

'Your nickname,' I replied, 'is Sylvia.'

This, as I say, was my final day at school. I was due back the following year but such was the extent of my injuries that it was thought best to keep me on a life-support machine.

XL

I thought back to this earlier acquaintance and was just about to follow Mr Scully for a nostalgic reunion when I noticed that the premises immediately adjacent were home to London's most celebrated Irish restaurant, The Great Famine.

This in itself was of no great interest to me but I was immediately drawn to a sign on the wall which said *Nightly entertainment. Performers wanted.* Fate? Perhaps. I would normally have run several furlongs from this vision of false jollity, but I had several copies of *Deep Probings* secreted about my person, and the curious twists and turns of Mr Scully's life seemed to have led me to exactly that place at exactly that moment. My star appeared to be on the rise.

It must be said in retrospect that the setting was not, perhaps, best suited to the subtle arts. The proprietor, one of my many compatriots willing to usurp historical facts in the mad pursuit of lucre, had established that the world is full of people willing to pay West End prices for the privilege of eating boiled potatoes. I soon found myself in the artists' enclosure with a piano accordionist and a drag artiste referring to himself as the Bootleg Singing Nun. The clientele included a smattering of preeners from the entertainment world laconically sipping buttermilk.

Any nerves I may have had were banished by the not unpleasing thought that if the restaurant lived up to its title the same preeners would have been lying across the tables in agonies of malnutrition. Reality, however, soon intruded on this uplifting image. I was summoned to stimulate the jaded palates of the potato eaters. I climbed aboard the rickety stage with a sense of foreboding, justified as it turned out. My arrival coincided with the front table arguing over the bill.

'Desist!' I exclaimed. 'Let the artist speak.'

This was intended as a rallying cry. A summons to lay down their forks and feast, instead, on a plentiful harvest of words. But no. They decided to use what remained of the potato crop as a form of visual criticism. Soon the whole room was at it, gleefully pelting me with a vegetable I have never since liked.

The Bootleg Singing Nun, in a misguided show of solidarity, leapt up on the rickety stage, but this only added to my troubles. A voice began screaming that The Bootleg Singing Nun had ruined her life.

'You ****ing abused me, you ****,' it roared above the splat of potato against my person and the back wall and, before my brain had articulated a response I was grabbed by the arm and yanked offstage. It was none other than cousin Rosemary.

'Let's get out of here, lover,' she said. 'This is no place for the likes of us.'

In a state of shock outside the restaurant, I was removing yet another Kerr's Pink from my jacket when Mr Scully emerged from the shop next door. He passed with a look of intense pleasure on his pink and bulbous face. Not noticing us, he danced a jig down Old Compton Street, whacking his generous thigh with a bullwhip.

XLI

My position in London was becoming increasingly untenable.

Cousin Rosemary's desire to have a child by an intelligent man was all very well, but I drew the line at being that man myself.

She made it clear as she stomped me through the streets of central London, however, that she was accompanying me back to base. When she confided in me that she had begun writing poetry herself, I must admit to an involuntary inward chuckle. Many young girls dabble in verse before settling down and I made encouraging noises while steering well clear of offering to read the stuff. Lavender-scented pink notepaper does not a poet make and if I have a fault – and I readily admit I am not flawless – it is a complete inability to dissemble. I am nothing if not forthright. I would be forced to confront my cousin with the yawning chasm which separates high art from juvenile tosh. Fortunately I was able to shift the conversation, with utmost delicacy, to myself.

Philomena was in bed on our arrival and Francis was watching the television. An overly familiar face was about to sing the title track from his eponymous recording, *Yours Truly, Brendan Gilhooley.* Unable to avoid the musical introduction I was at least able to reach the off switch before he burst into song.

Rosemary then decided to celebrate our little family get-together by rifling the drinks cabinet. She opened a bottle of anise brought back from the continent by Philomena on a honeymoon trip some years previously. Excellent stuff. It loosened Francis up and he began talking wistfully of the lone fellow countrymen staring into their pints at Ward's Irish House without a care in the world. By the time the anise was finished he'd produced a bottle of port which Philomena had been saving up, he slurred, for just such an occasion.

A superb ten-year-old, it was actually seventeen at the time of drinking and we followed it up with a six-pack of Beamish purchased by my estimable sister-in-law against an impending visit by her mother, a sachet of add-water-to-taste lager which had been shoved through the door, and a home-delivery take-away from Francis' favourite Balti house near his pre-marital address in Luton.

Apparently I used the latter as an excuse to extemporise 'Where Seventeen Shires Meet', ostensibly the clod Gilhooley's latest single, and I was struggling over Ashby-de-la-Zouch when I fell into a deep sleep.

Some time later I awoke with a pounding but sober head. In full control, therefore, of my estimable faculties. Whatever lingering traces of insobriety remained with me were banished when I returned to my room. Venus entered; Bacchus fled. On the bed, a generous sliver of moon caressing her ever present boots, lay cousin Rosemary, her clothes folded neatly on the bed-post. Now I may have seen my mother naked early on in life but the brain is capable of blocking out traumatic events. And what of Widow Bernelle? Who knows? The lights were as good as out.

But here was cousin Rosemary and here was I and here, irrefutably, was the moon. It bathed the sensual scene in shades of muted white. The walls. The bed. The mirror. I caught my reflection and noted that the moon lent a pleasing aspect to my masculine features. The strong jut of my jaw. The proud brow. The gravitas. The depths of my soul. The fish.

Christ, I reflected, spent forty days in the desert; resisting temptation if we lend credence to the official version. The scene I have lovingly described lasted nothing like forty days, more like five minutes; and when I decided at last to look away from my beautifully lit reflection to my cousin, the muse, that fickle mistress, struck. My hand reached instinctively for notebook and pen. The result? Suggestive, perhaps, that my muse was insanely jealous of another woman.

> *The moon has been about a bit*
> *It's Aphrodite's sister*
> *A naked wench, by moonbeams lit,*
> *Could any man resist her?*

> *The wench has been about a bit*
> *The less said there the better*
> *She'll roast your manhood on her spit*
> *Consume you if you let her.*

> *The bed has been about a bit*
> *Its mattress old and fusty*
> *It's wide enough for two to fit –*
> *Beware! The springs are rusty.*

The finished text, magnificent yet artless though it seems, nonetheless gave me deep pause for thought. What, I found myself fretting, if the springs *were* rusty? I needn't, however, have worried. No sooner had I committed this bawdy, rollicking masterpiece to my journal than I noted, with a poet's keen eye, that the sun was shining and that Rosemary and her clothes had long since left the building.

XLII

I would have to watch my step there. Rosemary had passed the sixteen-year mark but she was still sexually ambitious. Philomena, too, was becoming increasingly problematic, and things came to a head when she 'completely forgot' – her words – to lay a place for me at the breakfast table. Now I like to think of myself as an easygoing sort. It takes a lot to ruffle me. But consider the feelings of a sensitive man at this slight, whether intentional or no. I permitted myself the luxury of a dramatic sigh. That was all. I then sat in Philomena's seat as if nothing had happened and forgave her in my heart.

And yet London, as I say, was becoming a burden. The artist needs space in which to function at his – or, yes, yes, yes, *her* – best. The arrival of my parents' weekly contribution at this juncture seemed almost symbolic in its timing. As previously mentioned, they were presently residing in an old persons' compound within Derry's historic walls. This seemed an ideal place to continue my life's work. Old people are notoriously quiet and, in the odd case where they overstep the mark are much more susceptible than the average person to threats of violence.

I had been visited by the idea of building a performance, based on my life and art, to be offered to some of the more select venues in the English-speaking world. The coup de theatre would be to use the services of an uilleann piper to accentuate the more melancholic segments. I would, I concluded, return to my native land and begin work immediately.

I outlined this plan to Francis and Philomena over breakfast. No sooner had I mentioned the words 'returning', 'native' and 'land' than Philomena's head shot out of the butter dish.

'I'll buy the ticket,' she enthused with such joy on her countenance that I felt I might have seriously misjudged the woman. And true to her word she did so that very morning. I had to question her economic sense in that a return ticket costs no more than a single, but she meant well and economics, to be fair, is not a strong point with most women.

XLIII

So it was that I found myself searching for my parents' home the following morning. As I have already mentioned, they lived in close proximity to Heaney's fish shop and, as I had a small matter to thrash out with the same gentleman, I decided to go there first. Given the degree of study that would surround my person in years to come I had decided that my collected letters would be of invaluable use to scholars of the future. I had begun keeping copies, but had failed to do so when writing to Heaney. I wished, accordingly, to make a copy of the original.

Imagine my horror, then, on discovering that the shop in question was under new management. Perhaps Heaney found the world of traffic control more to his taste. Who knows? But it certainly left me in a difficult spot. I waited patiently in the queue and outlined my position to the new proprietor. Mr Heaney, he informed me sadly, had recently passed away. Odd, I thought. It doesn't appear to have stopped him writing. I kept this observation to myself and merely commiserated in what must have been a trying time. The death of a fishmonger, I suppose, reminds all other fishmongers of their own mortality.

I then asked what had become of my letter. He professed ignorance of such a letter. I began to detect a shifty look about his eyes. Fishmongers, not unlike the rest of the capitalist breed, are fine-tuned to the possibility of making money. A letter from one great artist to another? I could see he was already ordering several tonnes of mullet on the expected proceeds. I put it to him with great respect that he could either give me the letter like a good man or I would be forced to circumnavigate the counter and prise the damned thing from his mercenary grasp.

By this stage a long queue had formed, most of them, it seemed, as ever, pretending to want fish. They could wait, I decided. What was more important; perch or posterity? My fine friend behind the counter persisted with his ludicrous denial so it was one step onto the hand-rail, another into the tray of monkfish and a quick slide, complete with tray, into the freezer.

'Serve away. Don't mind me,' I said as I began searching through the fish carcases, and examining minutely every inch of the back passage. Nothing. He was a wily operator, I had to allow him that. I climbed back over the counter as the police arrived and left under armed escort with only half a kilo of bream – on special offer – to show for my efforts.

When I explained my position at the station the officer on duty looked suitably perturbed. He said nothing, but his look suggested that stealing artists' letters was on the increase and that there was little he could do about it. I was moved to remark that if the local constabulary didn't spend so much time apprehending bombers, polishing their moustaches and indulging in tea breaks, they might begin to make inroads into this most heinous of felonies. The officer at the desk promised to bring the matter up at the highest level but was doubtful it would yield results. It's the culture that needs changing, he said, and that, he concluded, would take some time.

XLIV

I left the station shortly afterwards, followed a gaggle of ancients round the city walls for several hours and was in due course led, unwittingly, to my parents' block of flats. A dank hovel when set against the bright expanse of my childhood dwelling, but it seemed churlish, if not downright pointless, to complain. I bade them both a curt good morning, requested tea and victuals and immediately set to work. I had resolved to establish myself as the pre-eminent poetic genius of my age through the crucible of live performance. There wasn't a moment to lose.

My first task was to enlist the services of Blind Cearbhúil. He would make me look stunning by contrast. He was home, he was available and by the following afternoon he was parked in the middle of my parents' living room helping me make preparations for an evening of light and shade, of high art and low noise.

Now it may be supposed that an old people's flat would be an ideal place to hold a quiet, uninterrupted rehearsal. Not so. The next door neighbours were listening to the shipping forecast at an unacceptable volume, but that was soon remedied. No. The problem lay closer to home, and if I seem to dwell in detail on what followed it is merely to dissuade other artists from returning to their roots.

There were several problems from the start. The flat was small. I silenced Cearbhúil's first blasting forth on his instrument by requesting that he tune up somewhere else.

'I'm not tuning up,' he replied.

My father, to add to the inconvenience, shuffled about in his Wellington boots to no great purpose. Fadharta the

Simple placed a couple of stones in the corner of the room and sat glancing at me defiantly. Even my mother was intent on disruption. Her raison d'être had been superseded by the invention of the dishwasher, and this gave her a licence, in her own mind, to wander hither and thither, offering beverages at will. I was busy collating my notes when her head appeared round the door.

'Would yiz like a cup of tea, lads?'

I replied, civilly, that I didn't wish to be interrupted.

'Sorry, son,' she replied. 'Well?'

In order to get the woman out of the room I relented. Two cups of tea. Thank you. Bye now. Blind Cearbhúil sat impassive throughout. Like me, no doubt, wishing the woman would just go away. No such luck.

'What about Cearbhúil?' she said. 'Does he take sugar?'

Now why she was asking *me* I have no idea. I responded that I was an artist. How could she expect *me* to know these things?

'But son,' she whined, 'I can't go making a cup of tea if I don't have all the details. Be fair.'

I looked at her in disbelief.

'Well why not ask someone who does?' I said condescendingly. 'Try phoning his mother.'

'My mother,' said Cearbhúil, 'is dead.'

'Back to square one, son.'

'Well then,' I suggested testily, 'try his Auntie Eileen.'

'Do you have an Auntie Eileen, Cearbhúil?' chirruped my mother nervously.

I closed my notebook in disbelief.

'Of course he has an Auntie Eileen. Everyone the length and breadth of this tragic little country of ours has an Auntie Eileen. For God's sake, woman, even Auntie Eileens have an Auntie Eileen.'

'Fair enough,' trilled my mother. 'I'll give her a quick buzz so.'

I might have been forgiven for thinking that would be the end of the matter, but no; my father chose the exact moment of her departure to shuffle aimlessly in, his Wellington boots totally incongruous in this cramped urban setting. I was beginning to wish the Brits hadn't bothered burning the old homestead down, especially when my father sat down and proceeded to ogle the television. On it a man was playing a melodeon at full volume.

I sighed dramatically at this fresh interruption to my tight work schedule.

'What ails you, son?' said my father.

I decided to deal with my grievances point by point.

'Oh, Mr Uilleann Pipes here for starters,' I snorted. 'How many sugars in his tea has kept us going since we started rehearsing.'

'Sure that's easy enough,' said my father. 'Wouldn't his mammy know?'

'His mother is dead,' I said testily.

'Fair enough. His Auntie Eileen?'

At this point my mother returned.

'There's seventeen Auntie Eileens in the phone book,' she said.

'I only have the one,' said Cearbhúil miserably.

'Is it 47 Kensington Gardens?' said my mother.

'No.'

'12B Cyprus Road?'

'No, no.'

'76 . . .'

'It might be quicker, mother,' I suggested wearily,' if you asked Cearbhúil where his Auntie Eileen lives.'

'That's exactly what *I* was thinking,' said my father. I examined his large peasant face and doubted it, frankly.

'What?' said my mother. 'You mean ask him where she lives and then match the address with the one in the phone book?'

That, I sighed, was substantially my thesis. My mother was happy again.

'Your Auntie Eileen, Cearbhúil.'

'What about her?'

'Where does she live?'

'Tallahassee.'

My mother's brain was working on this when the parish priest dropped by. He greeted me like the Prodigal Son.

'We don't see you at mass on Sunday, my child,' he beamed. I bridled at this fresh interruption.

'I've lived several hundred miles away for a number of years,' I said pointedly. 'And besides, I'm a committed atheist to whom the idea of a personal God, a God of Wrath and Hell Fire, an All-Knowing God, a God of Rage, of Ire, a Great God Almighty who can't be bothered to engage in the simplest form of correspondence with a potential client, is the ultimate absurdity.'

He chortled with false bonhomie.

'Well the Lord save us all,' he said. 'I've heard some excuses in my time but that takes the proverbial biscuit.'

This sort of talk infuriates me and I was happy to abandon my work momentarily on a point of linguistic principle. The family bible stood nearby. I opened it at the relevant section and thrust it at him with mounting fury.

'There's your proverbs,' I said. 'Perhaps you'd be so good as to locate this oft mentioned biscuit.'

He laughed nervously. Fadharta moved his stones. Mother brightened up.

'Speaking of biscuits, Father,' she said, 'I'm just this minute wetting the tay. Will you have a cup in your hand?'

He closed the book with relief.

'I will so.'

'And do you take sugar, Father?'

'Two spoons, thank you kindly.'

'Fadharta,' said my mother, 'would you ever go to the kitchen like a good boy and bring in the sugar for Father.'

Thirty-six-year-old Fadharta, stupefied by the magnitude of the task, lumbered off excitedly to do her bidding. My mother returned her attention to the priest.

'I only wish,' she pouted, 'that everyone was as easy to deal with.' She dropped her voice conspiratorially. 'We're trying to find out how much sugar Cearbhúil here takes and I'm afraid all the people in the know seem to be gone to a better place one way or the other.'

'Don't talk to me,' said the parish priest. 'We had the same trouble with a one-legged man on the missions. In the end he got a glass of yak's milk and lumped it.'

'That's all very well, Father,' said my mother, 'but where do you suppose we'd get yak's milk at this time of night?'

I'd had enough. Cearbhúil's disability was going to prove impossible to work with. I gathered up my effects, slipped Fadharta's stones into my bag and made a discreet exit while no one was looking, so I don't know, to be honest, if Cearbhúil ever got his drink.

XLV

There are those who would insist that my decision to part company with Cearbhúil showed a lack of compassion on my part. I admit it. Guilty as charged. But I would respectfully suggest that compassion and art don't mix.

A fellow poet, for example, was castigated for the following: *An old lady is chased through a North London park by a rabid dog. She is impaled on the perimeter railings as she tries to escape. He fails to intervene.*

If he had, however, how could he possibly have written 'Lines Composed upon Watching An Old Lady Being Chased by a Rabid Dog And Impaled on the Railings of a North London Park?' A lacklustre composition, admittedly, but that is hardly the point.

Further example featuring second poet: *Said poet goes rock climbing with his mother. He is inspired by the muse as he guides her up the last few feet. He is thus presented with the stark choice of grabbing his notebook and biro, or maintaining his hold on the rope.*

He chose as I would have chosen. And I'm sure his mother would have supported his decision had she lived, in spite of the fact that the finished product was later consigned to the bin. He couldn't possibly have known that at the time.

At any rate, when I returned to London Philomena seemed genuinely stunned.

'You're back,' she cried as I handed her the invoice for the return ticket, her look of dismay no doubt occasioned by the fall-through of my tour. She seemed deeply depressed on my behalf. Perhaps as a result of this, herself and Francis came to the parting of the ways some hours later, which led to Francis leaving the marital home. I don't care to dwell on the following weeks. Suffice it to say they were distressing in the extreme.

Now I am the last person to pontificate, but people should think more carefully before getting married. Had Francis remained single his salary would have been more than adequate for both of us. But there it is. He married in haste; I repented at leisure.

His leaving, I'm sad to say, led to a downward spiral which would have broken a lesser man. With the poet's gift of compression, of boiling language down to its essence, the facts can be briefly stated. As soon as Francis had gone Philomena put the flat on the market. I put it to her that I had no wish to move but she was beyond reason at this stage. As a result of her selfish action my life's work was interrupted by an endless stream of estate agents, an odious breed, followed by an equally endless stream of young couples.

I kept my head down and concentrated on my work but Philomena had developed an infuriating habit of showing these wittering galloots round my room. To make matters worse, she seemed to be displaying all the signs of mounting hysteria.

'This is the master bedroom,' she'd say, 'and that fine-looking specimen with the long jaw is the master.'

Much laughter.

Or 'Here's Fiachra, the sitting tenant. He comes with the flat.'

Much laughter.

The endless stream eventually became a trickle and we were left with one couple who insisted on turning up with monotonous regularity and redesigning my room without any consultation on the matter.

When lost in the muse I can work in any environment, but I must say I baulked at their notion of painting the room laven-der and 'putting the cot by the window'. I said nothing but was determined my personal space was not going to be used for storage, new owners or no. I said nothing, but gave vent to my displeasure when asked 'And what exactly do you do, Fiachra?'

'Generally speaking,' I replied, 'I wait for people to leave.'

XLVI

Philomena's outward cheerfulness, as I say, didn't fool anyone. She was obviously heading for a nervous breakdown. I came to breakfast one morning to find her tut-tutting over a copy of the *Irish Post*. I ate for some time in silence but the tutting continued unabated. She then placed the paper with great deliberation on the table and left the room whistling.

I waited till she'd gone, then glanced at the object of her derision and for once, I have to say, it was justified. A book launch, the same morning, by that staple of the poetry lists, the puffed-up amateur. Venue? The Irish Club. *Irish Post*? Irish Club? I had left Ireland to get away from these people, yet here they were, following me over.

The guest list read like a roll call of our country's most mediocre scribes. No Yeats or Plunkett (J 'M') for obvious reasons. Worse. No MacFiach. I looked up as Philomena came back in.

'Well?' she said.

''Obviously a bureaucratic oversight,' I replied, placing the paper back on the table. 'But don't worry. MacFiach will be there.'

I wolfed down what remained of my breakfast, gathered together the tools of my trade and bade farewell to my sister-in-law who, true to her worsening condition, was caterwauling with strident gaiety in the kitchen and wrapping newspaper around plates. The actions of a sane woman? Let me put it this way: I was glad I was going out.

Sometimes, however, we merely swap one set of problems for another. I arrived at the scene of the book launch to be met by a young lady with a clipboard. A steady stream of versifiers filed past as she ticked their names off her list. A rather vacant lot in the main which, given the level of talent, was hardly surprising. Within minutes I stood facing the usherette.

'And you are?' she said.

I was already peeved by the oversight on the invitation front, but that she failed to recognise me was beyond endurance. Do they teach them nothing in school these days?

'Don't be ridiculous,' I said, prising the clipboard from her grasp and ticking a name at random.

Proceedings inside began happily enough. I attacked the buffet with vigour and sped the victuals on their way with several glasses of warm white wine. While doing so I gave my rivals the once-over. None, of course, withstood the intense scrutiny of my piercing intellect. Pygmies! Minnows! Nitwits! I was on the verge of declaiming this point with Ciceronian vim when a woman in a three-piece suit joined me by the wine. I noted with interest that she was cultivating the left side of a moustache. The inference was hard to miss.

'Hello, Miss Plunkett,' I said.

An apposite guess. She winked at me in a masculine sort of way.

'Hello yourself.'

I launched into a vigorous defence of her great uncle and remarked that I was planning a biography when my own genius was recognised. I then went on to give her a detailed account of my life-in-progress. This riveting discourse was interrupted, I'm sorry to say, by the efforts of an earnest-looking poseur of inflated reputation trying to convince the young woman on the door that he couldn't possibly be there already as here he was, arriving. This altercation was distasteful in the extreme and it is to the credit of the management that he was physically ejected.

It did, however, have the negative effect of interrupting my flow and Miss Plunkett took this as a cue to trumpet her own accomplishments. In retrospect it was just as well.

'Oh,' she said, rubbing quiche from her facial growth, 'I don't go in for this poetry lark at all myself. I'm here for the wine.'

I felt myself cooling towards the woman.

'And what exactly do you do?' I enquired.

'I'm a senior civil servant as it happens,' she replied.

She was about to regale me with the intimate details of her tedious profession but I was rescued from this depressing vista by the commencement of speeches from the stage. Reflecting on how far the Plunkett gene had plummeted, not to mention how low the civil service now set its sights, I bade her good day, purloined a couple of glasses of tepid Liebfraumilch and moved closer to the forthcoming action.

Proceedings were opened by an Australian 'poet' of generous girth who spoke, at interminable length, about himself. I switched off, to be frank. 'Australian' and 'poet' fit together, I mused, like 'German' and 'wine'. I returned to the Liebfraumilch table and, reflecting that 'Waltzing Matilda' had a lilting melody, began humming it involuntarily. I was shushed by several people in the immediate vicinity and have to admit I took their point. The tune is as bland as the lyric.

When I returned to my place at the front our Antipodean friend had been replaced by the guest speaker. And the guest speaker turned out to be none other than the model used by the late Seamus Heaney for his publicity shots. If he had been introduced as such then fair enough. But this appalling chancer was masquerading as the man himself. I downed both glasses in mounting fury.

'Heaney' (sic) was just getting into his stride when I interjected to startling effect.

'You, sir,' I announced, 'are an impostor. A charlatan. The worst sort of con man.'

The room fell silent, stunned by my powerful rhetoric. 'If we must have Heaney,' I continued, 'then let us have the real Heaney and not this sop to the marketplace; this glamorous front.'

'I *am* the real Heaney,' said 'Heaney'.

I was ready for this.

'Aha!' I said, suppressing an almost physical attack of glee. 'In that case you'll have the answer to the following three questions at your fingertips. What is the present price of prawns?' Silence. 'When is the high season for rock salmon?' Silence. 'How many whelks, on average, in a tub?' The embattled mountebank looked visibly shaken. 'See? Quod erat demonstrandum. I rest my case.'

Knowing that my point had been proven with force, I withdrew with dignity. I am not a vindictive man. 'Heaney' had been unmasked. He would have to face the consequences. My work was done. I felt the warm glow of admiration on my back as I marched past my pseudo peers and out into the early afternoon sun.

XLVII

I wandered around for a while before getting my bearings and eventually arrived home around teatime. I noticed a skip outside the flat and, perched on top of it, my suitcase. On closer examination it proved to have been packed. Curious, I thought, but it was that sort of day. I retrieved it, struggled over the key-hole for a time, and let myself in.

If the suitcase-on-the-skip incident was odd, then locating a cot in my newly painted bedroom was puzzling in the extreme, especially as it contained a sleeping child. I was baffled but determined; I wasn't sharing my room with anyone. But I decided to check the lie of the land first. No sense in getting upset without having the full facts at my disposal. I opened the door to the dining room and there sat the Lavenders, as I called them, enjoying their evening meal. They seemed somewhat surprised to see me, to be honest. Perhaps they thought book launches went on all night. I decided to put them at their ease.

'No tea for me, thanks,' I said. 'I'm up to here with quiche.'

I pulled a chair up and gave them a scene-by-scene account of the unfolding drama and my central role in it, guffawing loudly when I came to the bit about the fish.

'The thing is,' I roared, thumping the table with relish, 'I didn't know the answers myself. The fool could have lied.'

I then made a couple of disparaging comments about Liebfraumilch, excused myself and went for a long walk to relieve my aching head. When I returned, a 'Do Not Disturb' sign hung on the front door, the locks had been changed and my suitcase had been relocated, still neatly packed, to the top of the skip. As Rosemary, apparently, had left no forwarding address – an oversight which was typical of the woman – I was temporarily homeless.

XLVIII

I spent the evening contemplating what to do. I could hardly return to my parents' house at such short notice. Cearbhúil, no doubt, would still be sitting there waiting to start rehearsals. I was also unwilling to retrace my steps to Dublin. Cousin Rosemary would, I felt sure, arrange to be there coincidentally, and I had begun to have grave doubts about my ability not to father her child. Falling asleep had come to my rescue on one notable occasion, but Morpheus might not always be so obliging in his timing. Not surprisingly, the following extract from my journal, which I don't remember writing, gave me serious pause for thought on this subject.

I fell victim to the most appalling nightmare which I propose to outline in detail as an insight into the troubled psyche of the creative artist: I am offered a lecture tour of the American Midwest as a great Irish artist. The contract stipulates that I wear faded tweeds with leather arm patches and am constantly inebriated for purposes of authenticity. I honour the contract in letter and spirit, returning to civilisation some months later with no recollection whatsoever of my trip, such has my degree of intoxication been throughout. When I finally sober up I find myself in a strange bed. A well-built

woman with a purple rinse lies sleeping ominously beside
me. Her passport sits next to her tooth mug. I open it with
trembling hands. One of the Minnesota Mermans as was,
she is now Mrs Ethel MacFiach. I note a pile of Midwestern
press cuttings.

'Irish Poet Blazes Love Trail Across States.'
'Irish Poet Weds Hooker In Reno Parking Lot.'
'Irish Poet Romances Post Box.'

I conclude that my resistance to alcohol has its limits and
am about to panic when a brace of large pre-teens with crew-
cuts and close-knit eyes lumber in.

'Hi, Mom,' they say. 'Hi, Dad.'

DAD?!

I leap out of bed noting, too late, that I'm wearing only
my scarf.

A dream, assuredly, but a warning too. Poets in their cups
are noted for waking up with different people, many of them
women, and the higher the number the greater the possibility that one of them will be called Ethel, or, to return to my
original thesis, Rosemary.

For this reason a return trip to Dublin was out and I was
pondering my other options – there weren't any – when the
problem was solved on my behalf. I was ambling along a side
street in a dejected fashion when two men with stockinged
heads sprinted round the corner. They were about to dash
past when the one in front stopped suddenly.

'Jayzus! Fiachra!' he said. 'I haven't seen you in years. How
the hell are you?'

I replied that I was fine as far as it went and was about to
ask if he could put me up for a while, whoever he was. But no!
He started reminiscing about the old days and how they all
had great hopes for my future and wasn't it terrible what the
Brits did to the house, while his friend frisked about beside
him in an agitated manner.

'Well anyway,' he concluded, 'can't stand round here chatting all day. Things to do. Places to be.'

At that moment a police siren started up and with a final 'Here! Hold this!' he was off. As the police car turned the corner I found myself holding an old acquaintance's pistol, which guaranteed a roof over my head for some time to come.

XLIX

If I had known anything about the conditions of my tenancy I might have thought twice about accepting the weapon in the first place. I refused to 'grass', as they put it, on my 'mates', for the simple reason that I didn't know who they were. The chatty one did a good impression of my brother Ferdia, but men who wear stockings over their heads usually do so for purposes of anonymity and I felt I had to respect their right to privacy. My principled stand led to an eventful couple of days with several interrogating officers which brought me back, not without nostalgia, to my years with Mr Scully. I didn't even have to draw a map of Ireland for this lot. I still remember clearly the three concurrent thoughts that preceded my first blackout.

That the pleasure they took in their work was almost infectious.

That a state of temporary homelessness approaches the idyllic when measured against the alternative.

That the ability to think three different thoughts simultaneously is perhaps at its most acute when a heavily moustachioed detective is sitting on your face.

I spent a lengthy period on remand awaiting trial and propose to gloss over this period for the simple reason that I failed to get one iota of writing done. I was livid and have since tried to block the experience from my mind. I was forced to share my quarters, it pains me to report, with a common criminal. If we had both been writers we could no doubt have come to some arrangement, but I felt my cell mate had within him the capacity for physical unpleasantness and was best given as wide a berth as our cramped conditions could afford. I also felt, instinctively, that divulging my profession might not work to my advantage. I kept a wary eye on him most of the time and, after a few attempts to draw me out, he left me to my own devices.

I had some writing materials hidden away and once or twice attempted a quick verse when he dozed off; but, although I concealed the notebook within a pornographic magazine or, failing that, *Stevedore Quarterly* in case he woke up suddenly, the conditions were hardly ripe for creativity.

L

Intellectually, then, a barren time. *Stevedore Quarterly* is not without merit – it is, for instance, well bound, and a series of colour prints of naked women in building-site helmets suggest that rugged, outdoor work is not the male preserve of popular myth – but I pined for a different sort of stimulation. And this came, when it did, from an unlikely quarter. A group of Irish prisoners soon got wind of my presence and it transpired that I enjoyed something of a cult status with same. I found this immensely gratifying. I seemed to remember some of them from school, mainly friends of Ferdia, and they began to make quite a fuss over me.

There's nothing quite like a period of incarceration to make an otherwise below-average intellect yearn for culture, and it wasn't long before my presence acted as the catalyst for a Celtic studies group which soon attracted sufficient numbers to warrant official recognition and a cell of its own. The scope, initially, was broad in the extreme and took the form of a general discussion overlooked by a couple of burly, moustachioed warders, both of whom dropped out of active involvement within minutes and took to wandering about in the corridor engaging in mindless prattle.

After a couple of months, however, a curious change began to take place. I had been treated with deference so far, and it was now being suggested that I give a poetic master-class, concentrating on my own work, with which some of the more enlightened were no doubt already familiar. Naturally I was pleased to do so, and discovered, in this collection of social outcasts, a responsive audience which pounced with delight on my every metaphor.

This, then, became our regular diet. A brief discussion, followed by a recital, always given by myself. The odd interruption was quickly dealt with. On one occasion, as I was about to begin, my cell mate drifted in, intrigued perhaps by the sustained burst of applause which greeted my opening salvo. I was frozen to the spot. This was the last thing I wanted.

My restless audience, seeming to sense this, turned and stared at him in silence until, cowed into submission he wandered, head bowed, back whence he came. I then returned to my reading with renewed vigour, my sonorous voice and dramatic gestures provoking involuntary and sustained applause in the unlikeliest places as the warders, unable to deal with the spiritual intensity of the experience, remained outside debating the simplicities of their own small souls and world.

Great poetry reveals itself slowly and it's hardly surprising that the group was keen to hear my work at every available opportunity. Perhaps because prison life accentuates the patriarchal, they developed a particular fondness for the image of my father digging. So they put it to the warders that the physical presence of a small amount of wet, brown clay would immeasurably further appreciation of the poem. The warders chuckled and stood on the balls of their feet.

'You find it, Pat, you can have it.'

Find it, I have to say with undisguised admiration, my companions did. And, in addition, from I knew not where, a spade. The gnarled tree, it was pointed out, they could live without. So it was that 'Lines for Seamus Heaney' became the focal point of our by now thrice-weekly meetings, and each reference to wet, brown clay was met by vigorous and sustained applause of such duration that I felt that here, at last, I had found my audience. I was often prevailed upon to render the poem in question, to an increasingly rapturous response and, as if in physical reflection of the concerns of my art, the volume of wet, brown clay began to increase. One of the warders, at the end of a particular session, quipped merrily that you never find an Irishman far from his shovel, but the leader of our group snapped that this was a racist remark and the warder was forced to retract his comment.

I was naturally delighted at the response to my work but was moved to point out that we might have sufficient in the way of wet, brown clay to illustrate the poem's main image. It was, after all, becoming increasingly difficult to find space for seats. I was somewhat reassured by the explanation that the volume of clay reflected, in physical form, the growing understanding of the work in question. And the seats were shortly to become redundant anyway.

A most odd occurrence. I had begun yet another rendition of our favourite piece when I became aware that the applause, though genuine and prolonged as always, seemed more muted on this particular occasion. I read it three times that evening and each time the response was less and less voluminous.

'One more time, Fiachra,' said the group leader and, when I reached the line about clay it was greeted by a solitary clap. Perhaps, I felt, I had peaked with that particular work. I am always wary of overdoing things. Looking at my audience I noticed that the seats were bare. The wet, brown clay was piled neatly to one side. Between the first and second row, the group leader waved farewell and disappeared down a hole which, it transpired, they had been digging for some time.

LI

The governor at first tried to hold me responsible, but it soon became apparent that I was an artist of the highest integrity and that culpability lay with a hard core of troublemakers intent on disrupting the cultural betterment of others. The explanation for the hole was that it formed the entrance to a tunnel through which the Celtic studies group had vacated the premises. I begged leave to doubt that they would find an educational facility to match it on the outside and that the brighter ones would be back.

The warders seemed to have forgotten granting permission for the clay – I jogged their memories, naturally – and the governor asked me to accompany them down the tunnel in case I had anything else of value to contribute. What we discovered was a narrow gap, scarcely big enough to walk two abreast, which led to a taxi rank half a mile from the main gate. The tunnel was fully lit and tastefully decorated in beige wallpaper. It contained, at its centre, an extended section with multi-channel television set, mini-bar and a comfortable if slightly shop-soiled three-piece suite.

The warders seemed quite upset by the whole business and embarked on a damage limitation exercise for the benefit of the media, which piled in from the taxi rank end. There was, they said, at least no aspidistra. I was happy to enlighten them on this point. The aspidistra, I explained, is a symbol of domestic harmony for the English lower middle classes. The closest Irish equivalent would be a statue of the Blessed Virgin Mary, one of which sat here in pride of place on the mantelpiece, directly under the three flying popes.

The governor was genuinely grateful for my co-operation but felt that it would set a bad precedent if he rewarded me with a spell in solitary confinement. I was back where I started. Common incarceration. The daily grind. The mind-numbing passage of days. *Stevedore Quarterly*. The spring edition had just been published but this was of little interest to me. Nor for that matter was the summer one that followed, nor the autumn or winter. They merely marked the inexorable march of time, the relentless ticking of the clock which hastens us all to our end whether we be king or commoner, poet or peasant, or, for that matter, editor of *Stevedore Quarterly*.

LII

I was rescued from inertia, oddly enough, by a surprise visit from the Clooney twins, Joel and Ethan. While I was honing my art in obscurity they, it transpired, had been working their way up in the world of cinema. I wasn't really listening, my views on cinema being well documented, but they appeared to be meandering towards some sort of point. Their most recent film – *Nine Hundred and Eighty-Six Years A-Growing:*

The Life and Times of Methuselah – had been, apparently, a palpable hit.

But what, I asked, had that to do with me?

I freely admit I was delighted – but not surprised – by what they had to propose. They wished, said Ethan, to use my life, elaborated Joel, as the subject of a film, concluded his brother. The development of my genius would supply the narrative thrust. They had followed my progress with fascination and had been given background detail by a host of interviewees. My parents. Philomena. Mr Scully. Bridie's father. They had even traced Assumpta the Ass to a field in Athenry.

And yet I still remained to be convinced that they were in earnest.

I had been captured on film once before and it had been a salutary experience. My journal – *Volume XLIV* – records this episode with limpid, stylish prose.

Philomena is in many ways a fine woman and I am happy to put my dirty clothes at her disposal. My scarf, however, is sacrosanct. I took it to the local launderette this afternoon and, as always, brought pen and notebook with me. Although locked in concentration my creative juices failed to flow. I sat impassive, pen poised above paper, while my scarf struggled ineffectually with the tumble drier. (This image of my scarf as reluctant prisoner is typical of my attention to poetic detail.) I returned home some time later and was naturally startled to find the scene replayed on a popular television programme.

'Have you seen this man?' the presenter was asking and, yes, there I was, pen poised, face set in an attitude of supreme concentration. Behind me a man with a knife was relieving the launderette's proprietor of his takings in a most aggressive manner, but such was my attention to the absent muse that I noticed nothing. This, of course, was the

raison d'être of the piece: to alert artists to the need for total concentration.

I was about to mention this incident, and the fact that I came away without my scarf, when the twins broached it themselves. They had seen it. They felt exactly as I did. So strongly did they feel about it, indeed, that a re-enacted version, entitled *Writer's Block*, had been shot by themselves as a short feature and had been shown to great acclaim out of competition, out of festival, out of season, at Cannes.

I was impressed by their efforts so far and finally decided to give them full access to my notebooks when they showed me a transcript of the opening scene of their proposed script. It was me to the life. I transpose it with due humility.

EXT. DAY. FIELD AT BACK OF COW SHED.
FIACHRA AS BOY STANDS IN FIELD IN PAIR
OF WELLINGTON BOOTS. TWO BOYS CHECK
CAMERA ANGLES AND LIGHTING.
FIRST BOY Hold it right there, Fiachra . . .
SECOND BOY We're just off to save up . . .
FIRST BOY For a box camera.
TWO BOYS WALK OFF. FIACHRA HOLDS POSE.
TITLES
DARKNESS FALLS. FIACHRA STILL THERE.
FADE.

Stunningly cinematic, but I had one final question, simply to put my mind at rest. Was this to be another Irishman-wrongly-imprisoned blockbuster? Nothing of the sort, they responded. They were both convinced that I was guilty. Which brings me to another curious point about this decidedly odd pair. Their assumption that I had some involvement with proscribed organisations can hardly be said to enter the realm of the comic. And yet both parties were visited by uncontrollable fits of mirth on this and other occasions, usually when I was in full flow. Far from wishing to ridicule a man of my exalted stature, however, it transpired that they suffered from an incurable medical condition: gelastic seizures, or the inability to refrain from laughing.

This unfortunate affliction hindered the progress of our conversation somewhat, and I was moved to remark, with dry and pithy wit, that if the medical profession spent less time rushing round hospitals interfering with artists' creativity, and concentrated on their work, they could rid the world of such pernicious ills twice over. I was about to expand on my thesis but was drowned out by fits of weeping and thigh slapping which are, apparently, regular symptoms of this vexatious scourge.

On the other hand, knowing that my life was to be the subject of a serious reappraisal was a source of great comfort to me throughout the period of my imprisonment. My inability to write rankled, but I was visited on a weekly basis by the twins and was able, in the brief moments when their affliction abated, to unburden myself of some of my theories and clarify points in the journals. I also basked in their obvious admiration at my ability to affect the lives of all I touched, in the pursuit of one small but glowing masterpiece.

'A rose,' began Joel,

'On the dung-hill of life,' concluded his brother.

Beautifully put, I thought at the time, and ideal for the foreword of my forthcoming memoir. I resolved to write the phrase down as soon as I was free.

LIII

I was also to make another, more far-reaching resolution. On their final visit the brothers gave me a small book bearing the Faber and Faber imprint. My initial response was one of profound shock. It was none other than the maiden slim volume of cousin Rosemary: *The Seduction and Other Poems*. I couldn't believe it. As soon as her brothers had left I shot to the back cover.

> *'Reflects a poet's sensibility. Taut and honed to the whim of word and image'*
> – Seamus Heaney, *London Review of Books*

> *'Word and image juxtaposed in a taut, honed reflection of poetic sensibility'*
> – Seamus Heaney, *Times Literary Supplement*

I was stunned. Cousin Rosemary: a poet. But as to being taut and honed, I rather doubted it. Heaney, of course, could be relied upon in matters of fish as long as you double-checked your change, but poetry is a different matter. I opened the book.

To my Muse – F it said.

Good God, I thought. Who was F? I glanced quickly at the titles.

'Nun'

'The Great Famine'

'Joseph "Mary" Plunkett'

'Algebra'

A blank page, the last. I turned frantically to the title poem and reprint the piece here in full to save people the bother of buying the book.

THE SEDUCTION

I had it all. The soft white flesh
The curving inner thighs
The moon was on my side
The night
The element of surprise.
My living sculpture lay in wait
To trap his burning eyes.

I rearranged my subtle limbs
The bed and I both bare
I lay in wait and heard his foot
Upon a creaking stair
Then I lay here
In silence
And he stood
Silent
There.

He stood
Transfixed and rooted
for hours in a daze
Behind me
cold and silent
In moon-enchanted ways
The mirror on the wall returned
His passionate
Longing
Gaze.

Not without promise, undoubtedly, but hardly meriting the hyperbole on the back cover. It was ever thus; mere talent is rewarded with the baubles and trinkets of the market-place while genius – brain-disturbing, mould-breaking genius – languishes on remand. Besides, it was a wardrobe mirror.

And yet . . . And yet . . .

While it is certainly true that she was a mere girl, and the fawning reviews undoubtedly betray a patronising tone on closer inspection, she was not, as I say, without promise. Under my tutelage she might even amount to something, especially if she could be encouraged to avoid the gaudy circus of inflated, publicity-seeking egos parading themselves as poets in the modern world. It was certainly worth thinking about.

I looked again at the dedication.

To my Muse – F.

My God! I, Fiachra F. MacFiach. It was I!

I readily admit that this new perspective began to have a profound effect on me. Perhaps I'd been wrong. Perhaps it was possible to pursue a wild romance and still be a great poet. I thought of William Wordsworth and Dorothy. Of . . . well, that was enough to be going on with. I began to visualise the scene. Cousin Rosemary rapt with attention as I read from my journal, guiding her ineluctably in the direction of minor greatness. Long walks by the river. Passionate couplings enveloped in a double-length scarf. Rosemary waiting on tables to bring in the necessary finance to propagate my work, and happily typing up my manuscripts in the odd lull.

Being a woman she would probably want children. Fine.

'But don't,' I found myself admonishing, 'expect MacFiach to weigh in.'

An affectionate pat on the head once a fortnight? Why ever not? The day to day mundanities? Sorry but no. Busy busy busy. Writer at work.

This, of course, is to look on the positive side. What, then, of the negative aspect? What if, as so often happens when poets marry, she committed suicide? This was not, on mature reflection, an entirely negative prospect. It would boost sales of both our books and no doubt spur me on to a fine study of bereavement. No. My mind was made up. Rosemary was the woman for me. I would inform her of my plans in person at the next available opportunity.

LIV

And that happy occasion, I am pleased to report, was soon to arrive. After some two years in detention my case was heard and my defence was able to produce a witness who had seen the whole sorry business. The judge eyed her beadily as she took the stand.

'I demand to know this woman's sexual history,' he said.

'With all due respect, my Lord,' said my defence, 'the witness is not in the dock.'

'I'll be the judge of that,' said the judge. 'I am, after all, the judge. What were you wearing at the time?'

'I fail to see what this has to do with the proceedings against my client,' protested my defence.

'It may have nothing; it may have everything. Well?'

The judge was eventually prevailed upon to deal with my alleged crime but seemed baffled when my defence came to the fact that I may have known one of the men.

'He may have been my client's brother, your honour,' said my defence.

'May have been?' said the learned judge. 'Surely your client might be expected to recognise his own brother.'

'He has sixteen brothers, my Lord.'

'Ah.'

'Besides, the men in question were wearing stockings at the time.'

'Stockings? What? Women's stockings?' He brightened up and peered at me. 'Is there a history of this sort of activity in your family, young man?' I was about to demur when he looked at his notes. 'MacFiach,' he said. 'MacFiach. Sweet Alis MacFiach. Nothing to do with you, I suppose?'

'My paternal grand-uncle,' I replied.

He mellowed slowly and his grizzled face took on a softer, more boyish look. 'How terribly interesting,' he said. 'D'you know I never missed one of his performances when I was studying for the bar. The gay nineties we used to call them. And so they were. So,' he sighed, 'they were.' He sat up. 'What sort of stockings?'

'One was black silk, the other more flesh coloured. Most likely nylon. Fifteen denier I would think although I didn't get that close a look.'

He peered at me over his glasses.

'You seem to know a lot about such matters, young man,' he said.

'I am an artist, sir,' I replied. 'I make it my business to know.'

'You're a credit to your uncle,' he replied, beaming. 'Excellent,' he continued. 'So we've established that you were set upon by two one-legged transvestites, one of whom may have been your brother. That much is clear.'

The case dragged on for some weeks. The learned judge, in his summing up, said that too often women, by their code of dress and brazen conduct, by their misplaced desire for equality and the fact that the words 'ideal' and 'home' seldom feature together in the feminist lexicon – he paused here until his laughter had died down – were simply asking for it. And it appeared that this brazen use of a come-hither style of dress was spreading, disturbingly, to the criminal classes. Whatever our personal views on the matter, he concluded, the law was the law and must be seen to be applied in an even-handed way regardless of codes of dress. I was, in a word, given two years for receiving stolen property.

Two years. That meant that I had precisely twenty minutes left to serve. Just sufficient time to gather together my effects, while my cell mate of those wasted days swung his feet morosely on the top bunk. As I was leaving, he looked sheepishly at me and asked if it was true I was a poet. With a moustachioed guard at the door, and further protected by the fact that we would never meet again – I don't make a habit of consorting with criminals – I answered that yes, I was a poet, a great poet, and that I was proud to declare the fact before the whole world if necessary. He extended a large tattooed hand.

'I like poetry,' he said. 'It's been a privilege to know you.'

LV

Aware that my brother and sister-in-law had failed in their familial responsibilities, Joel and Ethan met me at the prison gate. They had arranged a place for me to stay and when I saw it I was, as I recall, deeply touched. A one-bedroom flat in one of London's less seedy districts, it had been decorated in my honour. Pictures of me lined the walls. Blown up reproductions of my verse resided in glass cases. In pride of place on the shoe rack sat a spawn-flecked pair of child's galoshes (circa 1970). A full-length mirror greeted me as I entered the bedroom, where my best striped pyjamas lay draped over a chair, and I admired, in passing, the mature artist I had become.

Other than that the rooms were reassuringly spartan. A cooker. A bed. Table and chairs. Several full-length mirrors scattered about the place. The one odd feature was that two people, a man and a boy, appeared to be in residence already. As we entered they were wandering about with pen and notebook in hand, extremely severe of countenance, both wearing a pair of Wellington boots. We were not introduced and I was so taken with the general decor that the moment passed.

Joel and Ethan gave me their telephone number and a set of keys and left. The two residents stayed where they were. As I say, the moment had passed so I decided it might be best to ignore them. Besides, I had been too long away from my art and so, not wishing to waste time in banter, I sat at the kitchen table with great anticipation and set to work.

At least I would have set to work, but I had the odd sensation that the above-mentioned were examining me closely. They procured chairs themselves and sat down at the same table. I stared at the blank page of my notebook and tried to concentrate but it was impossible. I looked up suddenly. They looked away. I was right. For reasons best known to themselves, I exerted an enigmatic hold over them. All very flattering, I felt, but what if it carried on indefinitely? I resolved to phone Joel and Ethan on the subject.

This, of course, was more difficult than simply picking up the phone and dialling a number. People, after all, are notorious for listening in on private conversations, especially when conducted in the same room. They would be bound to notice we were discussing them. So I would have to wait until I was on my own, but they seemed content to sit where I was sitting and do what I was doing.

I sat. I couldn't write. They sat. They couldn't write. The boy raised his pen and glared at me.

'This is my pen,' he said. 'I'll dig with it.'

The man did likewise.

'I am an artist,' he declaimed. 'I demand sustenance in return for which I will entertain you with verses to delight the mind.'

This went on for some time. Hours? Weeks? Eventually I decided to break the deadlock and go to bed. I went to the lavatory, brushed my teeth, entered the master bedroom, shut the door, disrobed, put my pyjamas on and got into bed.

I lay still.

The lavatory flushed twice in quick succession. I heard two sets of teeth being brushed.

A short silence.

Then the door opened and my persecutors got into bed on either side of me, both wearing identical striped pyjamas. Exactly the same as mine, in fact. I had never, to my almost certain knowledge, been in a similar situation and could find no precedent in any work of literature I had read, whatever the language of origin. It was difficult, therefore, to know how to respond. I decided, in the end, to get some sleep and attempt to resolve the matter on the morrow.

It was a comfortable bed after my prison experience but I slept badly in spite of this. I tossed, they turned, and vice versa. It was difficult developing any sort of coherent rhythm, especially after the elder of the two, his black, intense eyes piercing mine, murmured 'Your nickname is Sylvia.'

I was quite relieved when morning came and enabled me to put an end to the proceedings. I sat up. They took this as their cue to rise. I abluted. They abluted. We dressed. I held back slightly, allowing them to finish before me. I thought they might slow up themselves, but they seemed to know what they were doing without my help. They finished dressing, loaded two pans up with the makings of Ulster fries, took possession of their notebooks and pencils and, with looks of preoccupation on both their faces, left the flat. As they did so the boy returned my glower with a glower of his own.

I was astonished and liberated at once by their departure. As soon as they had closed the door, I phoned my cousins for an explanation.

'Didn't we tell you?' they said.

'That's Fiachra Junior,' said Joel, 'and Fiachra Senior,' said Ethan.

'They're,' said Joel, 'the male,' said Ethan, 'leads,' they concluded.

I slammed the phone down in outrage. I had just, against all the tenets of morality, integrity and plain common sense, slept with a couple of actors.

LVI

Perhaps, in the end, though, it would all be worth it. I was aware that cinema, although a minor art form, was capable of alerting the world to the presence of a greater one, and the twins had a duty to perform. But the impending film made concentration difficult. I began to look forward to its release and the resultant increase in sales of my work; the queues round the block at my book signings; the pleasure of seeking out anonymity rather than having it thrust upon me; the feeling that posterity was going to honour me while I was still young enough to enjoy it.

I had also chosen the premiere as the ideal backdrop for my forthcoming proposition to cousin Rosemary. The anticipation of her delight made the delay more than worthwhile.

I had one further reading before being summoned to the premiere and if I describe it in some detail I do so merely to illustrate the contrast with my prison experience, a golden age in comparison. Here are the bald facts. A folk music artist named 'Dillon' – no Christian name if you please – was performing a concert in an intimate setting in north London. My cousins had met the man before and had mentioned me to him in glowing terms. The consequence? I was cordially invited to expand my audience by giving one of my celebrated readings at this same concert. Disarmed, as I say, by the twins' humility, and lulled by the reference to my other celebrated readings, I submitted graciously to their request. Someone had to fill the blessed hall.

It was only afterwards that the implications of my promise filtered through. I made some inquiries into the Dillon character's work and realised that I was acquainted with his songs. They blared out so relentlessly from every underground station around London you'd be forgiven for thinking there was more than one of him. He was employed to sing them in an effort, I imagine, to make people walk faster, and the notion that he would fill a hall with people actually wanting to sit still was, frankly, ludicrous. It suggests an all too common case of arrogance outstripping talent.

On the other hand, if he was foolish enough to hire a hall without bothering to publicise the event, I might as well benefit. I decided, for that reason, to publicise it myself. A few sheets of A4 attached to trees in the local park would alert a wide cross-section of the local populace so I set about the task with relish. I agonised, naturally, over the detail. The performance was, after all, Dillon's idea. Perhaps I should reflect this in the billing. But 'Dillon'? I wrote it at the top of a sheet of paper, and quite honestly it didn't work.

Some people can get away with only one name. Christ, for instance. 'Do you believe that Christ died for your sins?' No need here for 'Which Christ did you have in mind?' Dillon, however, is less specific. 'I hear Dillon is performing unpublicised at a small venue in north London.' This is hardly likely to set the pulse racing. MacFiach, on the other hand, has a certain ring to it. 'Have you read the latest MacFiach?'

My decision was made.

MACFIACH
(ARTIST OF THE SPOKEN WORD)
plus support

I forgot to bring sellotape into the park, but the gods were smiling. Someone had recently put a pitiful lost-dog notice up in several places and had been more than generous with the Blutac. It was the work of minutes to remove these – the dog, I felt sure, must have had his reasons – and replace them with my own. And I'm delighted to report that they produced the desired effect. The venue in question was packed.

I made several fruitless attempts to speak with the Dillon character before curtain up but he was permanently surrounded by others. Creditors? I had no way of knowing but was willing to bet it was his first full house. I had no burning desire to speak to the man. I merely wished to establish which of us was to open the proceedings, but the first sour note of the evening was struck when I was called to start the show without any proper consultation. This insult was compounded by the fact that Dillon must have been a party to it. Arrogance stroke talent? Point proven, I fancy.

I don't wish to dwell on my performance. Suffice it to say that the audience comprised thousands of paying customers, and whatever else they were there for, cultural enlightenment was obviously not on the list. I have since established beyond reasonable doubt that people who drink strong ale out of plastic glasses are rarely in pursuit of intellectual stimulation. This particular mob also appeared to find, in the same glass, an acceptable substitute for the boiled potato. As the first wave flew past I made my excuses and left.

The rather pallid-looking 'main act' (sic) was waiting in the wings. He mumbled something incomprehensible which didn't augur well for his chances with the mob. And yet I felt a certain sympathy. If they treated a bona fide genius to a hail of plastic what would happen to a man awkwardly plying his trade with a child's guitar?

'I wouldn't bother if I were you,' I said in a kindly, avuncular sort of way. 'They're a pack of animals out there.'

He mumbled something else I failed to catch and marched off to meet his doom, blatantly ignoring my sound advice. I had seen old news-reel footage of young men going over the top in the Great War and had no desire to be reminded of it. I had done my best to alert him to his fate; he had failed to take my advice. So be it. The roar that greeted his arrival on stage was frightening in its intensity and was, without doubt, far worse than my reception. The crowd, I felt, was after blood.

I have not seen or heard of him since.

LVII

I was well on the way to recovery from the above, and was planning my forthcoming nuptials with cousin Rosemary, when I was contacted again by my cousins. An official invitation, if you please, to the charity premiere of *The Genius* – an apposite title – in their native city. Car to the airport, chartered flight to Dublin, open top bus, that sort of thing. And, though unostentatious to a fault, I decided there might be a poem in it. Besides, the prospect of waving to the masses from a great height seemed, as I caught sight of my profile in a nearby mirror, entirely appropriate.

The great day finally came and, feeling distinctly peckish as I awaited the arrival of my transport, I placed some victuals on the stove, double-checked my profile in the mirror and looked out the window. An enormous black car had pulled up outside and a man in a peaked cap was getting out. I made sure I had everything, donned my best scarf and . . . what a time for the Muse to strike!

At least, I thought it had struck. I dropped everything and grabbed a notebook. I was sitting at the table and was about to give birth when the doorbell rang. It rang again, more insistent this time. I tried to put it out of my mind but no! My concentration was shattered. The Muse had fled. And so, as I discovered minutes later, had the man with the cap.

Inconvenient, granted, but fired up by the anticipation of greatness, not to mention the business with Rosemary, I stuffed my pockets with copies of *Deep Probings*, left the blazing stove to its own devices, raced outside and hailed a cab.

'Heathrow,' I cried, elated. 'And there's a hefty tip in it if you break the law.'

I felt sublime. Fame awaited. Cousin Rosemary awaited. I caught my reflection in the rear-view mirror and saw that I had metamorphosed, almost without knowing it, into Yeats' 'smiling public man'. The cab driver launched into the obligatory monologue as he raced towards Heathrow, but I wasn't listening. I was undressing cousin Rosemary, *a living sculpture to trap my burning eyes*, and basking in the warm glow of a nation's applause.

We arrived at our destination with commendable speed and I thrust six copies of my book into the talkative chap's outstretched hand. Six copies at five ninety nine. That's nearly thirty-six pounds' worth for a thirty-pound fare. Lucky man.

LVIII

I waved away the change, left the good man to the traffic police and raced inside the terminal building, but as luck would have it the plane had already gone.

The boat. I had to get the boat.

I raced back outside and hailed a second cab. A different driver this time, so imagine my surprise then when he launched into a plodding yarn – hilarious to the teller – of an unfortunate rival's fare being paid in books. I nodded politely as the car drove sedately towards Euston, but my mind was elsewhere.

Rosemary, at this stage, was without hat, gloves and trench coat. The applause, deserving to the last ripple, had spread to the European mainland. We arrived at Euston Station with the driver still chortling away. A low fellow, I decided, happy to spend the entire journey mocking his peers. The fare came to twenty-nine pounds and ten pence. Five books. No tip.

I raced into the station and was soon on my way to glory. Not to mention Holyhead. By which point, as I discovered some days later, the victuals were overdone. As, indeed, was the flat.

LIX

Rosemary's waistcoat and blouse came off during the course of the train trip and, as the boat docked in Dublin, I removed her boots with a shoehorn while the known world saluted my genius.

I had to walk from the boat to the city centre, since the cover price of *Deep Probings* was in pounds sterling, not euros, and arrived at the premiere examining Rosemary's lovely feet for the first time, while the entire universe exploded with adulation.

As I approached the cinema, situated pleasingly close to the river on Dublin's fashionable north side, I was heartened to see a sizeable crowd of onlookers, gawping at proceedings behind metal barriers. Huge neon letters above the brightly lit entrance broadcast the title, *The Genius*. In smaller letters underneath was the legend: *A Man. His Mother. Two Donkeys.* Quintessential MacFiach.

I tried to force my way through the broad shoulders and jutting elbows of the common herd but was distracted from my task by the sight of expensive cars disgorging celebrities. Guitar twangers, tub thumpers, board strutters and the like. Preening across the scarlet carpet to the flash of a thousand cameras.

Also disgorged were members of my immediate circle.

My parents, bent with age. Flash.

A slack-jawed Fadharta. Flash.

My ill-fated brother Francis, displaying a nervous twitch and a slightly disconcerting high-pitched giggle.

My weeping uncle, his wife and her female lover.

The bland crooner Gilhooley surrounded by a gaggle of simpering spinsters.

McAdoo, Bridie, Doody.

My fourteen other brothers.

A radiant Mr Scully.

The model for Heaney's publicity shot.

Flash flash flash.

I prised my way through the teeming rabble.

'Stand aside!' I bellowed. 'Disperse! Make way for MacFiach!'

Finally, after much prising and not a little bellowing, I managed to reach the barrier.

I braced myself. All would change when I was spotted. The paparazzi would pounce. I would be welcomed into my kingdom. I almost wished I had arrived on Assumpta, but it was not to be. Assumpta, I noted, was already strolling casually up the red carpet, happily munching the Heaney impostor's tweed jacket and casting her soulful, melting eyes earthward in a becoming display of modesty.

At this moment the preening thespian who played Fiachra Senior in the film strutted past. He waved foppishly to the gullible masses, who roared their coarse, idolatrous approval. Arm in arm beside him was cousin Rosemary. Fully dressed. Glamourised.

Rotund!

Yes! The woman to whom I was about to plight my troth was positively *corpulent*. In most respects, I grant you, she was much the same as before, but her midriff, or stomach area, had grown out of all proportion to the rest of her. Typical of many Irish women, I reflected sadly, she had blossomed briefly; and, while a certain *Rubensesqueness* round the abdomen might have been deemed attractive in peasant cultures, it was not to MacFiach's taste.

Excellent, I thought. That should thankfully put an end to unwelcome and intrusive dreams of a libidinous nature, and leave me to concentrate on my one prodigious gift.

Spurred on by the intense passion of this sublime epiphany, I began to climb the barrier. Within seconds I reached the top as a bevy of burly security guards rushed forward and barked obscenities from the other side.

'Do you know who I am!!?' I cried.

They didn't.

I asked them again. And yet again. Not once, not twice, but thrice; and thrice I was denied. I pointed at the huge neon sign.

'I. AM. THE GENIUS.'

They lunged at the barrier, snarling.

'That's me there,' I yelled, balancing precariously and pointing at false god Fiachra Senior, swanning up the red carpet with my former Muse Rosemary on his arm, and nonchalantly signing *my* autograph!

The crowd roared afresh as yet another limousine slid to a halt and my younger self emerged. Violin case. Gaffer tape. Arm in arm with Widow Bernelle. I pointed at him with delight as I leapt, spring-heeled, from the top.

'And so,' I whooped triumphantly, 'is that.'

1   *Heaney, S* – Fishmonger.

BOOK TWO
Posterity Now

I

I was thirty-three years old and back in London. My master-piece, *Deep Probings*, had sold four copies. This had involved a certain amount of arm twisting with my parents and the old couple next door, but the fact remained: at the time of Christ's untimely death *his* masterpiece, the Bible, had shifted – in the parlance of the publishing industry – zero units. I, MacFiach, was already four up on the best-selling author the world has ever known.

And I was very much alive.

I leapt out of bed, and was pondering the implications of the above, when I was interrupted by a loud banging on the door. I ignored it, of course. I am an Artist, not a gateman. I opened my journal with a view to elaborating on the Christ/MacFiach statistic, but the banging continued unabated. I relented, unlocked the Chubbs and Yale of my latest abode, and opened up.

Before me stood an irate male; possibly Glaswegian. Why only possibly? I am well aware that many people, when they lose their temper, adopt the Glaswegian accent; but this particular specimen was always angry so it was difficult to tell.

'The phone,' he snarled, 'is ringing.'

So it was, and I admitted as much.

'It's directly outside your door,' he continued.

I complimented him on his powers of observation. He went on to suggest that I might like to answer it occasionally.

'But what,' I rejoined, 'if it's not for me?'

'There are eight bed-sits in this accursed building,' he

replied, 'and only one person', not his precise noun, 'never answers the blessed', not his precise adjective either, 'phone.'

I let him have it with both pupils.

'I am an Artist, not a messenger boy,' I said. 'If I ever decide to embark on the latter profession' – and here I drew myself up to my full height for dramatic effect – 'you'll be the first to see the bicycle.'

Chastened, he picked up the phone.

'Yes?' A pause. 'I don't recall anyone of that name here. What does he look like?' A second pause. 'Ah. Grey hair. Gaunt. Eyes like a demented fish?' He thrust the phone at my chest. 'It's for you.'

A woman claiming to be my mother asked me, in hurt tones, why I had failed to attend my father's funeral. The answer was classic in its simplicity. I didn't know he was dead. I told her as much in words of one syllable and there, you might be forgiven for thinking, the matter should have rested.

'I told you last week,' she whined. 'I phoned you up special.'

Ignoring the appalling grammar, I was forced to gainsay her.

'You most certainly did not,' I countered. '*Phoned*, I grant you. *Told*, no no no.' She then insisted on quoting herself verbatim.

'It pains me, son,' she said, 'to have to bring you the sad news . . .'

Aha! A-*ha*! I cut the woman short.

'It pains me, son, to have to bring you the sad news of your father's debt. Unless I'm very much mistaken, Mother, those were your precise words.'

She agreed that this, indeed, was the case.

'Now forgive me if I appear pedantic,' I said, 'but debt and death are two distinct and separate concepts. *It pains me, Son, to have to bring you the sad news of your father's debt.* I naturally assumed you were on the make, which is why, Mother dearest, I hung up.'

She seemed reassured by this explanation and apologised for her less than perfect diction. Not wishing to indulge a lengthy outpouring of Catholic guilt – a greater source of pleasure to the giver than the receiver – I informed her that I had work to do and bade her good day. I quickly whipped out my notebook, located a blank page, and wrote across the top in firm, masculine capitals: LINES IN MEMORY OF MY FATHER

> *'But oh! Fleet time, thou subtle thief !*
> *How thou anaesthetiseth grief!'*

Wise words indeed from Anon, for no sooner had I committed the title to paper than all recollection of the deceased seemed to disappear, imperceptibly, from view. First to go were the boots. The old tweed suit. The gnarled hands and broad peasant face. Within moments all that remained was the thick fug from his ever-smouldering pipe. MacFiach, paterfamilias: embracing oblivion.

II

Now the death of a man's father is an excellent time to take stock. Unfortunately I had already taken stock twice the previous day. What to do? Take stock again as a mark of respect? Nonsense! There was work to be done. My stocktaking the previous day had suggested nothing less. It was as if the Gods of Poetry had said 'Arise, MacFiach. The time has come to find your place in the great scheme of things. PS Expect a call from your mother.'

The Immortals, I felt, were testing me. Nay, *teasing* me.

'Whither now, MacFiach? Your move.'

Good question. I mulled it over, and my mulling led to the following thought: it ill behoves a poet of genius to ignore his duty to the coming times. A smattering of slim volumes forms the bedrock of his reputation, granted. But what about the all-important 'version'? That masterpiece of Greek tragedy, for instance, relocated to Magherafelt?

My Irish *Oedipus*, however, had been doomed from the start. Irish men never sleep with their mothers. Marry, yes, in certain rural communities; but this is purely to quell malicious gossip. So. No version. But the ineluctable fact remained. The Immortals had thrown down the gauntlet. And I, MacFiach, had wittingly picked it up.

Such concentrated mental exertion, however, had taken its toll, and I sank back on my seat, exhausted. A quick glance at my journal – *Vol. LXIV* – revealed that I hadn't eaten for three days. I decided to rectify matters at once, but the rickety old cooker had other ideas and refused to ignite on demand. I gave it a damned good kicking, tweaked the offending knob till it snapped, and strode off in search of matches.

III

In Victorian times, of course, it would have been possible to apprehend a match girl under the nearest gas lamp and have the job done in minutes. Whatever about the merits or demerits of child labour – and it certainly gave those malnourished waifs a powerful incentive to better themselves – at least you knew where you stood on the match front.

I, sadly, was thrown on the mercy of the corner shop; the octogenarian sales assistant; the obligatory small child at the head of the queue; the ordering of a quarter pound of boiled sweets from the top shelf; the location, positioning and ascent of the stepladder; the boiled sweets brought perilously down; measured out; brought, equally perilously, back up; the procedure with the stepladder in reverse; the prising of the sweaty coins from the grubby little fist.

A lethal mix, the above, which brought me back to a sentimentalised view of the past – those blue remembered sweets – for what may have been several hours.

I awoke from this reverie to find myself being prodded in the kidneys by a withered crone who hadn't, as she informed me testily, got all day. An astute prognosis by the look of it. But neither, for that matter, had I. The prods, however, had been executed with malice aforethought and demanded, I felt, redress. An accidental jerk of the elbow would certainly have done the trick, and I was about to trace the curve for maximum impact, when I had a better idea.

I turned to the sales assistant.

'A box of your best budget matches,' I said. She placed a box on the counter. A price was agreed. I fingered the coins seductively. 'And while you're at it,' I continued, 'a quarter pound of your finest peppermint balls.' I smiled angelically at the crone. 'I don't know what it is, but I'm a terrible man for the sweeties.'

I fingered the matches with mounting pleasure as the ladder reappeared and was placed against the cliff face of jars. The assistant began her rickety re-ascent and had just passed base camp when a darkness came upon the land and an eerie silence prevailed. Not unlike the split-second silence before a mighty explosion.

And so it came to pass.

The silence lasted just such a second – split – whereupon it was followed by just such an explosion – mighty. The sweet jars rattled. As did the crone. I gave the shop assistant my best sympathetic look as she prised herself off the floor.

'Forget about the balls,' I said. 'And as for these' – I tossed

the matches on the counter and pocketed my loose change –
'I rather fancy the moment, dear lady, has passed.'

IV

Curious. Had I purchased the matches, I would have been
infuriated beyond belief by the stove's perceived revenge for
my earlier displeasure. As it was I surveyed the rubble that
had once been my living quarters without rancour. I say *my*
living quarters. The damage had been more widespread than
that, and small groups of the newly homeless huddled on the
pavement in various stages of preparedness for their new, and
possibly more modest, futures. But such is the world we live
in, and the homeless, I fancy, will always be with us.

Among their number stood the postman. Excellent. The
modest weekly postal order from my parents was overdue
and had been troubling me somewhat since the phone call. I
was well aware of my mother's peasant cunning. What if she
had used the excuse of her recent bereavement to halve my
allowance? I probably had no recourse to law as it was, strictly
speaking, a voluntary donation, but I would certainly lose no
time in asserting my moral rights if the woman in question
had succumbed to her baser instincts.

I put these thoughts to one side and approached the aforementioned postman.

'Anything,' I asked, 'for 13b?'

He clutched his bundle in a quasi-parental way.

'Sorry,' he said. 'It's door-to-door delivery. I mean, you
could be anyone.'

Fine. The door in question, I noted, had been blown free of
its moorings and rested, at a jaunty angle, in a nearby hedge. It

was the work of but a twinkling to remove it from the hedge, dust it down, and plonk it in front of the postman.

'Anything,' I repeated, 'for 13b?'

He rooted through his bundle and pushed a brace of missives, with ill grace, through the letterbox. I bade him hold the door for a moment, retrieved the missives and left him, and the door, to it.

V

Now I am happy to report that I count myself one of the more enlightened members of our sad species. Why? I incorporate the lessons of the past into plans for the future. This has served me well on the all too frequent occasions on which I have had to find alternative accommodation. The reasons have been multifarious. The list of disasters both natural and man-made would have broken a lesser man. Suffice to say that I await pestilence for a full house.

But such has been my level of adaptation to changed circumstances that I never venture abroad without

My journals
My notes
My work-in-progress
A few carefully secreted copies of *Deep Probings*
A liberal selection of pens
A large bottle of Stephen's best ink.

My point? Precisely this: my lodgings may have exploded, but I had what I needed for artistic sustenance. I was, in a word, a free spirit.

My possibly Glaswegian acquaintance, for his part, was buried up to his neck in rubble. I was about to suggest a career in existential drama when he cut across his own incomprehensible rant by questioning my legitimacy. I accepted the intended slur with equanimity. To be honest, I've often questioned it myself. I bade him a courteous farewell and made my way through the huddled masses to an as yet uncertain future.

VI

As I turned the actual, and possibly metaphorical, corner I passed a small girl cycling aimlessly round a street lamp. I couldn't help thinking that in another, and nominally less enlightened age, she would have been standing under the same lamp, consumptive but chirpy, dispensing matches to the local bourgeoisie. And that I, as a consequence, would by now have been happily eating lunch. An interesting thought. But her mother – it may have been her sister or granny; difficult to tell with the working classes these days – was watching from a nearby window, so I kept my own counsel and strode purposefully on.

To return to the missives. The more astute reader will have noted that I introduced their arrival in spare but elegant prose and then left them to their own devices. A well-known literary stratagem, this. There they rest in the crook of my hand and, simultaneously, in the reader's subconscious. So. I change the subject. The reader's conscious mind is momentarily diverted. Whereupon I whip them out – the missives, remember? – and all is revealed. The subconscious mind is satiated.

To return, therefore, to the letters. The first looked not unpromising on the outside. Handwritten address. Embossed envelope. Dublin postmark. And the contents? I could tell from the introductory greeting that it came, not from my mother, but from my estimable maternal uncle:

MacFiach, you blackguard!

A pithy opening gambit. I braced myself for a cold blast of his dry Dublin wit and was not disappointed.

MacFiach, I repeat, you blackguard!
I take it you remember Rosemary, my daughter and your cousin. You certainly ought to. I welcomed you into our house for matters algebraic. Tutorials, damnit! I don't recall advanced lechery being on the school syllabus. I mean God knows what went on inside those trousers of yours. AND YOU [his capitals] *AN HONOURED GUEST IN MY HOUSE!*
But enough. The Rosemary in question is to be married on the twelfth of this month at the Church of Our Lady of Perpetual Sorrow, London N. Fourteen hundred hours. Dress, formal. I mention the date, time and place for a specific reason. Because the very thought of you fills me with blind, bilious loathing, your absence from that place, on that date, at that time, would be excellent company. The alternative, I am more than happy to inform you, is certain death.

He signed himself off in typically waggish style with an extended improvisation on his blind, bilious loathing motif. That deadpan metropolitan humour wherein deep affection masquerades as unadulterated hate. I chuckled appreciatively and reflected, also appreciatively, that I had long since recovered from any foolish juvenile notions of the pleasures of the flesh. I then ceased chuckling and set out for the church in question.

The date, location and time could not have been more apposite: that very day; a five minute stroll away; and the time, as I tossed the crumpled letter at a passing road sweeper's brush, was precisely five to two.

VII

It may be worth mentioning at this point that I don't, as a general principle, endorse weddings. Noisy, vulgar occasions full, for the most part, of sexually repressed, sherry-fuelled maiden aunts. And yet my uncle had seemed pretty insistent in his pseudo-deprecating way. Besides, I was beginning to feel the effects of my enforced fast. I needed sustenance. I was wrestling with this particular dilemma – principle versus finger buffet – when I spotted the church. It nestled dolorously in its generous grounds, a sad-eyed Our Lady beckoning the faithful to misery.

No harm, I supposed, in taking a look. But all I could detect in the dark, forbidding interior was a smattering of professional geriatrics whispering to themselves in the pews.

'*Terrible sad.*'

'*Shockin' thing entirely.*'

'*Tragic waste.*'

Not exactly a ringing endorsement of matrimonial bliss, but they were certainly old enough to have given the matter their mature consideration. And this, I feel bound to report, unsettled me somewhat. I, MacFiach, appeared to be in broad agreement with the central thesis of a churchful of the post-senescent. The implications were unsettling to say the least. I sidled into a vacant pew and, in the absence of the soon to be unhappy couple, opened the second letter. *Stop press. Due to*

*tragic passing of groom, for wedding read funeral. Disinvitation
extended to same.*

I trembled with joy and relief. The pew huggers had been
referring, as I now realised, to matters funereal.

I, MacFiach, as always, was alone in my thinking.

Huzza!

VIII

With a spring in my step and a song in my heart I strode towards
the grave. Before me lay London in all its panoramic majesty.
A fine and fitting frame for a funeral. The funeral itself was in
full flow in the distance. Small black figures huddled together
in mourning. Priest. Coffin. Hole in ground. All the paraphernalia of grief. And, off to one side, a couple of gravediggers
swapping bons mots on their cigarette break.

In the midst of death, life. Spring had sprung. The sap was
rising. The first daffodil had opened its timid bud, luxuriating
in the warm caress of a benevolent April sun. Rejoicing in its
own uniqueness.

'Fair as a daffodil,' to paraphrase Wordsworth, 'when only
one is shining in the sky.'

I felt positively skittish. The caterers would no doubt have
had their instructions. *For wedding read funeral. Hold the
cake. Otherwise, as you were.* Excellent. As for the maiden
aunts, their rampant if repressed sexuality was likely to remain
dormant, in the early stages at least. Respect for the dead and
so on. As long as I was away by six I was probably safe there.

Such were my thoughts as I strode purposefully on, the first
daffodil of spring now basking, as I noted with some surprise,
in the dark shadow of my descending boot.

Squelch.

The yellow pulp attached itself to the treads of my sole with the consistency of dog excrement, and there it remained in spite of my best efforts to flick it off.

The funeral continued apace as I walked and flicked towards it, zigzagging through the snaggle-toothed gravestones of those long dead.

I negotiated the last headstone and positioned myself at the back of the crowd. Rosemary, I noted, took centre stage amongst the mourners, looking slimmer now and unbearably beautiful in grief. Or was it, rather, the devious wiles of woman? Difficult to say from this distance, but I, MacFiach, was inoculated now against her charms and turned my attention elsewhere as the pastor of ceremonies, so to speak, issued forth from the graveside.

'Indeed it is fair to say that our young friend, an actor at the height of his considerable powers, would still be alive today were it not for the contents' – and he whipped a sheet of white vellum from his cassock – 'of this letter.'

Curious. I recognised the vellum.

'"My dear fellow,' read the padre, 'you call yourself a thespian, and I own to having seen you in action."'

I also recognised the I. It was, well, *I*.

'"You once portrayed the present writer on celluloid,"' continued the priest, '"and I salute you on the accuracy of said portrayal. The overcoat, for example, was me to the life. Not your fault, I suppose, that the film was deemed to have comic intent. I followed your subsequent career with interest, and noted that you wisely chose a celebrated hunger striker as the next subject of your 'art'. Little chance of unintentional humour there.

'"As you purport to be a disciple of so-called method acting, however, I think you'll find the key to this particular character in his diet. Odd, then, that you have been spotted in the staff canteen partaking of its limited but generously subsidised menu between takes.

'"My point? Bacon butties and roly poly pudding – with or without custard – do not a hunger striker make."'

The corpulent cleric stopped reading and pointed at the open grave. 'The result of this epistle,' he concluded, 'you see before you.'

I braced myself for the inevitable critical pasting. I had written the letter in a furious single draft, and – my goodness! – it showed. Content, as it were, over style.

I was intrigued to note, however, that none of those who passed comment saw fit to remark on the uneven quality of the prose. No. Such reservations as they had, and there were several, rested solely on the letter's narrative thrust.

Whoever had penned it was a disgrace. A low cur. A murderer, if you please, as surely as if he had starved the victim himself. This collective outpouring of vitriol took some minutes before the mourners turned to the possible identity of the author.

'MacFiach,' slurred my lugubrious Dublin uncle. 'The pseudo bloody poet.'

The murmurs that followed this witty pronouncement proved the present writer to be the popular choice and I took enormous heart from this. Granted, the prosody wasn't up to my usual standard, but it was still recognisably the work of a genius. Perhaps I had been a tad harsh in my criticism. I lounged against one of the sturdier-looking gravestones and savoured the moment.

Or would, at least, have done so, but the prattling padre made the basic error of passing the letter on. Now I have no objection to this in theory. In many ways, in fact, I welcome it. It may, for instance, have given the more thoughtful among them a boastful tale for their grandchildren. 'I read one of his letters in the original, you know.' That sort of thing. But to pass a precious artefact around when its natural home is behind a glass case, or in a university vault, reflects a democratisation of the artistic process which makes a mockery of excellence and places a work of genius – I can think only of several examples of my own offhand – on a par with a child's drawing or the modern Irish novel.

Such were my thoughts as murmurs of discontent rumbled and spread.

'Disgraceful.'

'Ought to be strung up.'

'Did for Little Father as well, you know.'

Fortunately I stood at some remove from the proceedings, because the mood was in imminent danger of turning ugly. And the deceased's mother was not without culpability in this. Her attempt to act as judge, jury and executioner in the case of MacFiach versus the Deceased put me in mind of the Clonakilty Witch Trials of 1987. I was, it seems, to be tried, convicted and tossed in a microwave in absentia. And not one voice was raised in my defence. I was alone in this world. Alone and unloved. Alone, unloved and about to be crucified for my Art.

I felt fantastic.

The letter, meanwhile, wound its way back to the priest. The mob awaited further instructions. A vaguely familiar-looking man standing near Rosemary raised a hand for silence. As he did so a shaft of sunlight peeked from behind a cloud and bathed him in garish hues, from the top of his fools' gold head to the tip of his scarlet shoes.

The sun disappeared behind a cloud. The red-shoed man slipped back to rank anonymity. The priest coughed politely as a prelude to pontification.

'Let us pray,' he said.

I was stunned. The prospect of martyrdom was not something I relished, but the long-term benefits far outweighed any short-term physical discomfort; for what great Irish writer does not wish, with every fibre of his being, to be dead so that Posterity can scavenge his artistic corpse? But if I was upset by this last-minute reprieve, at least I kept it to myself. The deceased's mother had no such qualms about broadcasting her innermost feelings. A practice that owes not a little to the malevolent influence of our American brethren.

Now I am no expert in the psychological arts, but of all the methods of dealing with a hysteric in full flight, a sympathetic hearing is not even in the top five. The priest, however, thought otherwise. He appeased. He pampered. He reminded her, unctuously, that in the midst of death there is life.

'Look at it this way,' he soothed, waving a vague finger in the general direction of the middle distance, 'your son may be dead, but lo! The first daffodil of spring.'

A ripple of muted applause greeted this sentimental claptrap. At which point I could take it no longer.

'Not so,' I cried. A collective gasp. An almost choreographed turning of heads. I strode forward and, raising my boot triumphantly I pointed at the rotting yellow mush. 'I think you'll find that *this,*' I roared, 'is the first daffodil of spring.'

And I flicked it, with unerring accuracy, into the open grave.

IX

Rosemary's house, I am bound to report, was perfect for my artistic purposes. Admittedly it was full of funeral revellers on my arrival, but I put this down to morbid high spirits and thought no more about it. I resolved to inform Rosemary of my decision to move in at a later date, cleared a space for my journals on the victual-strewn table, and set to work.

I had just twiddled my quill in preparation and written the

personal pronoun as an aide-memoire, when I spotted the deceased's mother across a crowded room. I was pleasantly surprised by what I saw. I had been monitoring the festivities even as I wrote, with particular reference to the maiden aunt scenario. The representatives of this breed had, thanks to liberal doses of cream sherry, loosened up considerably and were currently roaming the living room in search of prey, habitually in packs of three.

But the mother. My pleasant surprise was caused by the fact that, surrounded by the clatter and general merriment, she had opted to sit on the couch re-reading my letter and weeping quietly. I was genuinely moved. I would go to her and give her comfort as follows: 'Weep not. Rejoice, rather, that your son has died in pursuit of artistic integrity.' And then I'd reclaim the letter for my files.

I ordered my papers and set off on the short stride across the room. Ten feet? Three strides? Would that it were so simple. The padre, alerted to my presence by a prying nature, beamed unctuously and blocked my passage with corpulent ease. I braced myself for small talk. The priest would demand it. Any effort to convince him that I was not of his faith, and therefore exempt from Romish banter, would be met by simpering condescension. He would smell the baptism off me.

'Delighted you could make it,' he beamed. 'Sad business. Sad business. Sad business entirely.' He extended a portly hand. 'Father. There you have it. Name and job in one.' He beamed in closer. 'So what exactly do you do yourself?'

I was about to answer that I minded my own business when the man with the golden hair and the red shoes ambled over, a painted female on his arm, and answered for me.

'He's in the same line of business as yourself, Father. Showbiz.'

I was further about to object to this vicious slur, which seemed to amuse the priest if his seismographic mirth and 'That's a good one all right' were anything to go by, but there was something about Red Shoes which intrigued me. The voice. The face. The demeanour. I felt as if I had experienced them all, in a curious sort of way, before.

He turned to me in a fine show of over-familiarity.

'Fiachra,' he said, 'let me introduce Dominique.' The painted lady fluttered her eyelashes in my direction. 'She's my sex therapist.'

Dominique laughed uproariously for no apparent reason.

'Don't mind him, Fiachra,' she trilled. 'I'm an actress. And Finn has told me all about you. He says you're a genius.'

Did he? I began to soften towards him.

'Absolutely,' he said, with a toss of his infuriating locks. 'Fiachra is, without doubt, the greatest genius the world has ever known. His name will live on when you and I, Dominique, and the church which Father here so touchingly represents are long forgotten. He told me so himself.'

Pithily put. And I may have said something to that effect. I softened further.

'And you are?' I said.

His female friend almost choked on her beverage.

'Don't be unkind, Dominique,' said Red Shoes. 'I think he means it.' He turned his attention back to me. 'Finn,' he said. 'Ring a bell?'

I examined his physiognomy. Riffled the memory cards of my brain. Nothing.

'I'm your twin brother,' he said.

The woman stared at me in patent disbelief.

'You mean you really didn't know?'

I stared patently back.

'I have somewhere in the region of one to two dozen siblings, madam,' I replied. 'I can't be expected to remember them all.'

I had just formulated a courteous, if brusque, dismissal when I was forced to dispense with the pleasantries. Whilst I had been engaged in unavoidable banter, it seemed, evil stalked abroad. The quietly weeping mother, forswearing the gentleness of her sex, had metamorphosed into a malignant double act with my inebriated, not to say meddlesome, uncle.

Now standing to attention, she held the aforementioned letter at arm's length, while my uncle fumbled with a box of safety matches. Not unlike the very safety matches I had rejected all those hours ago. My historic letter – this precious artefact – trembled like a captive bird. And I? I too trembled.

But there's trembling and there's trembling. And mine was the trembling of the righteous. As my gently swaying relative embarked on an elaborate and no doubt hilarious mime – *Drunk Uncle Attempts To Strike Match* – I steeled myself for action. I brushed past the sex therapist, and would no doubt have saved the letter for posterity had not fate declared an interest.

My eye fell on Rosemary, who had, at our last meeting, been so rotund. So corpulent. The bundle she cradled in her arms, I conjectured with a blinding flash of insight, had possibly been the cause of that corpulence but had now taken on a life of its own. It was at that stage where feet and hands seemed to act independently of any controlling device, and there I would have been more than happy to let the matter rest. Except that one tiny finger pointed unerringly in my direction.

The child looked straight at me. A brow-furrowed glower that belied its tender years. And, as the bereaved mother whipped the matchbox from my uncle with a wild cry and condemned my letter to the crematorium of Art, the infant spoke.

'Dada,' it said.

X

As I lay in bed that night I pondered the profound implications of what had come to pass, my thoughts interrupted only by the drunken bellowing of my maternal uncle and the thud and splinter of best mahogany as he tried to break down the door.

True, I had purloined his room, but as he was leaving for Dublin on an early flight the inconvenience was surely minimal.

And besides, I had placed suitcase, garments, airline ticket and travel wine rack on his side of the door, so I hardly see that he had just cause for complaint. Quite the contrary. They were all now several yards closer to the airport.

I say profound implications, and profound implications they most decidedly were. Not the rather upsetting scene with the deceased's mother, who failed to see that her public burning of the letter – my intellectual property, I need hardly add – put her on a par with the worst excesses of Hitler's Germany. Not the disturbing midnight encounter with the flying maiden aunts, although I must say in passing that I usually associate banisters with the under eights. And not the sudden appearance of my alleged twin.

No. I refer to the small child incident. The pointing finger. The proprietorial stare. The 'Dada'. I gave the matter some thought the following morning as I abluted, dressed, unlocked the door, and made my way downstairs. The banister rail, I noted, had been burnished to a glow by the bloomers of the flying maiden aunts. Alcohol? Dementia? The phases of the moon? By the time I reached the foot of the stairs I'd settled on all three.

On a happier note, the ladies in question had long since fled the scene; possibly, I couldn't help thinking, for a fresh infusion of blood. And the rabble had disappeared, as the old Scots' saying has it, like the snows of August.

All that remained was the detritus of their visit: empty bottles; broken glass; cigarette stubs and, sitting in the midst of it, Rosemary. Comatose. Her face, which may have looked positively carefree on a horse, was hardly best suited to suggesting gaiety in one of our own. Morose is as good a word as any, and her disconsolate state was caused, as I later discovered, by a mixture of bereavement, postnatal depression and adolescent angst.

But whatever the reason for Rosemary's current state it suited my purposes admirably. I required a quiet environment in which to work, and might expect no interference from that particular quarter, possibly for years to come.

A silent woman, I need hardly add, is both a contradiction in terms and the pearl beyond price.

XI

The child, sad to say, was a different matter. It was careering around the room on all fours as I entered and had, as previously mentioned, begun to explore the thrilling possibilities of language, albeit without transitive verbs at this early stage.

No sooner had I cleared a space at the table and begun arranging my papers than it parked itself at the feet of the master. Inconvenient, granted, but not unflattering. I could work with that. The tug on the trouser leg was more problematic however, and I found myself thinking back to my own childhood for a solution. My mother at the sink. Me tugging for attention. No response. I could yank at the maternal folds of either ankle for hours and she would carry on scrubbing. Mind, or whatever mothers possess in that department, over matter.

I decided to adopt the self-same approach toward the infant now tugging at *my* metaphorical folds. And it may have worked had I been deeply immersed in the soapsuds of creativity from the off. That I wasn't may have been in part due to the weight placed on these slim shoulders by the Immortals. They had set me a positively *onerous* task. And I hadn't heard from them since!

Enough for one pair of shoulders you might be forgiven for thinking. But that wasn't all. Add to this the mental exhaustion brought on by the not-untraumatic birth of my first slim volume. At any rate the intervening years had produced but one work of note, the movingly elegiac

Lines for Samuel Beckett

I sat for some time admiring the compressed vigour of the piece – so much contained in so little – and was toying with the idea of a quick edit when I noticed that the child had worked its way up my leg and now stared at me from a standing position, its chin clamped, limpet-like, to my knee.

'Dada,' it said.

That word again. Dada. Small word, two meanings. The child was, in human years, somewhere between the ages of nought and twelve. Unlikely, then, that it was referring to the early twentieth-century absurdist movement.

The alternative, however, was chilling in its implications. I most certainly wasn't the child's father, but the courts are notoriously eccentric on this particular subject. The child was present at the moment of conception, in spirit at least, while I was transparently not. So what if it hinged on the child's word against mine? The podgy little finger trained in my direction over the witness box. The accusatory 'Dada'. No jury in the land would find against the plaintiff. Next case.

I decided to keep these thoughts to myself, prised the offending head gently but firmly from my knee, and returned to my burdensome task.

Or would have returned to my task, but several seconds later the head was back in place. Reclamped. I put down my pen, re-prised the head from the knee, and placed its owner, with a look both stern and unyielding, at the farthest corner of the room. And then? I sat back down with a deep, involuntary sigh.

I had been visited, I freely admit, by a frisson of Stygian gloom. The child, did she but know it, had been clutching the trousers of greatness. Unhappy trousers! They were, it seems, condemned to wander the world, unrecognised in their own lifetime.

And so, by inference, was I.

But wait!

I felt a quickening of my pulse. A twitching of my nib. A girding of my artistic loins. This, I reflected, would be the first flowing of my genius for no small time. So be it. Let the floodgates open!

I raised the pen. I steadied the page. The child was back.

Stern and unyielding obviously hadn't worked. I decided to adopt the scientific approach and laid down my pen. Temporarily, I hasten to add.

I am well aware of the dangers posed by infantilising children; indeed I have often thought that if my mother had flicked me off her leg at an early age she might, at the very least, have washed more dishes. Perhaps she recognised the prior claims of my genius but, given the limited intelligence of her gender and class, I somehow doubt it.

But to return to the scientific approach. I was resigned to the fact that the infant in question would be deemed worthy of full board and lodging for some years to come. The human animal, it seems, is alone in expecting to be seen through tertiary education. It seemed reasonable, then, to lay down some ground rules for peaceful co-existence. The erection of a wall, for example. Theoretically seductive, but a quick inventory suggested I would need bricks, mortar, a selection of tools and an easily affordable crash course in plastering. I decided, instead, to relocate the couch. Complete with present occupant.

Minutes later, the deed was done. The couch sat jammed in the corner. Rosemary sat facing the wall. She murmured something inaudible as she was wheeled across the floor, but other than that accepted her new location, and its admittedly restricted view, with good grace; the strict pattern of the wallpaper, in fact, proving not unsoporific. The child, for its part – and a nametag at this point would have been helpful – was afforded a generous triangle of varnished floorboards to explore at its leisure. Problem solved to the greater good of all.

I was about to congratulate myself on my ingenuity and give the still blank page my undivided attention when a small head appeared over the top of the couch. It was followed by a whirling succession of limbs that powered the main body over the top. This, in turn, crashed to the floor, righted itself, and scurried towards its prey: MacFiach.

I was reminded of old war footage, with particular reference to the Sherman tank: progress of. True, instead of blowing me to smithereens it contented itself with saying 'Dada', but the effect was much the same: it interrupted my work. So I did what any intelligent person would do in a similar situation. I placed it on the front porch with strict instructions to keep well away from the road and approach strangers with caution. With that I closed the front door gently, as befitted the occasion, but firmly.

Game, set, over and out to me.

XXII

A moment, then, for reflection. Later that day, as I settled at my desk, I caught sight of myself in a strategically placed mirror. I caught sight, simultaneously, of Rosemary. Catatonic on the couch. Odd, I mused. We were beginning to look like a married couple. Time, I thought, to 'go to the pub'. I'm being deliberately humorous here. Lightening the tone, as it were. The notion of MacFiach going to the pub (sic) is risible, but only if we accept the narrow definition of that statement. I had indeed resolved to go to the pub, but not, I hasten to add, to imbibe and flatulate and moan about 'the wife'. No. My motives were altogether more cerebral.

I was, at this stage, several months into my weekly residency at the Gnarled Tree public house. I had, in market research terminology, maintained my lack of audience with commendable consistency. I had been excluded from several other establishments on grounds of elitism – mine, not theirs – but the Gnarled Tree served my purposes well.

A dark and imposing mausoleum of the Irish persuasion, the landlord was democratic in his dislike of people. This was reflected in the clientele, which was select in the extreme, particularly after the last light bulb blew. On my last visit, to add to the deepening pall of gloom, the landlord, a non-syllabic individual from county Roscommon, appeared to be dead. And I had every reason to suppose he still was.

So thinking, I donned my scarf, stiffened my gait, and headed for the great outdoors. It was a glorious summer evening. The sun shone blithely on saint and sinner; on king and commoner; and, closer to home, on Rosemary's first-born, cavorting happily with a stray and mangy cur. Contemplating the fact that, in an age of rampant consumerism, children are often happiest with the simple pleasures, I left her matching it snarl for playful snarl.

The Gnarled Tree, as I've intimated, would have graced to gloomy perfection those appalling Gothic comics that find favour with the adolescent classes. It certainly made its presence felt in an area which, in all other respects, reflected the somewhat dubious architectural preferences of the present century. It stood, in a word, out.

And yet, in spite of the fact that I had exercised the creaking hinges of its front entrance on numerous occasions, I couldn't find it. Had it ever, in fact, existed? Had it been but the figment of a voluminous imagination? Or – and it's a big or – had it, perhaps, been bought, dismantled and shipped home by a wealthy American who had once imbibed there and thought he was in Ireland?

Wrong on all counts.

No. The truth was prosaic in the extreme. It had merely been bubble-wrapped prior to refurbishment. I was about to stride past in search of a more welcoming hostelry, when my eye was caught by a fluttering as of angels' wings above me. I looked up. A white banner rippled in the breeze.

GRAND REOPENING
UNDER NEW MANAGEMENT AS . . .

I could scarcely believe what I saw.

MACFIACH'S

(Sic), (sic), a thousand times (sic). I, Fiachra MacFiach, poet, perambulator, bon viveur, was to be immortalised in neon. I yodelled involuntarily from the sheer pleasure of my own company, edited

Lines for Samuel Beckett

with the insouciant flourish of a finger on the balmy air, and sauntered homeward revivified.

XIII

On my return home I was accosted by a neighbour, who was 'terribly sorry about my daughter'. As I didn't have a daughter I could afford to be magnanimous.

'Think nothing of it. Could, whatever it was, have happened to anyone.'

And there the conversation might have ended on a semi-agreeable note.

Sadly, however, I suffer from seven-pockets-one-key syndrome. Front pockets of trousers. Back pockets of same. Outside, and inside, pockets of coat. Breast ditto of ditto. The pedant – and I put pedantry on a par with playing the melodeon in public on the list of human failings – will have counted eight pockets. True. But the breast pocket is out of bounds for keys, coins, objects larger than a breast pocket and, indeed, any and all of the paraphernalia of our daily existence. The breast pocket on my coat is, in a word, sewn up. Hence, not to labour the point, seven.

I mention this because it took me some twenty minutes to establish the absence of a house key, during which time the long-winded neighbour imparted the following information: the child had emerged unscathed due to the fortuitous arrival of the bereavement counsellor.

Now I don't wish to appear, well, pedantic, but I don't recall acquiring the services of a bereavement counsellor after the sad news of my father's tragic passing. No. I simply got on with it. What was it Jesus Christ – God's alter ego in his much-filmed novel the Bible – said on the same subject? 'Let the dead bury their dead.' A mite impractical, perhaps, but crisply put and possibly worth a try.

No mention, at any rate, of bereavement counselling.

Rosemary, however, had to have the full works, and the party in question was just leaving as I opened the unlocked door. I gave her the cold stare that brooked no banter and out she shuffled. Silent, sheepish, cowed.

But the damage had already been done. The back of Rosemary's head seemed on the verge of animation. Her cheeks, on closer inspection, were flushed, a sure sign of impending fever. I calmed her down somewhat by ignoring her, and soon enough things had returned to normal. I was well aware that the last thing Rosemary needed – if she was to make a full recovery from her present malaise – was undue excitement, and I resolved to monitor the situation with a paternal, but not uncaring, eye.

XIV

Things settled down into a not displeasing simulacrum of married life. Much like the wallpaper that Rosemary had begun studying with renewed interest, there was a strict pattern to the day. Mornings, for instance, were devoted to matters creative, and I am delighted to be able to report a breakthrough on the gauntlet question. My historic pact with the Immortals.

Typical of the insecurity of the genuine Artist, I had been agonising – internally for the most part – over the Beckett piece. Pithy. Pointed. In many ways perfect. But would it – *ah, the eternal but!* – merit inclusion in the definitive anthology of Irish verse?

No sooner had I thought this than the Immortals were back with a whump.

Definitive anthology? We know of no such book. Is there such a book? And if so . . . who wrote it?

'Relax,' I replied. 'There is no such book.'

An oversight surely. But who now living could compile such a book?

I had no idea. That, at least, was the official version.

Then think, man. Think. There must be someone, they implored.

I blushed prettily and awaited further developments. At which point I heard them muttering excitedly among themselves. This was followed by the sound of heavy footsteps fading across a marble floor, and further followed by much far off murmuring.

Silence. A pause. The footsteps returned.

We don't suppose . . . no, no . . . couldn't possibly . . . too much to ask of one man . . . giant among his peers though he be . . .

I gazed, as if distracted, into the middle distance and settled, as if fated to do so, on a second strategically placed mirror. Which relayed back to me an image of myself.

'Giant among his peers, you say? Heaney,[1] perhaps?' I ventured.

The distant sniggering which followed this spurious advocacy was like unto the music of the spheres. And, though modesty forbids a detailed account of what followed, the result was as stunning as it was unforeseen. The giant in question had acceded to their demands, and in so doing had committed his energies for years, perhaps decades, to come. His brief? To compile the definitive, all-encompassing compendium of Irish poetic output. And already he was planning it out. Seven volumes in all. First volume . . .

But hold! His, *my* foremost task was to locate a publisher and I decided to approach, in the first instance, Messrs Faber and Faber.

Rosemary was snoring gently on the sofa, the child snoozing likewise on my left leg. I could look forward to several minutes of uninterrupted work. Perfect. I laid paper, pen and ink on the table and set to with a flourish.

Esteemed Sirs,
  You may recall rejecting my slim volume Deep Probings. *No matter. I have no doubt whatsoever that streams of publishing houses were kicking their talent scouts when Gideon snapped up world rights to the Bible.*
    There was no Bible 2 – the all-important second book proving a step too far for that particular Messiah – but MacFiach is one for the long haul. What say you to The MacFiach Anthology of Irish Verse from the First Rhyming Grunt to Last Tuesday Week? *A slightly unwieldy title I admit, but I think I can promise a slightly unwieldy book.*
  Yours ever, MacF. No first name, I fancy, required.

Now certain readers might well protest as follows: surely the title should include the name of the publisher. Tosh, bunkum and balderdash. Who does the work? The Artist! The publisher, a glorified printer, basks in the reflected glory. And besides, *The Faber and Faber Book of etc.* might be acceptable up to a point. But what if this venerable firm expanded to include succeeding generations? *The Faber, Faber, Faber,*

Faber and Faber etc.? Out of the question. The spine just wouldn't take it.

In spite of the agitation engendered by this thought, and the resultant muscle spasms in my left leg, the child slept on. As, in her own way, did her mother. I allowed myself a sigh of no small satisfaction. The letter written, I was now committed to the task.

After which it was almost a relief to deal with my correspondence in-tray. Item. A postcard from my maternal uncle threatening to kill me at the earliest opportunity. This had been posted from his home address where he had been happily reunited with his drinks cabinet. I replied to the effect that his sense of humour, in the face of his many and obvious flaws, was a lesson to all.

I also received a letter from three maiden aunts – North Dublin branch. It mentioned, among other things, that I was a very big boy for my age. Enclosed was a postal order for two and sixpence in old money with strict instructions to splash the lot on my sweeties of choice. *Our little secret.*

And finally, a long and tedious missive from my 'poor' widowed mother.

Poor? Allegedly poor at any rate. Pleading reduced circumstances she enquired if it would be permissible to halve my weekly allowance. I had no intention of capitulating on the monetary front and derived a good deal of satisfaction from writing a curt note to that effect.

Might set a precedent.
Matter now closed.
Your loving son.

XV

Little wonder, given the tedium of the above, not to mention the omnipresent, catatonic Rosemary, that I cherished my afternoon walks. This usually took me, by one route or another, past the Gnarled Tree as was.

MacFiach's as would shortly be.

Nothing gave me greater pleasure than overseeing the work – I was there anyway, so why not do my bit – and engaging in gay banter with the work force. The linguistic mismatch of the ages, granted, but I like to think it gave them something to aspire to as they hoicked their hods up ladders and gestured at passing women. I exhorted them to greater things as they laboured, pointing out that I was the eponymous MacFiach, and that their involvement in the refurbishment guaranteed them a sort of immortality: think, for example, of the slaves who built the pyramids.

Thus we would pass the time of day until, brain-tired, they would revert to type and become as one with their Neanderthal forebears. This usually involved much ribaldry and the hurling of bricks. Whereupon I would leave them jabbering happily till the morrow.

Evenings were more relaxed. Me grappling with the word; Rosemary staring at the wallpaper. Odd way to pass the time, I often thought. Perhaps she just liked yellow. But whatever the reason it seemed to have a calming effect, and this was all to the good in her progress towards wellbeing.

The child was a different matter entirely. Wilful, persistent, and beginning to struggle with the myriad complexities of sentence structure. She continued to home in on my knee, and I continued to resolve the matter with a subconscious flicking movement; but she invariably landed, regrouped, and homed back in. I finally settled on two pairs of trousers as a makeshift buffer zone, and with this we achieved an uneasy peace. The Dadas continued, of course. Dada. Dada. Dada. I was ground down by the metronomic regularity of its repetition.

One evening, however, all change. She was clamped tight to my outer trousers, her cheek pressed close to my knee. Our eyes met. Weakness on my part? I think not. I was merely alerting her to my intention to stand up and reclaim my leg. Our eyes, as I say, met.

'Me uv oo, Dada,' she said.

Three small words, if we exclude the ever-present noun. But what was their import? What, in a word, did they mean? 'Me' I took to be exactly that. Misuse of the personal pronoun. So far so comprehensible. But 'uv'? Possibly Gaelic for egg, which would make her first sentence bilingual. And what about 'oo'? An egg-related suffix is my best guess. So what exactly was she trying to say? Something about paternity? I pointed out that she might be better advised to try something a mite less – how to put this delicately – *ovulatory?* – till she'd got the hang of things. Then I stood up and flicked her across the room.

No sooner had I repositioned myself than my ears were visited by the following: 'Me want bockle.'

Ah. This one I understood. Me want bockle. I want bottle. Understandable, perhaps, that she persisted with her inaccuracy on the personal pronoun front, and she seemed to have mislaid her indefinite article, but at least we had something to work on.

'I want a bottle,' I enunciated.

She chortled at this. Some misunderstanding surely, so I tried again.

'I want a bottle.'

'*Me* want bockle,' she giggled.

It took me some time to work out what the problem was, by which time we had developed a call and response which included, for no apparent reason, the odd 'Hallelujah'. But I wasn't, of course, meaning to imply that *I* wanted a bottle. So I tried over-enunciating.

'I. Want. A. Bottle,' I said. 'Now you try.'

A simple enough request, you'd be forgiven for thinking, and her initial attempt had been close. But the all-important first lesson in sentence structure was about to be interrupted by none other than her own mother. I was almost certainly approaching a breakthrough on the indefinite article front when Rosemary staggered to her feet, shuffled into the kitchen and returned some minutes later, exhausted, with a bottle.

I was, at the very least, nonplussed. Why had she done this? It had merely encouraged the child in her belief that sloppy language gets results. Is it any wonder that our schools, universities and, indeed, all buildings where people congregate in groups of more than one, are filled with people trying to destroy their mother tongue? I made this point to Rosemary in clipped and modulated speech, and stormed upstairs to my room.

XVI

This was perhaps as close as I was likely to get to marital bliss, but all was about to change, and not necessarily for the better. The blame, if we are to apportion blame – and I think we are – lies squarely with the fragility of the female psyche. The inability of women to bottle their emotions. There. I've said it. Not a fashionable sentiment in these dark times, but let history judge the truth or otherwise of my observation.

Picture the scene. I had taken the precaution of hiding all writing paper not pertinent to my own lofty purpose. Rosemary had taken to dabbling in the black arts of women's verse, and it was having an adverse effect on her otherwise placid nature. She became, at times, positively frisky and, although not a trained physician, I was well aware that over-excitability, in one so mentally delicate, could lead to cerebral havoc. Ergo, I hid the paper. And would that it had ended there. But wait.

The pattern of this particular day had been routine in all respects.

Work.

Correction of grammatical inaccuracies in child's tentative exploration of language.

Constitutional.

The latter had ended on an untypically sour note. I had merely pointed out to the refurbishers, as I called them, that the MacFiach sign might benefit from a modest enlargement. This led to my head being inserted into the cement mixer, which I accepted in good part, and being told to *quote* 'Go and MacFiach yourself' *unquote*.

This, as I say, I accepted with good grace.

Until, that is, the cement began to dry. Fortunately, however, they had poked a couple of holes for my nose, so no harm done.

Enough, you might be forgiven for thinking, for one day's work. But I arrived home to find Rosemary's counsellor-ess woman slinking guiltily out the back door. Infuriating? Decidedly. But also instructional, her premature departure enabling me to monitor the effect of outside interference on the delicate balance of Rosemary's mental state. It was exactly as I feared. Agitation replaced placidity. Sporadic noise replaced the healing power of silence. She even muttered a

sentence at one point – noun; transitive verb; seemingly obligatory expletive – which cut across my dialogue with the child.

The sentence?

'Her name is ****ing Aoifra.'

It had, on the positive side, cleared that small matter up,
although a name tag would have been perfectly adequate.
But I was, not unnaturally, deeply concerned. I am a genius,
but I am also a human being. My dearest wish was to with-
draw from society and ply my modest trade, but here was
a woman in freefall. There was work to be done. And I,
MacFiach, would countenance no shirking, nay, nor derelic-
tion, of duty.

I immediately put my own selfish (sic) needs on hold, and
put my modest (sic again) gifts completely at this fragile creature's disposal. I thought about wrapping her in a warm blan-
ket, toyed with the idea of soothing her troubled brow with
honeyed unguents, and even considered making her a pot of
nettle tea. Short-term solutions all, but I – a male trait this
– take the long view. So I penned several furious letters to
the national dailies, the Institute of Psychiatric Medicine and,
due to a slight terminological misunderstanding, a local health
food outlet – 'The Nut House' – on the subject of mental
illness. There. Pen down. That should do the trick.

On raising my head from my furious task, the first thing that
struck me was the eerie, doom-laden, mid-hour-of-night hush.
Not even the silence of a fellow human being brought relief. I
was alone. The room was strangely ordered, as if in preparation for . . . I knew not what. In the hours I had spent writing,
it appeared to have been rendered spotless by an unseen hand.
I patted my hair to check for spit and a centre parting, in case
my mother had dropped by. But no. It remained exactly as
before: pleasingly tousled to suggest loftier priorities.

Not so the moon-brightened room. There was something
different about it. Something almost imperceptible. I decided,
by a process of elimination, to find out what.

The furniture remained much as it was. Table. Chairs. The couch of Rosemary's prolonged recuperation facing the wall. No. The almost imperceptible change lay behind the couch. Behind, indeed, everything in the room. The wallpaper, which up to now had suffered only the ill effects of Rosemary's fingernails as she tried to claw her way inside it – I filed this under women's interests and left her to it – was covered from floor to ceiling in frantic scribblings.

And Rosemary's scribblings to boot.

I graced her handiwork with a quick perusal.

> *In my withering widow's weeds I wail*
> *I weep and wail*
> *Waiting, waiting*
> *For the deathbell toll*
> *The darkening sleep*
> *To free me from this hell*
> *This sterile hell.*

That was quite enough for me. Schoolgirl existentialism, nothing more, nothing less. To be honest, I blamed myself. Why? I had hidden the paper. I had refrained from hiding the wall.

I stifled a wry chuckle. She'd be sorry in the morning. And yet there was little to inspire laughter in the whole sorry mess because, once seen, the scribblings became impossible to *un*see.

But enough of this frivolity! Time, I felt, to return to my own lofty pursuits. I picked up my pen, but the walls seemed to close in on me, taunting me with disparate words and phrases. She had even given the blessed thing a title – 'Suicide Note', if you please – almost as if she intended a linear reading. This really did smack of adolescent angst.

XVII

I decided, as an act of compassion, to remove all trace of the offending scrawl, and leapt straight into action. I began phoning all-night paint shops to compare prices, and was locked in earnest conversation with a squeaky-voiced trainee manager when – horror of horrors! – I smelled gas. I was, I admit, hypersensitive on the subject, and not without reason. It's easy to be blasé about your house blowing up if you haven't lived through the experience yourself, but I was understandably none too keen on a repeat performance at such short notice, particularly while I was located in the same building as the boiler.

But the paint. My needs, as I've said, were simple. Matt emulsion. Black. Not off-black or hint-of-black. Not seriously-decomposing-apple black. No. *Black* black.

'Sorry. We don't do black. There's no call for it,' squeaked the trainee manager.

'But there is,' I countered. '*I've* just called for it. And what,' I continued, 'if a group of Satanists moved into the area? Why, you can be pretty d**ned sure they'd take their trade elsewhere.'

At this stage the smell of gas was beginning to pervade the room, and I had just decided to terminate the conversation on this pertinent and witty aside. But wait for this!

'I certainly hope Satanists *don't* move into the area,' giggled the trainee manager. 'But if they did they'd have a wide range of pastel shades to choose from like everyone else.'

I pointed out, in measured tones, that the Satanic movement had never done *me* any harm. Unlike – and I was fuming at this point – the opposition. I then launched into a diatribe about God and his earthly henchmen which ranged far and wide and was about to segue neatly from the general to the specific, when the intensity of the gaseous fumes became almost too much to bear. I slammed the phone down in mid sentence and phoned the gas board emergency service instead.

'I wish,' I said, 'to be put through to the complaints department.'

And what, pray, was the nature of my complaint?

I had suffered greatly at the hands of their nauseous product in the past, I explained, and was fast running out of places to stay. I wished simply to record that fact and suggest they cease their apparent vendetta forthwith. Was I constantly, I concluded, to be hounded by errant gas?

No complaints department at that number, it seemed. They simply dealt with emergencies. That was why it was called the emergency number. And there were calls waiting. I bit my metaphorical tongue at this point. There's no point arguing with these people. I contented myself with the observation that one of the less attractive features of the modern world is the constant rush, the seeming inability to converse for conversation's sake. I then went on to conjure up the spirit of my dear, departed father who would often lean over the electric fence for days on end, chewing on his ever-present pipe and chatting happily with his latest helpless victim.

And the receptionist's curt response?

Name and address, please.

I was, it seems, to be denied the casual civilities of a more relaxed age. So be it. I left my name and address and, almost before I had put the phone down for the umpteenth time to complain of their late arrival, the doorbell rang. And yes, the gasman agreed that there was indeed a smell of gas. He pushed past me with unseemly haste. See? Modern world mores again.

'Christ,' he expleted. 'Where's the meter?'

'I have no idea.'

'Well, where's the b****y kitchen then?'

The present volume will assuredly grace the school syllabus in the fullness of time, yet I must, I feel, record proletarian speech, when forced to report it, with a reasonable degree of accuracy. B****y he said, and b****y I bl**ming well write.

'The kitchen?' I replied distastefully. 'Do I look like a woman?'

His expletive at this point may have shocked even his proletarian peers but before awaiting my response he rushed through to the back of the house. Seconds later he reappeared, shaking his head and smiling that rueful seen-it-all smile that marks out people of a lower caste who have one skill, one tiny little skill, that they know you don't possess. I knew exactly what was going on. He was about to give me the idiot's guide to his particular area of expertise. Irony most certainly intended.

I followed the back of his boiler suit, mentally running through my vast store of *Do you tell me sos?* and *Is that a facts?* and *Isn't the world a wonder and you the most wonderful wonder of all its wondrous wonders?* By which time we had arrived at the cooker. He pointed a stubby finger at the oven dial; twisted it clockwise.

'On,' he said. He then repeated the process in an anticlockwise direction. 'Off,' he said. 'On. See? Off. On. Off. And this, as it 'appens,' – he gave as theatrical a flourish as his stocky frame could muster – 'is your actual kitchen. I'll see meself out.'

And with that he stepped gingerly over Rosemary's seemingly lifeless body and left.

XVIII

On a more mature appraisal of the facts it appears that the word *seemingly* might have been judiciously pruned from the last sentence.

'Suicide Note' turned out to be exactly that. And if I deal with the following days in a brief cameo, the reason is simple. I don't wish to be thought to have an unhealthy obsession with gas and funerals. True, both have loomed large in the thrilling narrative we call my life, but each episode in turn has yielded diminishing returns on the Richter scale of disruption.

Item: gas stove-induced fire at my parents' house.

Result: singed eyebrows (magnificent regrowth of same to twice their former length); loss of blank notebook (still missing – search discontinued).

Item: gas-induced explosion at London base.

Result: condition of homeless, stateless person for rest of morning; all notebooks intact.

Item: gas-induced noxious fumes at present address.

Result: very little writing done that evening.

The pattern, I feel, is obvious, and certainly bodes well for any future episodes involving this useful, yet potentially lethal, natural asset.

XIX

This latest turn of events, it goes without saying, led to a different sort of disruption. I was to be taxed, for a start, with the arrival of my supposedly droll Dublin uncle, who insisted on getting personally involved in all matters relating to his daughter's forthcoming funeral. No doubt he had his reasons.

On which subject, difficult to know how to put this: I'm a great believer in the healing power of laughter, but jocularity has its place, and as the day of the funeral progressed my uncle's inebriated death threats bore all the hallmarks of a one-joke act. I laughed dutifully but mirthlessly along for several hours, however, by which point I had what can only be described as facial rigor mortis. So acute was the paralysis, indeed, that I used it to facilitate the extraction of a couple of troublesome teeth.

One funeral is much like another, but Rosemary's was not without its positive aspects. The undertaker, for instance, was the very man to approach on the subject of black paint, and I waited for an appropriate lull in proceedings in order to do so. He proved to be courtesy itself. Reputable firm. Mention my name. Possible discount. He was about to search for his card when the priest, with a fit of pique that bordered on professional jealousy, suggested he lower the coffin first.

But that's funerals for you. There's always someone to put a damper on proceedings, and I was greatly relieved when the whole thing had blown over and I found myself back at the house alone. Except, that is, for the *poor little orphan child* (my italics) Aoifra.

Now the more ascetic reader will be thinking 'Whoa there. Dangerous', and will probably refer to a rather alarming entry in my journal – *Vol. CCIV* – of some two years previous.

On my return home I tripped over a small wicker basket which some idiot had placed by the front door, almost rupturing my spleen in the process. Normal procedure, when inconvenienced by an inanimate object, is to give it a damn good kicking. I noticed, however, that the basket contained a newborn infant, so I contented myself with a curt note to the landlord asking to have it removed forthwith. And the child with it.

Stepping gingerly over the basket the following day I posted the letter and that, I assumed, was that. Not so. Even allowing for the fact that I had used a second-class stamp I would have expected the recipient to spring into action by the next afternoon but one at the latest. Three weeks later, it pains me to report, the wretched thing was still there.

My point, and I can't make it forcibly enough, is that I had managed to avoid the greatest single threat to artistic achievement. I am referring, of course, to 'The Wicker Basket in the Hall'. And yet here I was, to return to the present, the sole custodian of a small, and transparently female, child. Was I *insane!*?

A moot point. But how's this for positive thinking? It was a big house. We probably wouldn't see each other for days on end. Why, in time she might learn to cook and type and be of some use to a stern but not unloving father. A dutiful daughter. I rather liked the sound of that.

XX

Buoyed by this thought I repositioned the sofa and established the fact that little Aoifra was elsewhere engaged. I then returned, after an unavoidable break, to my – *the* – anthology, and began to tackle it with vigorous rigour.

I first set about countering any charges of nepotism. As witness the following. I had, in my youth, rather foolishly agreed to an interview in the local Catholic monthly. On the editorial page of the following issue? This.

Dear Sir,
The violence and terror of young MacFiach's schooldays
as described in your magazine certainly brought this reader
back. A verse on the subject neatly encapsulates the era:

I taught in schools for forty years
The work was never boring
My leather belt soon brought the tears
I loved to hear them roaring

I taught them nothing for I knew
'twould send their spirits soaring
Instead I beat them black and blue
I loved to hear them roaring

I'd bounce their heads from wall to wall
Or off the lino flooring
In Dublin, Cork and Donegal
I loved to hear them roaring

And then one day the belt was banned
A law there's no ignoring
I joined the Guards instead; 'tis grand
I've got to hear them roaring

I'll carry on when I retire
For when I'm old and snoring
Asleep and dribbling by the fire
I'll dream about them roaring

I wrote the following some years back and had all but forgot-
ten it with the onset of senile dementia. Thanks to 'The
Parish Review Interview', then, for a nostalgic trip down
memory lane.

Scully, that scourge of my middle youth, had obviously antici-
pated my magnum opus and decided to court the sympathy
vote.

Foolish fellow.

XXI

Rejection, then, for the newly fawning Scully, but the all-
important first step had been taken on this mammoth undertaking. Which is why I left little Aoifra doing whatever it is
that young people do these days in her bedroom and stepped
out of doors that evening with a fresh coat of polish, metaphorically speaking, on my elbow patches. It was, I could
hardly bring myself to believe it, the grand opening night of
MacFiach's. Such *eponymity*. I felt so light, so carefree, so
indescribably jaunty that I almost splashed out on a bus.

Extravagant? Perhaps, but life was on an upward spiral. My correspondence over the past few weeks, for instance, had elicited some tantalising replies. The Nobel committee would debate, with utmost seriousness, my 'tentative' proposal to award me the prize in perpetuity; and nullify, in so doing, all previous awards. Gideon was also giving earnest consideration to replacing its current best-seller with *a certain anthology* in the more select hostelries. And the celebrated Writers' Museum of Ireland, to whom I had offered the complete contents of my room as a posthumous shrine to my genius, would look for bigger quarters and get back to me. Large bureaucracies are notoriously conservative and resistant to change, so this was promising. Highly promising. Why, so skittish and euphoric did I feel, I almost splashed out on a *second* bus.

This was turning into quite an expensive night.

But d**n the expense, I thought. I turned the corner into what would surely be called MacFiach Street when the local elders caught the public mood, and there, majestic, awe-inducing, bubble-wrap-free, it stood.

MACFIACH'S

MacFiach's. I repeat the name for its sheer poeticity! The new sign dominated the landscape. A magnificent neon facsimile of my signature in glorious Episcopal purple.

I walked slowly towards it, savouring the moment. I felt serene and, in a curious sort of way, humble. Synthetic humility, granted, for I had nothing to be humble about. As I approached the cathedralesque edifice, an ageing pedestrian apologised for banging into me and called me, in so doing, 'Your Worship'. I blessed her as I passed, collected a small donation for the church, and left her – final proof of my apparent vocation – to pick up her own shopping.

But the sign. Below it, to my almost dread amaze, a queue. This, it need hardly be said, was a notable first for MacFiach, and brought to mind my final artistic event at the Gnarled Tree of blessed memory. A select little meeting of minds that particular evening, as I recall. In the absence of an audience *I* filed out.

But now this! My humility expanded to incorporate the queue's indisputable *queueness*. Oh, how the mighty are elevated! And yet I was troubled withal. Popularity, that foul debaser of talent, had decided to come a-courting.

XXII

I eased my way down to the cellar, past the teeming masses, with magisterial poise and unaffected grace. The menial on the door affected not to know me. Perhaps he didn't. Perhaps, as I pointed out with not a trace of rancour, that was why he was a menial. I decided to clear the matter up, for his benefit, in plain English.

'MacFiach,' I asserted, 'c'est moi.'

'Et je suis le first woman pope,' he replied. 'Ticket?'

I chuckled wryly and decided to let him have his little moment. With a parting quip that his travail was sur le line I made my way back to ground level past my would-be acolytes.

And I must admit to vague stirrings of unease. From the back, on the way down, they looked merely hirsute. You can't tell what a man is thinking from the back of his or, in the case of him being a woman, her head. On the return journey, however, it was pretty obvious. Not a great deal. They didn't look the brightest, to be honest, and had obviously flocked to the opening night expecting a diet of my less challenging, which is to say lighter, verse.

Nor did they appear acquainted with my public face. Not a glimmer of recognition as I walked past, so I braced myself for the coming fray and decided to regroup in the main bar with a glass of my regular tipple, the establishment's finest eau du tap.

I breathed deeply and entered. All was changed, changed utterly.

Gone were the creaking hinges; the blown light bulb; the reassuring gloom. A glittering silver bar had replaced the nicotine brown original, while the aged and possibly dead landlord had given way to a job lot of scantily clad floozies.

I braced myself, prepared to embrace the new order, and was about to solicit my usual when I heard a voice I recognised from my youth. I looked around. The face, however, drew a blank. But the voice. It sounded so familiar. I strained to catch snippets of conversation.

War over . . .

Decided to go legit . . .

Good money in extortion . . .

Bought pub on proceeds . . .

And then it came to me. Ferdia. My ex – it seemed – paramilitary brother stood at the far end of the counter. I hadn't recognised him without the balaclava. And I must say he had an aggressive mien without the softening effect of the headgear.

I turned my collar up to avoid detection, crossed to the other side of the bar and positioned myself in front of a barmaid.

'A glass of your excellent tap water,' I said and, as it was turning into quite a night, 'best make it a double.'

Seconds later I was about to sit down and smoulder over a beer mat – tap water was off – when, upturned collar notwithstanding, Ferdia spotted me.

'Fiachra,' he growled affectionately, as if greeting a long lost brother. Which, come to think of it, he was. 'Glad you could make it. Big night for the MacFiachs.'

I felt strangely touched. Perhaps Ferdia wasn't so bad after all. I couldn't help thinking back to all those little incidents from the past which had sorely tested my resolve to stay alive. I have, thankfully, managed to relegate the details to my subconscious mind, though the faint whiff of tar and feathers remains, and I often wonder if my kneecaps are the ones I started out with. But to be fair to my psychopathic sibling, he had to learn the trade somehow and, as a writer uses paper, he used me.

Yet here he was, extending – thanks to an uncooperative timing device – the stump of peace and reconciliation. I was about to grasp the proffered limb and congratulate him on his espousal of, well, *me*, when a man rushed in, frantically undoing his trouser buttons. He charged into the gents' urinals, which provided an explanation of sorts.

'Ferdia,' he bellowed en route, 'that brother of yours is on in a minute.'

Now bear with me for a moment. This is not a conventional, plot-driven narrative. Who, for instance, after its histrionic and frankly implausible denouement, could possibly want to read the Bible twice? But what happened next beggared, and still beggars, belief. Which is why I describe the experience in some detail, and encourage the reader to experience vicariously my slowly unfolding sense of horror.

I took leave of my recently reformed relative and made my way back downstairs. The queue had dispersed. So had the menial. Closed door. 'House Full'.

I pressed my ear to the same door and tried to listen in, as if to a radio broadcast, but I couldn't hear, or indeed see, a thing. A whoop here, perhaps. A holler there. And then? A sustained burst of wild applause. A muffled introduction. I steeled myself to my purpose. Time to cast off the superannuated robes of anonymity. Time to embrace the smiling, public MacFiach. Time – at last! – for the dramatic entrance. I braced myself, burst through the swing doors and there, straight ahead of me and spot-lit in a blinding pool of light, stood Finn, my red-shoed, flaxen-headed, so-called twin. In full flow.

Now I tend, as a general principle, to eschew low culture, but the novelist that every Irish household used to produce has been supplanted, it seems, by the dreaded stand-up comic. And this self-satisfied preener was their titular cock of the walk.

His patter, if that is not to dignify his performance with unwarranted gravitas, seemed strangely familiar at first. A line here, a parent there. And surely that teacher was none other than the psychopathic slubberdegullion Scully? I watched in mounting horror as scene upon scene flashed before my eyes in a remarkably sustained episode of déjà vu and, as he began to describe his first sexual encounter with one 'Widow Bernelle' – Yes! *My* Widow Bernelle! – I could contain myself no longer.

'Impostor!' I bellowed. 'You have stolen my life!'

A stunned silence. My brother caught sight of me at the back and graced me with an adolescent smirk.

'Christ!' He ejaculated. 'There's two of us.'

He gave me a low bow, then turned to face his public.

'Ladies and gentlemen,' he rejoined. 'My estranged twin.'

He went on to inform the rabble that we had been insep-arable in the womb – loud applause – but that I'd taken advantage of a twelve-second start on the dramatic entrance front and he hadn't seen me since. This the audience took to have comic intent, although it was accurate enough as far as it went.

I informed him, in clipped tones, that nine months spent examining the back of his neck in a confined space with no prospect of early release was hardly a sound basis for later intimacy. He replied, to general hilarity, that I made it sound like a couple of hostages incarcerated in our mutual mother.

He then insisted on driving his point home with an elaborate conceit, spurred on by the mob, chronicling our day-to-day activities as we burrowed, if you please, an escape tunnel. Complete with the supposedly squeaky badinage of the Irish foetus.

I listened till I could take no more and informed him, with mounting anger, that I found his words offensive. He paused momentarily. He even had the good grace to look sheepish.

'You're right,' he said. 'Point taken.' He hung his head in shame, as well he might, and then he addressed the mob. 'Like all good Irish boys, Fiachra is fiercely protective of the good name of the beloved mammy. Mea culpa.'

I was, understandably, withering in my scorn.

'I am not thinking of the offence to my mother,' I rejoined, folding my arms and raising myself to my full height. 'I am thinking,' I declaimed, 'of the offence to *me*.'

But instead of the silence and respect my words merited, the audience hooted and hollered until I could take no more. Apoplectic with inner rage I stormed offstage. I had been consigned, it seemed, to the Seventh Circle of Hell. I made my way past the leering masses with their Howaya Fiachras, their vulgar familiarities, their close-set eyes, and arrived home in high dudgeon.

XXIII

Little Aoifra lay sleeping on the couch, her tiny black coat buttoned up to her tiny black scarf, an embryonic scowl lending high seriousness to her child-sized puppy-fat face. I gazed upon her, and not without a certain quasi-parental pride. Unlike me, she had an excellent role model in the present writer, and had managed, despite her limited vocabulary, to transmit this vital information to her tailor.

So deeply was she cradled in the arms of Morpheus, the gentle nest of slumber, that it took a full five minutes to rouse her. I had matters of import to impart and so, as she sat rubbing her eyes and yawning herself awake, I paced the creaking floorboards and laid the facts before her. I, the man she called Dada, was a genius. I had been ridiculed, pilloried and wilfully ignored, while my alleged twin had been lauded by the rabble. But what cared I for the rapturous applause of the mob? The gaudy trappings of celebrity? The ephemerality of fame?

There was work to be done. Work of timeless perpetuality. Of enduring indestructibility. Of sempiternality. I was referring, of course, to the anthology but didn't want to confuse her with high-flown concepts. 'Dada', in short, would be otherwise engaged for several years, I explained patiently. In the meantime I would leave her with the essential tools of survival in a harsh and unyielding universe.

I then introduced her to the grandiose, not to say grandiloquent, theories of Jean-'Jacques' Rousseau, the eminent French philosopher whose ideas on child rearing fell into disrepute when it was discovered, on the mortuary slab of all places, that he was a woman. I rather thought the Jean would have given it away myself, but that's the French for you. Too busy twirling their moustaches and cherching plaisir to grapple with the cold facts.

Latterly, for possibly cyclical reasons, women's theories on raising children have come back into vogue. Hence the renewed interest in M'selle Rousseau. And whilst feeling somewhat uneasy at encouraging the intellectual (sic) involvement of the female in this most formative of areas, I feel that her writings on the noble savage bear renewed scrutiny.

I laid them before my rapt child-pupil in a three-hour dissertation that rendered the theories comprehensible to a twenty-first century audience. I then turned to my still rapt, if droopy-eyed, charge with a dramatic sweep of the arm.

'And all *you* have to do,' I concluded, 'is put theory into practice. Well?'

Her tiny frame shuddered at the magnitude of the task.

'Me want bockle, Dada,' she said.

'Excellent,' I replied. 'Achievable goal. Nothing too ambitious to start off with. I wish you every success.'

With that – and the not unwistful wish that I'd been given the same encouragement at her age – I bade her a fond adieu and returned to my work.

XXIV

So much to do, so little time. And yet, conscientious to a fault, I decided to deal with the not insubstantial pile of letters that had built up during The Inconvenience, as I now referred to Rosemary's tragic but prolonged demise. The letters, after all, had amassed on my desk, unopened, as I dealt with the illness, the funeral, the grief. But that was yesterday. Time to move on.

I began by opening the latest missive from my mother. The woman in question had taken to dabbling in the epistolary arts, and my weekly postal order had begun to arrive surrounded by her barely legible witterings. Worse, she also inserted clippings from the Irish print media, which developed a seemingly obsessive theme.

Irish author, 30, gets 4-figure advance for novel.

Irish author, 27, gets 5-figure advance for three chapters of novel.

Irish author, 24, gets 6-figure sum for synopsis.

Broad hints in the margin – Aren't we Irish great? All that money for a bit of oul' scribbling – suggested a sustained and bitter subtext too obvious to require elucidation here. My readership at this point is, I think, not lacking in sophistication. The opening paragraph of this memoir was carefully crafted to see off ripping yarnites, the legions of the unbright, and aficionados of the one-syllable sentence.

Those still grappling with my muscular, unyielding prose will, no doubt, think as follows:

'The Great Man's grasping and acquisitive birth mother mistakes the ever rising tide of Ireland's verbal effluence, and its conversion into grubby lucre in the marketplace, as somehow indicative of excellence. Make no mistake about it. The woman is trying to evade her responsibilities as a leading sponsor of the Arts.'

Well done. I could, no doubt, have put it better myself. But only because words are my life.

I formulated a curt and appropriate response – a brief dissertation on the difference between High Art and low entertainment, followed by a renewal of my request for a standing order – and sat back on my chair with a weary sigh, my administrative work done.

The child, I noted with approval, had opted for the healing powers of the quick nap. Excellent idea. It had, after all, a hard life ahead.

XXV

My journal of the following day – *Vol. CLXIV* – makes for interesting reading:

> *I finally managed to locate a registered stockist for matt black emulsion. The Satanists in question informed me that they were recent converts from the Church of England, that Beelzebub didn't exist as such, and that they'd abandoned human sacrifice since turning vegan. Excellent paint, though.*

As I applied said paint with deft brush strokes to the desecrated wall I was, in my usual selfless way, acting in loco literary executoris. Rosemary's feverish juvenilia would destroy her reputation, which, at the time of its removal, was that of a feisty young suicide who dabbled in verse. And I was determined to protect her claim on posterity such as it was. Or, indeed, wasn't.

Which was probably just as well, for no sooner had I applied the final stroke to my handiwork and achieved total blackout, than the front doorbell rang. I assumed it was the latest in a long line of religious zealots or, failing that, my uncle indulging his increasingly unfunny running gag of waving a revolver in my face. Not so on both counts. The reality, I fear, was far, far worse.

A woman smiled at me from the doorway. Severe in black. Hair and face scraped back in a bun. She peered at me over the top of a pair of owl glasses. Her name was Thesaura, if you please, and she was here, if you further please, to research 'an exhaustive profile'. I was flattered but not particularly surprised. The women's glossies, as I believe they're called, were bound to get in on the action eventually.

Now my more high-minded acolytes will assume I sold her a signed first edition of *Deep Probings* and closed the door gently but pointedly on her full-blooded, ecstatic yelps – my own involuntary reaction when I see a spare copy lying about. Would that it had been so. But no. I can only assume that I had become light-headed from the inhalation of paint fumes, but I invited her in, sat her down and then, only then, did I offer to sell her a copy.

She brushed my offer aside. Feisty, I'll give her that.

'The fact is,' she continued with a ladylike snort, 'there hasn't been one single obituary, which is quite frankly shameful.'

Interesting angle, but that's modern journalism for you. I decided to play along.

'Well I must say, my dear,' I chuckled, 'I'm not altogether surprised.'

She bridled. Possibly a nervous tic.

'Sorry? I don't follow.'

'It may have escaped your notice,' I replied, with the merest hint of edge, 'but I'm not actually dead.'

To illustrate the point, I paced the room languidly, my hands abstractedly fingering the stuff of my trouser pockets. She gave me a quizzical look over the rim of her glasses.

'So I see.'

As she rummaged in a bulging valise for the tools of her trade I chuckled again. The mock obituary. A journalistic gimmick, granted, but clever with it. She had certainly got the Great Man's attention. Time perhaps, I thought, for magnanimity. I positioned myself in front of her chair and gazed benevolently at the top of her head.

'My papers, young lady, are at your disposal. Princeton can darned well wait.'

She snapped her valise shut and stood up.

'I'm delighted to hear it,' she said. 'And you are?'

We faced each other, nose to chin. My nose. Her chin.

I stood on the balls of my feet and laughed heartily. A self-deprecating, sardonic laugh tinged with steel.

'MacFiach,' I replied. 'C'est . . .'

But before I got to the moi bit my interrogator, with a sharp intake of breath, whipped her spectacles off, polished and replaced them in a matter of seconds and stared, mouth agape, at the wall behind my head. Transfixed. If it hadn't been for the fact that they shared no distinguishing features whatsoever, she could have been mistaken for Rosemary. The wall. The stare. The quasi-equine face. It was uncanny and, in its summoning up of my tragic cousin, curiously nostalgic.

But why the seemingly inexplicable change of mood? I observed her closely in an effort to find out. Perhaps, I conjectured, it was simply an aversion to black. But this was hardly the case. She was, after all, dressed neck to toe in it. More likely, however, her actions betrayed the nervous flitterings of a woman's unfathomable mind.

I was about to leave her to it and return to my work when my eye fell on the corresponding stretch of wall behind *her* head. Ye Gods! There was method in her seeming madness.

The paint – Ye Other Gods!! – was drying!!! The writing was seeping through!!!!

Now students of the period will note my brief descent into nineteenth-century melodramatic cliché. Worse, I fear, was to follow. This, though, is no penny dreadful. I was not, for instance, about to enter the murky world of the undead. Rather that of cheap paint. Paint that fails to do what it says on the label.

One coat.

The need for a further coat having been established, I first ushered my young friend to the door with avuncular courtesy. She seemed slightly peeved, to be honest, and informed me, as I frogmarched her down the path, that the subject of her profile was Rosemary, that she herself was neither my dear, particularly young nor, for that matter, a lady; that she was, in fact, a 36-year-old feminist academic with a seat on the editorial board of Sappho's Rib, a fellowship at Trinity College, Dublin, and a mission: to rescue Rosemary, a poet of the greatest depth and talent, and long overdue for inclusion in the canon, from the Curse of The Invisible Women.

Oh, and her name was Thesaura. And I could be 'darned sure' she'd be back.

XXVI

I pointed out that Rosemary had always been perfectly visible to me. Assuming, of course, that I'd cared to look. I then returned to the safety of the house, battened down the metaphorical hatches and retrieved the paint tin from the bin. Hoping to find sufficient for my needs I prised the lid off. Full! I began to suspect the Satanists of taking cheap shots as I applied myself to a vigorous second coat. And I pondered the folly of hospitality as I applied a last lick of paint to Rosemary's final full stop. For which, oblivion being preferable to ridicule, she would thank me.

I should have returned to my great anthology a happy man, but the excitable Thesaura woman had cast the seed of doubt. What if she was right about Rosemary? What if her work merited inclusion in the anthology of anthologies? What – horror of horrors! – if mine didn't?

Such thoughts are sent to torture genius. I was riven with self-doubt. *Riven.* There was nothing for it but to lose myself in my momentous task, and I set to with a will, disturbed only by the removal of Aoifra's cot and its replacement by a small pine bed. I seem to remember her signing something and introducing Rousseau to a puzzled-looking man in overalls, but apart from that I was immersed in the therapeutic consolation of work.

Oral poetry before the invention of the phonograph was out for obvious reasons, but apart from that I had reams of the stuff. Before me nestled a veritable mountain of verse. Now for the easy bit. The pruning. The whittling. The weighing, sifting, rejecting. I found this, in most cases, remarkably easy.

Verse before 1650 I binned. Much of it is Christian in character, which may have had a certain contemporary resonance: the Bible, after all, was still hot off the press at the time. More damningly however, early verse is, almost without exception, in Gaelic, and everyone hates a show-off. As for the stuff in English, most of it was written by blow-ins who couldn't get picked for their own anthologies, so they thought they'd invade ours.

There are, of course, honourable exceptions to this. Shakespeare, for instance. I'm willing to accept that he downplayed his Limerick childhood for success on the London stage. In his position I would have done the same myself. Sadly, however, this condemned him to describe a world about which he knew little, and his relevance to his own people – unless we accept the theory that the Dark Lady of the sonnets was, in fact, one Mick Duhan, a hedge-school caretaker from Aughnacloy – is consequently minimal.

Shakespeare, therefore, was out, and I scribbled a quick note to the Duhans to that effect. Old wounds were not about to be reopened. Present day Aughnacloy is justly celebrated for its inclusivity – at the last census the population was 112% Brazilian – and its thriving gay community, but back in 1588 you kept your sexual orientation to yourself.

From Shakespeare, then, to the celebrated Borris-in-Ossory school of Taghd Dall Ó'Cadhain, Taghd Uasal Ó'Cadhain, Taghd Láidir Ó'Cadhain, Taghds Rua, Dearg, Bán, Glas, Buí, Dubh, Dubh Glas, Dall, Mór, Beag, Óg and Aosta Ó'Cadhain and, perhaps most notably, Sid Phelps.

An understandably anonymous pamphlet, *Inbreeding in*

Late 17th-Century Laois, deals with the above poets in greater detail, although no mention, curiously, is made of Phelps. British literary historians have recently claimed him as one of their own – a sure sign of renewed popularity. One such even goes so far as to question Phelps' Roscommon roots, simply because he was born and raised in Pontefract.

It is doubly unfortunate, then, that none of Phelps' oeuvre has been handed down to posterity. Phelps was a performance poet. His Art consisted, not of words, which he felt restricted the potential of his poetic utterance, but in lengthy bouts of screaming, while simultaneously juggling potatoes and balancing an egg cup on his nose. Attempts to transfer his genius to the printed page were disastrous and Phelps died a broken man. He has not performed since.

My point? He may have merited inclusion in the anthology of all anthologies. Difficult, however, to tell.

XXVII

Immersed I remained for some time. And would that I had stayed in that happy state! What caused me to surface into the real world I know not. But my senses became gradually alert to their surroundings. The toxic odour of newly applied paint. A steady banging on the door. And Rosemary's mad rant of a suicide note seeping, nay, *bleeding* through the black. A scarlet gushing. A viscous, blood-red ooze.

Ignoring the persistent banging I closed the curtains and retrieved the paint tin, yet again, from the accursed bin. Hoping to find enough for a further coat I prised the lid off. Full! I was pretty certain at this stage that the Satanists were practising the dark arts in direct contravention of the Trade

Descriptions Act, but applied myself to a vigorous third coat, intending to visit them with the full majesty of the law on the morrow. Yet no sooner had I reached the final full stop than the paint had begun to dry on the introductory lines.

> *There's no way out*
> *I cannot hide*
> *My soul is on the other side*

I began again. And again. And, yes, again. There was something absurd, yet curiously profound, about the perfect circularity of the experience. The beginning. The ending. The beginning again. Yet again the ending. Did I say the beginning? The ending again. And on and on and on and yes, yes, on.

I began beginning at the end and working my way back to the beginning. This oriental approach led to a transcendental or hallucinatory phase, which further led to a glut of exclamatory entries in my journal. Wow! Awesome! Or, during the oriental phase,

!

t

u

o

r

a

F

And still the walls oozed scarlet rant. My clothing and person were stained with blood, sweat and paint. I also appeared to have grown a full-length beard and matching shock of shoulder-length hair, matt black with streaks of darkest red.

And still the banging continued. The walls seemed to close in on me. And then retreat. Close in. Retreat. As if they were trying to tell me something. But I wouldn't listen. I simply would not listen. I pressed my fingers to my ears and was about to clamp my eyes shut when the living-room door opened and Aoifra stood on the threshold. She wore what looked like a tiny school satchel – which suggested that she had possibly opted for a formal education – and a gaudy yellow badge which said, in simple terms, 'I AM 4'.

Good to know. She stood, at any rate, on the threshold.

'There's 47 ladies at the window, Daddy,' she said. 'I think they've come about Mum.'

XXVIII

I was reminded of the disembodied, 47-faced gorgons of Greek mythology as I battened down the physical hatches and double-bolted the door. I then sat back exhausted, surveyed my handiwork, and was struck by a sobering thought: perhaps I should have switched to pastel.

But then a curious thing happened. I began to engage with the wall and the artless ramblings thereon. The female narrator, referred to as Rosemary throughout, was tedious in the extreme. Prone to fainting fits, melancholia and bouts of self-pity bordering on schmaltz. The central character, however, was made of sterner stuff.

> *He glowered down*
> *from the lofty heights*
> *of his patriarchal perch.*

> *'Oh, don't upset your silly little head'*
> *He said*

There was a certain mean, moody magnificence about the portrayal that made me, I don't deny it, think of myself. Particularly as she had opted, in her artless, not to say witless way, to call this fabled character Fiachra. And yet the portrait, if crude and badly drawn, was not unflattering. Rosemary had unwittingly scribbled a flawed but unaffectedly charming vignette of the Great Man at work and play.

Enough. My mind was made up. I searched the house for any other scribblings or jottings which might shame my dear departed cousin if subjected to posthumous scrutiny. Apart from two dozen sheaves of light juvenilia, a so-called verse play complete with patronising acceptance letter from the Royal Court, and several hundred pages of an alleged poetic novel, nothing. I attended to this particular bonfire of the vanities in the empty grate. Finally, ready to re-enter the world of the living, I left the smouldering remains, strode out to the hall, and flung the front door open.

What I saw before me filled me with shock and stupefaction. The garden was littered with matt-haired women, stalls groaning with feminist literature and, on the small green patch that passed for a lawn, a couple of medium-sized canvas tents. As word spread that the Great Man had finally relented, Thesaura called the troops to order and turned her loudhailer off.

I smiled genially and stepped aside to avoid the impending stampede.

'Ladies, ladies, ladies,' I positively trilled. 'Pray enter.'

XXIX

Big mistake? In retrospect, I would have to say, yes. I had expected, at the very least, discreet adulation. Awestruck glances in my direction. The odd stifled squeal.

Once ensconced in the front room, however, the women seemed to take on a life of their own. They also seemed to harbour an obsession with Rosemary. Seminars, lectures and the like milked this unhealthy fixation, and all under the self-styled fellow Thesaura's strident tutelage. That I managed to accustom myself to the constant noise says much for my forbearance, although I must say I found the use of a microphone ostentatious to say the least. But they seemed, on the surface, content to leave me to my own devices. Their raucous laughter I took at first for girlish awkwardness, their whispered asides for deference.

Within days, however, I was introduced to chaos theory in living practice. The place was awash, wall to bleeding wall, with women. Not to mention their infuriating offspring. It was as much as I could do to locate my work surface, let alone use it.

One particular child, who appeared to labour under the prefix Quentin, sat on my work table with the express purpose, it seemed, of urinating on my notes. I offered to bury him down the back garden but this only gave vent to his mother's latent hysteria. Under fierce interrogation I was forced to concede that I only meant up to the neck. This ability to seek compromise in the face of seemingly entrenched positions is one of my less trumpeted character traits. But I was dealing, as I say, with a hysteric. And judging by the response of her screaming offspring, she had passed the condition on.

Thesaura, as termagant-in-chief, stepped in at this point and assured the horrendous woman that I did, if you please, but jest. The pinch-faced fury unclenched her features in the light of this monstrous untruth, but the whole episode had put a much needed damper on proceedings, and ten minutes later I saw mother and son off the premises, scrubbed the appalling Quentin's stench from the liberated table, and reflected that Herod may simply have suffered the fate of visionaries throughout the ages: an unsympathetic press.

XXX

The remaining women, however, did just that: remained.

I often thought of engaging them in light banter, but such an enclosed space would hardly bear the weight of hormonal expectation, so I held my peace. And therein lay the crux of the problem. The proximity of just such a torrent of female hormones, raging or no, began to exert a powerful influence, insidious and malign; for a man, even a man stamped with greatness, has perforce to sleep.

And my sleep was fitful and troubled by hideous dreams. Example:

I am trying to write but my pen has run dry. Thesaura, scantily clad, taunts me with an inkwell held just out of reach. I lunge for the inkwell to no avail but, as Thesaura finally relents, my pen metamorphoses into a sexual organ, definitively male and possibly mine.

But this is no A–Z of the erotic arts. And besides, my point is this. If the admittedly shameless Thesaura was prepared to invade my dream world in such a fashion, think what she might get up to in real life. And so it was that I chose to immerse myself in the anthology and practise the Buddhist technique of the vertical catnap. To no apparent avail. My catnap was fitful and troubled by hideous dreams. Example:

> *I am pursued relentlessly by a scantily clad Thesaura across the Bacchanalian hell that is modern Ireland.*
> *Temple Bar.*
> *Galway.*
> *17b Mother Teresa Memorial Gardens, Moate.*
> *I manage to escape to an uninhabited island where a monastic order of ancient times has built a retreat accessible only by climbing along an icy, windswept ledge jutting out over the raging torrent below; crawling through a tunnel built for humans fond of a good 49-day fast; clambering up to a pinpoint of rock upon which a solitary monk would sit in ancient times contemplating the nature of existence in excruciating pain. But far from the devious wiles of women.*
> *I awake screaming when I reach the old monastic resting place. There to be met by my three flying aunts who flap in on harpies' wings, land atop me on the overcrowded pinpoint with a clatter of stilettos and shrieks of wanton lust, whereupon . . .*

But this is no pornographic textbook. I penned a quick postcard to my grotesquely libidinous aunts suggesting it might be best to keep the details of our little 'dream experiment' strictly en famille.

And then I hid the sherry in case they dropped by.

XXXI

On my somewhat tousled emergence from several nights of the above, the raucous laughter from my fellow female residents had, I noted, grown more raucous. The whispered asides, too, had grown more raucous. Easy enough to see why. The unlovely coven had spent too long immersed in, and surrounded by, the Rosemary version of MacFiach. It had finally begun to exert its insidious influence.

Now up to a point I would have to say that yes! I was that man! The Byronic, Heathcliffian archetype. In the parlance of popular culture, The Hunk. I am large. I am multi-faceted. I repay endless revisits. Enough.

These women, however, were positively – if covertly at this stage – lascivious. I would issue them, on their return to some semblance of normality, with a stern warning. I, MacFiach, had no wish to be mythologised as a dark, brooding genius linked forever in the public mind to a beautiful but tragic dabbler – female – in the art of verse. Indeed, so insistent was I on the urgency of my cause that I penned a furious missive on the subject for immediate despatch to one of the less scurrilous broadsheets.

A slight over-reaction on my part? Possibly, but we live in dark times, in which female sexuality is encouraged to compete on equal terms with that of man and beast. What chance, then, for a man-beast like myself, cursed with the smouldering intensity of a latter-day Byron, if he was further glorified as 'Muse of the Dead Lady Poet'. Spurred on by this thought, I managed to post the letter without incident, although I did take a lengthy detour to avoid a tavern frequented by the

Irish Countrywomen's Association on their bi-monthly forays abroad in search of human flesh.

I say lengthy detour. I appear to have passed the same landmark on the North Circular Road twice, but at least my perambulations allowed me to plan my strategy. The house had been overrun, as if by a plague of locusts. It was imperative that I act. With this in mind I fashioned a speech of wit, passion, but no unnecessary erudition, designed to clarify the following: I, the Great Man, was strictly out of bounds. I made mental notes as I avoided the ever increasing packs of feral ladies on the prowl, and arrived home with a beautifully balanced speech fully committed – witty asides included – to memory. Thesis. Antithesis. Synthesis. Relevant quotes. Suggested reading list. No slides.

Having made my point I would then rid the house of this bestial plague of female desire. But how? I toyed briefly with the Pied Piper approach, luring them to their doom with selected readings from my work. I abandoned this idea, however, in favour of a modern rendition of Christ and the moneylenders. Apoplectic with rage at yet another hike in the already prohibitive interest rates, he drove them from the temple in typical Christian fashion. I opted for the self-same Christ-like approach as the more likely to achieve the desired result.

As soon as I entered the house, however, I realised something was amiss. I stood drumming my hands in the generous folds of my trouser pockets for some minutes before, on the advice of a passing constable, closing the door. I was flummoxed. Something had changed. Subtly. Imperceptibly. Indiscernibly.

But what?

It was only when I decided to enter the living room that all became clear. The women had vacated the building.

And they had taken the living room with them.

XXXII

I stared in wonder. The ground floor was now open plan. All vestiges of Rosemary and her demented scribblings had been removed. Brick by seeping brick. I was stunned. So stunned, in fact, that I almost forgot my speech. But what use is a speech, no matter how magnificent the oratorical flourishes, without an audience? A moot point. Judicious use of the full-length mirror has often spurred me on to flights of invention impossible to replicate with mere people. But this was different. No full-length mirror had ever offered me, as Thesaura had done in the shocking intimacy of her dreams, 'the friendship of her thighs'. No. This particular speech required an audience. And a female audience to boot.

Fortunately for my purposes a lone woman remained. Old to the point of perpetual dodderation, she pottered about as if she came with the lease. She also assumed a degree of intimacy, first name terms and the like, which has been the hallmark of old women since records began.

'Just the two of us left now, Fiachra,' she beamed over her knitting. Curious. The voice was familiar. Had I closed my eyes I would almost certainly have solved the puzzle in seconds, but I had a speech prepared. I had an audience. Old, certainly, but women are prone to lustful desires well into their fourth decade, and she may well have appreciated the flattery of my knocking the same again off her present age.

And so I began. I spoke of the apparent therapeutic effects of fornication. Of how I had often longed for the sweet release of coupling. For was I not a man? And did I not have fleshly desires? But this, I thundered, must never be! I had foresworn

the fabled pleasures of the flesh, and would continue so to
foreswear in perpetuous perpetuity.

'So begone!' I implored the crone above the rhythmical
clacking of her knitting needles. 'And offer me not . . .'

I was paraphrasing the siren Thesaura at this point but the
last line, I noted, was surplus to requirements. Typical of her
gender in moments of high drama, my audience rushed into
what I now knew, courtesy of the gasman, to be the kitchen. I
was momentarily thrown, having reached a stentorian climax
of sorts, but there were further peaks to scale. I followed her
in and there she stood, back turned, furiously unblocking the
sink.

Which solved, in one serendipitous meeting of woman and
sink, the secret of her identity.

'Mother!' I ejaculated. 'About that standing order.'

XXXIII

Her furious task completed, I packed my mother off with a
wry chuckle, the standing order negotiated. And yet, I freely
admit, the surface bonhomie masked a not un-nostalgic pang.
Why? A younger generation may well have been intrigued
to learn that I recognised my mother from the back view
alone, and only then in earnest communion with her beloved
kitchen sink. I can only say in mitigation that this was the way
of things in the Ireland of those bygone times and that I, for
one, mourn their passing.

I had packed Mother's suitcase myself and watched with a
son's affectionate gaze as she lugged it along the road, around
the corner and out of sight. Another wry chuckle, leading
this time to the healing powers of outright mirth. For there

is something about the sight of a diminutive lady of great age with a large, heavy suitcase which reminds us of our common humanity, and the absurdity of the human condition as it pertains to the common herd.

I was closing the door on this thought, and preparing to embrace the solitude of the Artist with renewed intensity, when I heard the scrape of nib on vellum. Curious. I had only two hands, and neither of them was writing. And yet there it was. Scrape scrape. Scrape scrape scrape. Tiny and yet distinct, like a mouse with a fountain pen. I peered into the far-flung open-plan corners and there, scribbling furiously at a tiny desk, was an equally tiny version of, well, *me*. Tiny black coat. Scarf. The radiant glower of total concentration. I flicked the light switch on and d*** the expense.

'Who are you?' I said. 'And kindly state your business.'

The figure put the pen down and giggled.

'Don't be silly, Daddy,' it said.

So. Not an incubus after all. Well, that was a relief.

Of sorts.

XXXIV

In all the unfolding drama of the women and the wall, I may have skirted round little Aoifra on occasion. Difficult to tell. Once seen in open-plan, however, she became impossible to unsee. And the fact remained. She might, who knew, grow into an excellent typist. But she would also grow into a woman. And with women there is always, *always* a price. She had, in short, to go.

Despatching your ageing mother is one thing. But a small child who has possibly just weaned herself off nappies? It didn't bear thinking about. So I didn't. I simply set about achieving my objective with as much compassion as divesting myself of a tot would allow. I toyed with the idea of depositing her under the nearest gas lamp with a tray of matches and a crash course in Cockney, but this was merely nostalgia on my part for a kinder, gentler age. And besides, I was out of matches.

The solution, when it came, was classic in its simplicity. Wicker basket. Bulrushes. The Tiber. I couldn't guarantee bulrushes on the nearest available river, but perhaps they were intended as a period detail to suggest that this was a true story and not the result of one goblet too many of the Biblical spirit of choice.

As we made our way to London's own Tiber at a cracking pace for a minor, I entertained her with the age-old story of Romulus and Remus. Vestal Virgin mother. A bit like her own mother, in fact. Well-known god for a father. Ditto there, although I did admit to being less of a household name at present than my mythical counterpart, Mars. Suckled, to return to the story, by a she-wolf – although Aoifra, I noted with approval, had brought her bottle. And finally raised as his own by a kindly shepherd. Little chance of that around here, although she might have better luck with a sentimental cabbie or, failing that, a purveyor of whelks to the masses.

I deposited her, in a word, on a Thames pleasure cruiser, excused myself with the observation that I'd be back forthwith – best keep it vague – and marched briskly off. I recalled, not without sorrow, an almost identical scenario not twenty years previously. True, Assumpta was an ass, her eyes were bigger, and I was less in control of my emotional hinterland. But my head had ruled my heart on that occasion, and must ever continue to do so. So I walked away with nary a backward glance.

And returned, you might be forgiven for thinking, to the melancholy pleasures of an empty house. Not so. My

perambulations abroad had become increasingly circui-
tous of late as my attempts to circumnavigate marauding
bands of frisky females became ever more ingenious. A
Religious Retreat for the Sick and Dying, for instance, may
have been just that. But as the Catholic Church strains at
the leash on the celibacy question it would take a brave
man to run the gauntlet of a hospiceful of libidinous nuns.
I gave it, in short, a wide berth and made my way back via
Gravesend.

I eventually arrived home three days later, closed the door
with some relief on the increasingly dysfunctional outside
world, and prepared for that most precious state of solitude:
silence, broken only by the far-off scratch of nib on vellum.

And the scream of delight as Aoifra charged the length of
the open-plan floor.

'Hurrah,' she shrieked, as she clamped herself lovingly to
my left leg. 'Daddy's home. Aoifra was starting to get worried.'

XXXV

I had little difficulty omitting Swift from the anthology of
anthologies. His Modest Proposal was nothing less than a
calculated attempt to cash in on the inexplicable fad for cookery writing and, just as his culinary ideas never caught on,
neither, for this reader, did his verse.

I was still some way short of a full complement for Volume
One – no one had yet merited entry – and I sat at my desk
most nights in contemplative, not to say melancholy, mood.
My own writing had suffered during my sojourn in London,
and this problem was compounded by the relentless scratch-
ing of Aoifra's relentless nib.

I had moved to the self-styled world capital of culture to be rebuffed at every turn. And if Rosemary – sad, tragic minor talent Rosemary – was receiving a good deal of unwarranted attention, my alleged brother was simultaneously lauded for his low patter. Inference? Mob culture ruled. London had succumbed to ephemera. Time, I instinctively knew, to move on. To embrace, wherever they had settled, the cultural elite. And this time I would pack my journal, my spare scarf, a change of underwear and a set of medieval eyebrow tweezers inherited from great uncle Alis, which I have found to be exceptionally useful in the repulsion of small children.

But where to go? I had tried the pin on the map treatment before, but all pins led to Limerick. So this time I opted for a more scientific approach.

No pin.

No map.

Just a foolish poet's dream.

I am referring, of course, to Oxbridge. For is there one who does not secretly yearn to breathe, untrammelled, the rarefied air of the groves of academe? To traverse, unhindered, those legendary teeming spires? I decided to hie me thither. No point in explaining the situation to little Aoifra; I might, after all, be back for the odd weekend. And so, packing a bag with essentials – the eyebrow tweezers, sadly, had attached themselves to a passing guttersnipe – I betook me to King's Cross station.

To be brutally honest about it, I didn't weep for the tweezers. I had taken to fondling them in my trouser pockets, a nervous habit according to the surgeon who removed them after they had become clamped to my fundamentals, my Jasper Conrad slight imperfects, and the left-hand pocket of the abovementioned trousers. At any rate they were gone, so – given that every area nowadays has its child problem – I packed a staple gun instead.

XXXVI

King's Cross, loveliest of stations.

I was in ebullient mood as I tripped gaily past an ageing guard, his lugubrious old face a picture of misery. I was, as intimated, in skittish mode, and decided to cheer him up.

'Pardon me, boy,' I all but crooned, 'is that the delayed 6.59 to Peterborough?'

This playful reference to low culture, delivered in a pleasing tenor, succeeded in raising him from his torpor, and I stood in line for a ticket marvelling at his firm grasp of post-war slang. He also appeared to think I'd engaged in sexual congress with my mother. Astute fellow. He was very nearly right.

A small vignette, then, of proletarian etiquette and perfect light relief for my journal. To be honest, I may have been slightly carried away with the mood of spontaneous gaiety. As I approached the glass partition protecting me from the menial within I was happily humming an old staple of the Irish dance halls of my youth.

> *Brothers*
> *There were never such devoted brothers*
> *God help the mothers*
> *Who get between me and my brothers*
> *And God help the brothers*
> *Who get between me and my ma.*

Excellent stuff and, proof that MacFiach can oscillate his kneecaps with the best of them, I accompanied the ditty with my own private dance: an internal experience; a form, shall we say, of mental choreography. On this occasion, however, the climax was marred somewhat by the menial rapping on the glass.

No matter. I was off on a one-way ticket to Academiaville. I stopped singing and raised my hand for silence.

'A one-way ticket, my good man,' I declaimed. 'Destination? Oxbridge.'

Little did I know it, but four seconds later I was about to enter a nightmare from which I could never, not being technically asleep at the time, awake.

'Single to Uxbridge,' he said. 'Free fifty.'

I decided to abstain from commenting on his cavalier use of the English language in view of the more pressing issue of place.

'Not Uxbridge,' I replied. 'Oxbridge.'

With a flourish he produced a well-thumbed directory and perused it for several minutes.

'No such place, mate. Don't exist. Next.'

Two points. I wasn't his mate in either sense of the word. As I explained with a polite nod to the ever mounting queue. I also took issue with his obvious lack of training.

Oxbridge not exist? I almost laughed in his face.

'Not for you it doesn't,' I replied, 'but what if you had foresworn the low expectations of your class and applied yourself to your studies?'

I gave the queue a conspiratorial wink. It shifted uneasily on its collective foot and muttered in collective agreement. With my adversary! It was at this point in the proceedings that I began to comprehend that there were dark forces at play. Oxbridge not exist!? Not for the lowborn ignoramus behind the glass, perhaps. Not for the ever lengthening file of fellow travellers. And not for the two officers who deposited me on the city's nether boundary with what they referred to as friendly advice.

True, there had been a mild bout of fisticuffs with one particularly truculent member of the queue, but the ill-tempered party in question persisted in ramming me with her wheelchair. Old age? The fact that she was late for her daughter's funeral? In my book there is simply no excuse for bad manners.

XXXVII

But this is to ignore the wider issue. I wish to buy a single ticket to Oxbridge. I make polite enquiries. Oxbridge? There's no such place, guv. To return with some relief to the past tense, I knew exactly what was going on. Vested interests! The old boy network! He's not, in a word, 'one of us'!

Good God, even the cap-doffing plebeians were in on it. I negotiated the North Circular several times in high dudgeon, arrived home some days later, and exorcised my wrath with a pithy missive, full of asides and addenda, to *The Times of London*. The letter – and I am hinting, yet again, at those dark forces – was returned unopened. *The Times of London*? No such publication apparently existed!

The plot thickened. I was naturally furious, but perhaps history had set a precedent. According to my sources, Jesus Christ's celebrated crowd pleaser, The Sermon on the Mount, caused quite a stir, but a quick perusal of the Jerusalem Post of the day would seem to suggest it never actually took place. So it was with my 'Oxbridge: Conspiracy of Silence' speech. Impromptu it may have been, but the sizeable crowd in the British Library's reading room attested to the people's hunger for truth. And yet press coverage was nonexistent, if we exclude a brief mention in the local *Advertiser*'s court circular.

But the search for Oxbridge continued. With, I am bound to report, increasingly bizarre results. Take the following: MacFiach's of bitter memory was located within walking distance of my habitation. This much I have made clear. That I haven't been more specific may suggest a lack of attention to detail. Not so. Unlike the alleged novel *Ulysses*, this is not a local street finder. Joyce, of course, was somewhat curtailed in his literary ambitions by the vast sums of money he received from Dublin Corporation, which must have been mightily disappointed with the result. No index, for a start, and the finished product takes piddling account of fundamental changes to the city's landscape in the several decades prior to publication.

But I digress. Unlike the slipshod *Ulysses*, this is a work of monumental integrity. The author was beholden to no one in its structure and content; he stands, metaphorically speaking, tall in his twelve-league boots. So, no free advertising for MacFiach's, which was, at the time of which I write, located in one setting. I, simultaneously, was located in another. Several miles thence!

Yet there, directly in front of my face – you may be ahead of me here – MacFiach's. For reason or reasons unknown, it appeared to have done, in the parlance of its clientele, a bunk. I gave the matter no further thought until, some days later, I passed the original site. Unbelievable! It was back! Now you're hardly *still* ahead of me. To be honest, I was hardly ahead of myself. By applying the left side of my brain to the conundrum, however, I came to the following conclusion: it was following me about.

Not so. As I discovered some time later there were, in fact, two entirely separate and distinct MacFiach's. Or, if we include the MacFiach's in Cricklewood, Ilford, Balham, Streatham, Hams West, East and New, Monken Hadley, Chipping Norton, Chingford, Chigwell and Cheam, a profusion of MacFiach's. London had fallen foul to a lethal cocktail of drinking dens and low culture. Such was my weary thought as I made my way home past the rubble-strewn sites of the Sidcup MacFiach's, the Catford MacFiach's, the Barking, Tooting and Balham MacFiach's.

Planning permission sought.

XXXVIII

London, as I have previously stated, was patently no place for a man of letters. It was imperative that I leave at once. But if not Oxbridge, where? It took me several months of trial, error and the North Circular Road to find out. By which point my – *the* – anthology was developing apace.

Time stood still as I pored over ancient manuscripts, deciphered ancient scrolls and pondered long and hard over the merits and demerits of Ireland's first transsexual poet, Joseph 'Mary' Plunkett. Tough one this. Plunkett's cross-fertilisation of the two known genders was bordering on the heroic at the time, and certainly led to the acceptability of cross-dressing among the Catholic hierarchy in an otherwise repressive state. But does this excuse the blandness of his verse? His place in the psycho-sexual history of his native country is assured, but that history has yet to be written, and I, whatever the blandishments on offer, am not the man, or woman, to do it.

Having said which, I admit to an early obsession with Ireland's first solo husband and wife team. An interesting footnote to a highly controversial career was his proto-feminist anthem, *If* . . .

Such was its controversial nature that it was given its first, and last, airing at Opus Dei's 1887 celebration of the Arts, 'Burnt Offerings'.

If you can set your goal and then pursue it
If you can stand your ground with any man
If you can say 'I'll do it' and then do it
Or say 'I know I can' and know you can

If you can see the truth and when you've seen it
You spread that shining truth both near and far
If you can say 'I must' and really mean it
If you can say 'I am' and know you are

If you can say 'I will' because you will it
And cause whate'er you will, my son, to be
If you can take the cup of life and fill it
If you can face the world and say 'I'm me!'

If you can say all this and never doubt it
If you can say all this and know it's true
If you can climb the highest hill and shout it
Yes! Shout 'I'm me!' and know that 'Me' is 'You'

If you can say all this most resolutely
Poor child! You only fool yourself because
This much is true, my son, yes, absolutely
You'll never be the man your mother was.

Sound familiar? Kipling 'borrowed' the idea, removed the sexual politics, and sanitised the whole into a bland, homo-incestuous confection. Which possibly explains its enduring appeal to the English.

Having consigned transsexualism's finest to the growing out-tray of history I was now ready to tackle the big one. The modern era. Yeats. Heaney. And who knew – *I* knew! – who else. But the alleged real world was about to interfere with my major undertaking for some time to come. Plunkett despatched, I dealt quickly with my correspondence.

Irish author, 21, gets 7-figure advance for interesting concept.

My mother had obviously begun to waver on the standing order front. I steeled myself for the psychological battle ahead. I then laid my pen down to a silent house. The child, Aoifra, was obviously in bed. Good. Time to return to the ticklish question of MacFiach – Whither Now?

I paced the open-plan vastness of the ground floor for some time and found myself, at last, seated at little Aoifra's unnervingly minuscule desk. Fondling, if you will, a correspondingly tiny child's globe. Pondering, reflecting, musing.

Whither indeed.

By a process of elimination I arrived at nowhere, but decided I was setting the cultural bar too high. I dithered for some time over Paris, but my long-held theory concerning the French language eventually won the day. Said theory posits the thesis that French is nothing more than a medieval parlour game that went disastrously wrong. The object of the game? To see who could sustain a conversation composed solely of arm waving and mindless gibberish for longest, without recourse to a single syllable of sense. Sadly, no time limit was set, with the tragic result that the more strong-willed contestants, unwilling to concede defeat, persisted through generations of inbreeding, which resulted in the France we see before us today; in which no one understands a word anyone else is saying but no one is willing to stand up and say 'Assez! Ça suffit!'

So Paris was out.

I was considering the merits and demerits of Malmo when I noticed a magazine lying open on the desk.

SWOT – the monthly periodical for the abnormally gifted child.

I flicked through it with casual abandon, and here is a brief selection of what my flicking unearthed.

'Burnt out at Six – A Case History.'

'Readers' Mothers'.

To be frank, I abandoned the casual approach at this point. The sexualisation of mothers in the pursuit of lucre is one of the less agreeable facets of modern mercenary practice. But I digress. The article of pertinence to my present situation read, in essence, as follows:

> *Sure to be a front-runner for biggest controversy at this year's Edinburgh Festival is Kiddipus, a version of the Oedipus myth for 3–6 year olds.*
>
> *'I don't honestly see what all the fuss is about,' quipped director Damian (5½). 'I've been sleeping with my mother for years and it's been a deeply loving and mutually rewarding experience.'*

Damian had further taboos to break on behalf of the above-mentioned grubbers, but they were of no interest to me. The sentence that caught my eye referred to 'Other Shows of Interest At *The World's Biggest Festival Of Arts And Culture*' (my italics).

It was a sign.

For what was I if not Arts and Culture and, although I might not merit coverage in *SWOT* on grounds of age, I began to see 'Ireland's Greatest Living Genius At World's Biggest Festival of Arts and Culture Exclusive' replacing 'MacFiach Moves to Malmo' as my headline of choice.

I began to pack my things. Toothbrush. Materials of my Art. Spare staples. And with that I made my way, as quietly as a pair of reinforced leather brogues would allow, to the front door. As I was about to leave, a distant church bell bonged. Twenty-one times.

I waited precisely six hours.

3 a.m. Perfect.

Only then did I open the door.

XXXIX

Now the more alert conspiracy theorist will need no explanation. If the establishment had gone to such lengths to deny a lowborn genius his rightful place in the Oxbridge elite, what might it not do to deny him the artistic delights of the frozen north? Best to catch them off guard. I decided, therefore, to leave at the most inconvenient time possible.

And as I waited, I heard little Aoifra, from her bedroom, singing herself to sleep.

I lie in my jim-jams all cosy and warm
And dream of my daddy who keeps me from harm.

I tiptoed upstairs and closed the door, as may be imagined, deep in reflective thought. I admit to a small twinge of I-know-not-what as I espied her little face peeping over the quilt, but normal service was resumed as I descended the stairs and began to dissect her girlish offering. Warm? Harm? Sadly, this feeble effort at rhyme suggested that she had inherited her mother's talent, not mine.

Some time later a distant bell clanged thrice. I went outside as quietly as the steel toecap of a leather brogue coming into violent contact with a precariously positioned metal bin would allow, and planned my next move. I had decided, naturally, to foreswear any mode of transport which might alert adversaries to my imminent departure. For which reason I had need of a bicycle.

I knew for a fact that the garden shed next door contained the very latest in bicycle technology. An embarrassment of gears. Weightless frame. For all I knew it possibly had a Corby trouser press facility and mini-bar, but all these newfangled gadgets went for naught when set against one insurmountable fact. It was a ladies' bike. No crossbar. I had to look further afield.

Four doors down I eventually found my man. Tall, black, masculine. Rusted on one side from what may have been dog urine, but otherwise ready to roll.

As, indeed, was I.

XL

One of the positive aspects of my decision to quit London was the distance it would place between myself and little Aoifra. Cruel? I assert not. It was, I think, Joseph of Nazareth who once remarked, in an unguarded moment, that some people become fathers, while others have fatherhood thrust upon them.

As with the celebrated Nazarene, so with MacFiach. A child had come into my life, I had introduced it to the ground-breaking if unfashionable theories of M'selle Rousseau, and was now about to leave it with a signed first edition of *Deep Probings*, a well-thumbed copy of the *Noble Savage Cookbook*, and two twigs.

And yet I was curiously troubled withal and was unable, as a result, to stem a flood of quasi-paternal memories.

Example: a day spent with Aoifra in the park. I had gone there to create and she must have toddled after me. I well remember taking time off from my work to point out a group of fathers playing with their children. Was there one among them who might qualify as a great Artist, I wondered aloud.

It was a rhetorical question as Aoifra, at that stage, possessed not the gift of intellectual discourse. I remarked to the rapt child that happiness, as exhibited by said fathers and their offspring, was a much overrated virtue. Whereupon I returned to the present.

The bicycle, as I soon discovered, had a flat tyre. Which brought me back to the garden shed next door. I had some difficulty working my way through the adjoining gardens – a bicycle and a privet hedge seem designed for mutual antagonism – but I eventually managed the task and purloined the pump from the ladies' bike on the assumption that, technically speaking, a pump is ostentatiously male.

By the time I had set the bicycle outside the front door, pumped the offending tyre and removed pigeon droppings from the spacious saddle, several windows had been opened and slammed. Typical. I had met almost none of my neighbours during my brief four-year tenure, and yet everyone had disregarded the earliness of the hour to bid me farewell. Gruffly, perhaps, and veering towards rudeness in some cases, but that, I'm afraid, is the way with the modern city. We've forgotten how to talk to each other.

On a more personal note, as I clambered aboard my trusty steed I spotted my erstwhile charge Aoifra at her bedroom window, clutching a lopsided teddy. She waved with her free hand; tiny and porcelain white. Was that a tear trickling down her cheek, illumined by the palest of moons? Difficult to tell from a distance. I waved gallantly back, turned to face the soon-to-be rising sun, and cycled out of her life.

Perhaps forever.

XLI

My short monograph, *Life on the Hard Shoulder*, deals eloquently and passionately with the dictatorship of the motorcar, and I'm afraid the main road out of London was overrun with same. Fortunately I had three lanes to choose from so I decided to give the lorries a wide berth. This seemed to upset the cars trying to negotiate their way past the same lorries so I thought 'Fair enough. I'll switch to lane number three; possibly even get some quality time to muse.'

It was not, sadly, to be, which is why I found myself, seconds later, metaphorically hugging the crash barrier. At which point, wouldn't you just know it, the police arrived. After a slightly crusty 'you again' they mellowed somewhat, and seemed quite pleased at my decision to decamp to Edinburgh. They graciously accepted a signed copy of a certain book for auction at their next Policeman's Ball – 'That should pull 'em in', they chortled delightedly – and we parted on the best of terms. Sadly, they said, I was about to leave their jurisdiction, but they would happily alert 'the Thames Valley lads' to my impending presence and await the evening news bulletins with interest.

At this point, however, events took over. A buckled wheel. A unilateral decision to throw myself at the mercy of the travelling public. The hospitality of a lift.

The car in question was compact, and obviously not used to having a bicycle in the back, but the driver managed to dismantle it with some difficulty and we set off in jocular mood, although he seemed more than a little obsessed with the oil on his suit. As he appeared to be from the

American subcontinent I remarked, testily, that I thought his sort couldn't get enough of the d**ned stuff. He took this to have comic intent and bellowed heartily for several minutes.

'That's a beezer,' he hooted. 'Okay if I use it?'

Use it? It transpired that my chauffeur was a comic 'artiste' on his way to perform at the Edinburgh Festival. It was now my turn to laugh. The Edinburgh Festival? The greatest Festival of Arts and Culture in the world? Low comedy? I rather thought not. I said nothing, of course, and, managing to internalise my glee, informed him that I too had plans for the Festival, if of a higher sort. His response?

'You should go to the States, man. You'd kill 'em.'

Now I am not, I hope, an intellectual bigot, but a country which can neither spell, nor pronounce, the word aluminium, has little to offer a man of my particular caste. As I duly informed him.

'And besides,' I concluded with ever-mounting hauteur, 'why should I go to America? Let America come to me.'

He fell silent; began smoking incessantly; listened in shocked awe as I described my exalted place in the grand scheme of things. And, as he stubbed yet another unfinished cigarette out on the dashboard, he cracked, as I secretly knew he would. He screeched to a halt and deposited me, and my bicycle parts, on the hard shoulder, his parting words pathetic in the extreme.

'Did I say I was performing at the E'bro festival?' he said. 'Fat chance. Hell, I'm just a lowly spot welder from Warwick and this is my turn-off.'

I informed him, curtly, that I was hardly likely to have a spot that needed welding and that, if I did, it was inconceivable that I'd be in Warwick – second W silent – at the time. Inference? So long, buddy, but not au revoir.

The bicycle at this point had been disassembled to such an extent that, if used as a mode of transport, it wouldn't know which way to go. Fortunately I was offered a generous sum by a passing conceptual artist in search of objets trouvés. And so, with a not inconsiderable sum in my pocket, I continued my journey north.

I accepted several more lifts and a curious pattern emerged among the drivers. All boasted of heading for the Edinburgh Festival. Purpose? Mirth. On being subjected to my incisive cross-examination, however, they turned out to be a short order cook from Ripon, head of the psychiatric wing at Newcastle General Hospital, and a trainee seamstress from Berwick-upon-Tweed.

As I was deposited on the hard shoulder on each succeeding occasion, I marvelled at my almost supernatural ability to prick the over-inflated balloons of the pompous.

XLII

Edinburgh, loveliest of cities.

Often referred to, I believe, as the Glasgow of the North.

I entered the city gates in ebullient mood. I was about to inhale the rarefied air of culture. I had naturally brought a copy of my work-in-progress for the delight and edification of my peers. Who knows, I might even meet someone from Oxbridge. Ask directions, that sort of thing.

Unfortunately, however, I had obviously entered the city well past the witching hour. My first port of call, then, was a lodging for what remained of the night. As I made my search I felt confident that my sojourn in this noblest of cities would be highly fruitful. I was sure to be in great demand for readings and the like when news of my forthcoming anthology circulated. I resolved, therefore, to err on the side of ostentation.

I would have to hold court, and would be ill advised to do so from a hovel.

The Caledonian Hotel looked eminently suited to my purpose, from the outside at least. And, to be fair, from the vestibule and main lounge. As to the executive suite of choice, however, I never actually got that far. I had given myself over to the notion of luxuriating in a foam bath while the trouser press went about its work, when word came back from the reception desk. They were fully booked for the duration of the Festival. I must look elsewhere.

'You'll be lucky to get anywhere at this juncture,' said the receptionist.

'And what juncture would that be?' I quipped.

'A plethora of people,' replied the receptionist. 'A paucity of places.'

I noted that the young lady in question was trying to match me with the breadth of her vocabulary and wondered, aloud, if she was perhaps a student at this historic city's venerable university and if, in that case, she was studying English literature.

'I am,' she replied playfully, 'and I am.'

'In that case,' I bantered, 'you'll have heard of the great MacFiach.'

'Funny you should say that,' she replied, 'but I have indeed. My thesis references *The Seduction and Other Poems*, a seminal post-feminist classic, and I believe the great MacFiach merits a footnote.' She leaned across the counter. 'But even he would have difficulty finding a place to stay.'

The mood darkened as she turned to a fresh customer.

'Yet another case,' I muttered dryly as I headed for the exit, 'of no room at the inn.'

I need hardly mention the precedent, but the receptionist seemed unmoved by my reference to Joseph of Nazareth. Of his dignity in the face of rejection. Of his stoic acceptance of the need to book in advance. And yet, I concluded, as I negotiated the revolving doors, his reduced expectations were hardly on a par with mine. He may have been denied the pleasures of the foam bath, granted, but he can hardly have mourned the absence of a trouser press.

XLIII

No inn then. And not a stable in sight. But my needs were simple, my expectations, at this stage, none. I passed a walled kirkyard. I went in.

Such atmosphere. Such mausolea. I have often thought that death is wasted on the dead, and here was living proof. I wandered from grave to grave in silent raptures of morbid ecstasy. And yet. And yet. I was weary. I had need of sleep. Not, yet, the sleep of eternity – time enough for that – but a good eight hours nonetheless.

To this end I laid my burden down before the burial mound of a city notary who wasted his life in good deeds, wrote no poetry as a result, and was therefore of no further consequence. Except – I am projecting forward here to give him the benefit of hindsight – that his gravestone was about to shelter a genius. So perhaps he had not lived in vain.

Here lieth the body of
Farquharson Hogg
Ecclesiastic
Righteous in the unwavering cause of Truth
Staunch in Religious Observance and Fear of the Lord
Both Gracious in the bounty of his Expatiation and Majestic
in Peroration

Scourge of the Iniquitous and Fleshly
Steadfast Patron of the Destitute in the Munificence of his
Counsel
Here also lieth
His unblemished offspring Duty
Released by the Almighty from Sin in the Glorious
Circumstance of her Birth
His unswerving mastiff Repent
And

And? Curious. The inscription seemed remarkably unfinished. Perhaps friend Hogg had run out of money to pay the stonemason. Or perhaps, and I say this with the great Artist's commendable lack of humility, the inscription was waiting for *me*.

I decided to do some work on my soon-to-be-groundbreaking opus, and noted that I had arrived at the nineteenth century. *Mise Raifteirí An File.* Now here was an interesting conundrum. The poem is in Irish, but I had already done a version myself. *I Am Raftery The Poet* became, in translation, *I Am MacFiach The Poet* – one has to make the imagery live for a modern audience – and was understandably rejected on the grounds that I didn't want to draw unwarranted attention to myself.

Raftery binned, I was about to bid the estimable Farquharson goodnight and join him in sleep when I became aware of a small group sitting in a huddle beside a nearby crypt. Naturally keen to lay me down, I was nonetheless intrigued by the presence of this close-knit gathering, and decided to approach them in a spirit of conviviality.

They were obviously in celebratory mood, if the quantity of bottles in the vicinity was any signifier. I announced myself.

'MacFiach,' I declared. 'Poet.'

That was as far as I got. A flaming redhead with matching hair staggered to his feet.

'This is Poets' Corner, pal,' he slurred. 'And I'm Hamish-h-h . . .' – he was having some trouble with the words – '****ing Sheaney.'

And such was their delight at meeting a fellow practitioner that they all laughed with uproarious pleasure for some minutes after. I must say I was greatly heartened to see them take such obvious delight in their poetic calling, but found it nigh impossible to establish the cause of their celebration. Their self-appointed spokesman informed me, however, that I might be permitted to join them if I cared to replenish their depleted resources and put my worldly goods at their disposal. He then embraced me with wild Celtic abandon and informed me that Hamish ****ing Sheaney was, from henceforth, my blood brother.

I delved into the deep pockets of my coat, and at that moment we – this motley convocation of versifiers and I – became staunch and steadfast friends. I was a fine fellow and a great poet to boot.

> *But time, foul time, thou fickle thief,*
> *How thou replaceth joy with grief!*
>
> *– Anon.*

As I pulled the pockets out to reveal the emptiness within, this fleeting bond of friendship turned to bitter enmity, and I returned to my sleeping quarters alone, unsung and with my former champion's bitter words echoing through my skull.

'I *have* no brother!'

I fell into a troubled sleep and awoke, some hours later, under a thin layer of early August snow. My erstwhile brother sat glowering at me with brooding, black-browed contempt from a nearby tomb. I fell into a deeper and more relaxed sleep and felt, in an odd sort of way, curiously at home.

XLIV

I awoke revivified, and with no obvious signs of gangrene. Sheaney, I noted, slept in the glowering position, and the debris of the previous night's revelries lay strewn on saint and sinner, king and commoner, and a generous smattering of city elders, deceased. I bade the amenable Hogg a cheery good morning and decided to dispense with work on my great project for that morning at least. There was the small matter of settling in to attend to. I might, after all, be here for some time.

The grave itself was perfect for my purposes, lacking only a bedside cabinet to give it that extra star. Serendipitously, a generous growth of grass grew around the headstone, so I secreted my papers in the lush greenery and made my way, past the loudly snoring Sheaney, to the exit.

Oh happy day! No sooner had I quit the walled repository of Death and Poetry than a postman approached from the opposite direction. I was in ebullient mood and decided to save him the trouble of going in.

'Anything for Poets' Corner?' I ventured merrily.

'Where?'

Where?! It was his confounded route! But he was young. Possibly new to the post. I decided to elucidate.

'Poets' Corner,' I chortled, in skittish mood. 'Affordable accommodation for the artistically afflicted. Spartan in its lack of facilities, but on the positive side, no gas.'

I made a note of my change of address and told him I fully expected to be woken by the plop of at least one item of redirected mail, chez Hogg, on the morrow. I was referring, of course, to my long-awaited response from Faber, with particular reference to an advance against projected sales. I also expected word from the Irish Writer's Museum, which must surely have located larger premises by this stage. But no point in taxing the postman with that now. I left him to address the contents of his groaning sack with a cheery dismissal, turned to face the metropolis, and strode briskly from the confines of the dead.

Edinburgh, it seemed, was basking in a Mediterranean glow, and I had been strolling along the cobbled streets of the Royal Mile for some time, rejoicing in the freedom of not being recognised, when I passed a large party at a pavement cafeteria munching and quaffing in unison. The cafeteria was agreeably shady, so I had a quick glance at the wall menu, set to pleasing effect in a glass case and describing exotic dishes in ornate language with a liberal use of the curlicue. To this reader, at any rate, it didn't make a great deal of sense. I was reminded, curiously, of female attempts at poetry.

I was, however, hungry, so I sat at a vacant seat the better to rest my weary limbs and – instructive, this – the woman at the adjoining seat sensed my essential otherness at once.

'Excuse me,' she said by way of introduction, 'but are you one of us?'

I placed an avuncular hand on her outstretched blouse.

'Certainly not, madam,' I replied, 'for the true Artist is an outsider. He must plough a lonely furrow. He must endure ostracisation, penury and the agonising throes of a solitary death. He is, in that most poignant of phrases, beyond the pale. Not for him the cheap laughter of the stalls. The comfort of women. The holiday home in Buncrana.'

And with that I raised an empty glass and rapped the marble table with a fork.

'Waiter! More wine! And I'll have the braised mullet.'

Some time later – and yes, you may be sure I recited for my luncheon – I was off. I bade adieu to my new-found friends and left them to stare in wonder at my disappearing back. Their lives, I suspected, would never be the same again.

XLV

At this point it is, perhaps, meet and fitting that I should pause and reflect for a moment on the momentous tides of fortune which had brought me here. By dint of perseverance and hard work, and as a result of shaking off my parents, background, false gods of the Heaney variety and native land at the earliest available opportunity, I stood on the verge of greatness. And things certainly augured well. I had homed in on Poets' Corner as if destined to do so. I had settled in, redirected my post, slept and eaten well, and was now ready to walk among my peers and feast on a diet of culture.

But as I strode further and further from the kirkyard I noted, with alarm, that the sunshine appeared to have attracted the worst aspects of trash culture. The streets of the city were plagued by strutters, fretters, preeners and unicyclists. So where on earth was the much trumpeted, so-called cultural feast?

I was beginning to think that the very word Festival was a construct of my wild imagination when I finally located it, emblazoned in neon on, to my dismay, an upmarket fleapit. Festival, yes, but of the categorically wrong sort.

The Film Festival proved a cultural feast too far for this particular aesthete. My views on the cinematographic so-called arts are too well documented to merit a further outpouring of bile. Suffice it to say that I almost bumped into my maternal uncle staggering out of the main auditorium, ubiquitous glass in hand. His parasitical offspring Joel and Ethan, for those interested in such matters, were the palpable hit of the festival, according to their own publicity, with *Shotgun Wedding – The Irish O'Edipus*. But this need not concern us here. Also showing, and I mention this in passing, was *Kiss My Ass 2*, which suggested that the formerly unspoiled Assumpta had carved out a pitiful niche for herself in the adolescent market.

That this minor art form should have its own festival says much about the times in which we live, but this is not an editorial feature and serves merely to distract us from my uncle, into whom, as I say, I almost bumped. And we would definitely have collided if both of us had been sober, or both, conversely, drunk. As it was, my own straight line and my uncle's zig-zag criss-crossed with mathematical precision and I was well nigh out of the danger zone when he spotted me.

'There you are,' he slurred, 'you . . . *towering blackguard.*'

Wit, as always, at any price. But by the time he had got a member of the public to hold his drink, drawn a revolver from his trouser pocket, and begun the execution of a no-doubt hilarious mime, I had very wisely vamoosed.

XLVI

Things could only get better? Unbeknownst to myself, I was about to subject this particular cliché to a rigorous analysis. To prove, in fact, the converse. Cutting a path through yet another unicyclist, I chanced upon the hallowed grounds of the university sector. The pleasing austerity of the architectural offerings augured well, and I entered a magnificent courtyard intending to apply for cultural asylum.

But wait. The courtyard was packed with the very strutters and fretters, the self-same preeners and unicyclists I had just relinquished to the street. My keen poet's eye absorbed the scene with a curious mix of clinical detachment and mounting fury. If I wish to see a clown – and I unquestionably don't – I go to the circus. Ditto with preeners and their ilk. But this venerable seat of learning had seemingly metamorphosed into a decidedly *un*venerable seat of trick cycling!

And there, as if to compound matters, I beheld the spot welder from Warwick, the short order cook from Ripon, the head psychiatrist from Newcastle General Hospital and the trainee seamstress from Berwick-upon-Tweed in riotous conversation at a nearby courtyard table. What could this possibly mean? My brain, true to its cranium-bursting complexities, juggled with three simultaneous thoughts:

That they bitterly regretted passing up the opportunity to purchase a signed copy of a certain slim volume and had clubbed together so to do;
That inferior signposting in the North Yorkshire area meant they were lost;

And, proof that my brain works in mysterious ways:

That the ability to think about thinking about two concurrent thoughts is, in itself, the third thought.

XLVII

I absented myself from the distinctly unhallowed grounds of the courtyard post-haste.

Not that I felt able to relax. I had singularly failed to locate the Festival, and as I traipsed around the swarming streets, genius in search of peer group, I was dogged by a condition without a name. Lord Byron Syndrome, perhaps? My brooding looks, at any rate, attracted unwarranted attention, although I managed to ignore it for the most part. Until, that is, I chanced upon a large theatre of the sort dedicated to all-prancing, all-trilling extravaganzas. And what particular offering had this particular edifice brought to the cultural feast?

Irish Sensation! World's First Catholic Lesbian Musical!

'17 Brides for 17 Sisters'

The matinee audience from this appalling spectacle had just begun to blink into the sunlight. Lesbians all, no doubt. And I have no quarrel with that. Au contraire; as a leading feminist I embrace them. But I had already noted a tendency for ladies of this persuasion to heterosexualise in my brooding orbit. Indeed I've written several monographs on the subject which suggest that sexual preference is, contrary to pseudo-scientific 'proof', a movable feast. At any rate I wasn't taking any chances with the gentlewomen now clogging the pavement in front of me as I marched resolutely on my way.

Intending to circumnavigate the Sapphic throng and continue, unmolested, on my way, I strode down a side street. Hah! Would that life were so simple. But if the same life has taught me one valuable lesson it is this: things can only get worse. No sooner had I reached the back of the theatre than the stage door opened. I had reckoned without the thirty-four lesbians on stage, and here precisely fifty per cent of them were, blocking my forward passage with gay abandon. The Brides? The Sisters? I had no way of knowing. Nor did I have time to enquire. They seemed intent on cutting small talk to a minimum by knowing my name in advance.

'Fiachra!' they shrieked, and their voices, in the confined space of the laneway, were as coarse and shrill as seagulls on sewage. I gave them a frosty look.

'I'm terribly sorry,' I said, 'but I don't believe we've been formally introduced.'

Now I have re-examined that sentence since. It was delivered with perfect gravity. It contains within it no concession to mirth. And yet their hilarity was unconfined. They roared! They hooted! Oh, how they hooted!

'That', apparently, 'was a good one all right'.

'That', apparently also, 'was the business entirely'.

I double-checked for possible visual humour, but no. Trousers present and correct. Zip ditto. I was about to bid them good day and prise my way through their serried ranks when one of the pushier members of the troupe linked arms and manhandled me along the laneway.

'Come on,' she said. 'We're late enough as it is.'

'Late?' I all but yelped.

'Oh for ****'s sake, Fiachra,' she snapped. 'The Book Festival. Surely you don't want to miss you-know-who?'

Book Festival? I-knew-who? I write this in full possession of the awful facts as they emerged, and it is with no small difficulty that I withhold same for dramatic effect. But that's narrative thrust for you. I could, I suppose, have begun this biographical masterpiece with the triumphant denouement. The glorious vindication which placed me in my rightful position, a giant on the shoulders of pygmies.

So why not do this? Drama. Simple as that. Will he succeed or won't he? There's a clue in the fact that I'm writing the blessed thing in the first place. But forget I said that. Back, for the moment, to the present.

There I was, being jostled along the streets of Edinburgh by seventeen lesbians towards a Book Festival about which I knew nothing. And perhaps this festival of books was nothing of the sort. Perhaps, perish the thought, it was rhyming slang for . . . But no! Surely not! Seventeen soon-to-be-former lesbians and the present writer? As one of the more outlandish plotlines of the modern musical theatre it may have had a certain decadent merit, but the real world was decidedly not ready for an all-singing, all-dancing sex slave MacFiach.

Fortunately, however, I was spared the worst of what these Amazons may well have had in mind. The Book Festival turned out to be just that. A book festival. Had I known what tribulation awaited, however, I might well have opted, in the seedy hostelry of their choice, for the rhyming version.

The close proximity of books, however, lent me wings. I had no intention of sullying my reputation by consorting with such wanton escorts, so I bade them good day with curt civility. I then ducked round the side of one of the many tents in the vicinity and disappeared into the nearest gents' toilet, a safe haven from even the most bullish Sapphite. And so it proved.

I commandeered the solitary urinal and was about to bemoan my fatal attractiveness to women when I heard applause from the nearby tent and made out the microphone-enhanced introduction to – and this beggars belief – the celebrated, Nobel Prize-winning 'author' Seamus Heaney.

The Nobel Prize!?

For Fish!?

XLVIII

I froze. Or, rather, my urinary tract froze. Unable to block out the sound of this appalling dilettante by humming loudly, I stood my ground for a good hour, brushed past the ill-tempered queue with regal disdain, and blinked back into the daylight. Just as the lesbians emerged from a long and wearisome but thankfully muffled dissertation on matters piscatorial.

And true, there will be those who say, 'Fiachra, be reasonable. Why should not a lowly fishmonger grace or, if you will,
*dis*grace a festival of books? Not literature, mark. Books. And
by the way, what's this about the lesbians?'

Fair questions. I propose to deal with the first by ignoring
it. Heaney may have tossed together a slim volume of recipes
on his day off. Good luck to him, say I. On the small matter
of the lesbians, however, I can only say that no one was more
surprised than I at the shocking revelation of their true identi-
ties. Fiona? Fionnuala? Fidelma? Felicity? Franny? Fanny?
Faith? Flannery? Frieda? Florence? Floella? Flossie? Flora?
Fauna? Fern? Fifi? Fay? Not to mention – and I haven't
included her in the final tally for obvious reasons – Fatima the
Apparition?

Had I delved into MacFiach's *Little Book of Aphoristic Wit*
I may have noted my own anticipation of this understandable
oversight.

> *To mislay one sister is careless. To mislay seventeen*
> *downright Catholic.*

True, I wasn't aware that I had such a large number of sisters
– *any*, in fact – but this was hardly surprising in the segregated
Ireland of those repressive times, where male and female occupied different countries of the mind, and a husband *spake not*
unto his wife lest he know sin.

XLIX

I reprised my curt good day, returned chez Hogg forthwith
and applied with great liberality the therapeutic balm of

work. I had now entered what might be called the foothills of Yeats. For such was his towering influence that his shadow is cast both ways across the centuries.

Take, for instance, the following, dealing with his old friend and mentor, the celebrated post-Plunkett transsexual Lady 'Gregory':

> *The playwright Lady Gregory's*
> *Remembered for Kiltartanese*
> *A style developed with some mates*
> *Like poet William Butler Yeats.*
> *Alas this style would not enthral*
> *A modern audience at all*
> *(At all at all); the theatre*
> *Would fall about in glee at her*
> *Whose sentences, although well meant*
> *Read like a speech impediment.*
> *For instance she would call a fog*
> *'The mist that does be on the bog'.*
> *In 1910 they thought this odd*
> *But now it's obsolete, thank God.*
> *Kiltartanese is long since dead*
> *And that does be all that does be after remaining*
> *   to be said.*
>
> *   – Anon.*

Interesting piece, but oh dear! – that last line. Scansion! Scansion! Bin! And so it went. Many days I laboured in the mighty shadow of Hogg's tombstone, consigning recent developments to the nether regions of my voluminous brain, where dark thoughts festered like a suppurating boil. This I could take. I had one on my left testicle once. Far worse.

Meanwhile I continued luncheoning at a wide variety of pavement bistros with not unpleasing results. The secret of my success? I never chose the same establishment twice. In this manner I met, and royally entertained, a cross-section of the population of this sad planet and, after the initial conversational ice breaker – 'Are you one of us?' 'Is he one of us?' 'No, no. I distinctly remember booking for twelve,' and so on – my easy charm and sociable good nature made many new friends from around the globe, and even resulted in some cash orders for my forthcoming anthology, post and packaging extra.

The anthology was proceeding apace. I had reached, as previously mentioned, the modern era, and I began to sense, one dark and Sheaney-glowering night, my great work drawing to its close. This energising assessment buoyed my spirits and I sauntered forth the following morning in ebullient mood. I dined with an excitable group of Japanese tourists. At least I assumed they were tourists. They might have been from Edinburgh's possibly bustling Japanese quarter. I also assumed, come to think of it, that they were Japanese. I didn't register with them for some time as they seemed more interested in photographing each other across the table. But once they had noted my appearance in several snaps, and babbled excitedly to each other as a result, they were courtesy itself and seemed genuinely sorry to see me go. Indeed they registered their sorrow with impeccably Oriental courtesy – they left before I did.

They also left a considerable repast and several unopened bottles of Basmati rice wine.

I appropriated a bottle of same, and was about to wish the manager good morning in Japanese when my Dublin uncle staggered past brandishing his revolver. The manager, little realising that this was simply my estimable relative in customary skittish mode, backed away from the outside tables and dived for cover inside. I pocketed my bottle, pleaded a prior engagement, and left my swaying uncle training his pistol on the scattering passers by.

L

As I indulged, that afternoon, in a post-prandial nap I was, as I say, in excellent spirits. I had eaten well. I had extended the hand of friendship to our Oriental brethren and female equivalent. I had also lain down a bottle of the previous year's vintage – a good year for rice, I believe – against the imminent completion of my magnum opus.

Things, otherwise, had returned to a state approaching normalcy. The odd can bouncing off my cranium. Ribald laughter from my erstwhile champion Sheaney and his pards. No mail.

The latter, actually, is not strictly accurate. I did receive an invitation to apply to American Express, several items of junk, and a misdirected gas bill. Wrong Hogg. I also received, and this infuriated me beyond apoplexy, a cheque from my crooning classmate Brendan Gilhooley to the effect that '"*The Night We Sold Shilelaghs Down The Shankill Road*" done (sic) the business all right. Here's your cut.' Tainted money. I naturally shredded the cheque. Finally, I opened the obligatory letter from my mother.

Irish author, 17, gets 12-figure advance for synopsis of limerick.

Nothing, however, from Faber. And I was bemoaning the fact that the publishing world had relinquished the old world courtesies when the festering boil, merely suppurating until now, began to throb incessantly, announcing its imminent intention to erupt like a Vesuvius of the mind.

This, I need hardly add, is a metaphorical reading. The reality, as ever, was marginally less benign. I began to hear voices. Well, *a* voice. Incessant at first, insistent, mingling with the sounds of ribaldry as I reassembled Yeats from memory.

And would that it had been Yeats' sonorous declamations I heard from afar. Sadly, however, I had mislaid my ouija board.

So all I heard was a disembodied voice, definitively external, which boomed and echoed off the graveyard walls as if heralding me to my doom. I felt compelled, as if by some hidden force, to follow it. I organised my papers for the off; leaned the bottle of rice wine gently against the carved stone of my lodging; and prepared to sally forth, yet again, into the world.

My fellow poets had evinced a marked restraint in respect of the privacy of my writings, and could therefore be expected to extend the same courtesy to my other effects. As I left the sanctuary of the graveyard, the voice rebounded off the magnificently austere buildings, not to mention my magnificently austere cranium, and I wandered for some time in a state of extreme confusion. The voice: whence, in a word, did it come? To whom, in another word, did it belong?

Not Yeats.

Heaney, then? I waited in vain for some mention of mullet, sturgeon, perch or pilchard, or, indeed, a passing reference to the Nobel Prize for same. Nothing. So not, then, Heaney.

But if not Heaney – who?

LI

The voice followed me through the streets and wynds of this historic city; beneath the historic cliffs of its historic castle. Eventually, as I was circumnavigating the historic castle walls, the voice increasing in volume all the while, I traced its infuriating source far below me.

A green sward sported a huge outdoor stage nestling in the lee of the castle. I have set the scene with broad yet precise brush strokes. Huge stage. Sward. Enough. I slalomed down the cliff face and approached the former via the latter, passing as I did so the statue of a city notary. Farquharson Hogg? Possibly. At any rate he looked pleasingly stately, if we except the ubiquitous traffic cone atop his bronze, unyielding head. A large screeching gull circled the statue, confused perhaps by the presence of the cone, which sat tilted at a raffish angle, suggesting a music hall turn or other low type. I mention this in passing as it had some bearing on what was to follow; but I, and not the unfortunate erection, am the subject of this piece.

To recapitulate: circumnavigate; slalom. I adjusted my trousers and strode past the statue in the direction of the stage. Many a head turned as I cut a swath through the audience in all its summer frippery. A black-clad figure of Byronic aspect is a delight to the eye at all times, and I was at least one up on the Byron who gave Byronic its name. No limp. Byron may well have remained stationary to achieve the desired Byronic effect – he was indisputably motionless any time he sat for his portrait – and he may well have suffered in the era of the moving image.

Not so MacFiach. I moved evenly to the front of the stage bestridden by my *accursed gag merchant brother*. For he it indisputably was, microphone in hand, patter tripping from his ever open maw. He seemed unaware of my impending presence, as witness his failure to quake in his scarlet boots, and as I reached the steps at the front of the stage he regaled the audience with yet another limp quip about his – nay *my* – childhood.

Emboldened by righteous fury I marched up the steps to the stage and stood, immobile, a matter of inches from his face.

'Christ!' he smirked. 'There's two of us!'

Now it might be remarked upon that he was repeating himself here. His followers, however – a mass outbreak of Goldfish Syndrome, perhaps? – had obviously forgotten. They broke, at any rate, into wild and spontaneous applause at the brilliance of his mental arithmetic, which illustrates how far standards have fallen since the introduction of the calculator.

But enough nostalgia. The scene's crowning image is imminent.

As I stood there, glowering but immobile, the gull, which had tired of waiting for the cone to dislodge itself, wheeled away from the statue, described an arc, began circling the stage and *splat!* Its white excretion, reserved for the ennobled and the mighty and the long since dead, landed on the crown of my head in full view of the stunned and muted mob. Time itself stood still. As the white fluid trickled down my luxuriant locks, I heard the wild cry of the gull as it rose in the heavens and disappeared behind a dark and Gothic spire.

'Bide a wee, MacFiach,' it seemed to cry. 'Your hour will assuredly come.'

Time resumed its onward journey. The crowd roared. My brother shrugged and graciously ceded the stage.

I was the anointed one.

He knew.

LII

This great omen signalled my impending elevation to the ranks of the immortals. For that, I was convinced, was the import of the seagull's message. And the crowd, as if sensing this, roared on. I raised my left arm in recognition of its mass devotion.

They roared louder. I raised both arms. They erupted. All I could see below me was a vast sea of humanity. Hands. Faces. Bodies. Joined together as one in this glorious celebration of MacFiach. I felt curiously humbled.

I would reach out to them with my poetry in sublime communion. So deciding, I was about to declaim from memory when I noticed, for the first time, Blind Cearbhúil – my erstwhile collaborator – standing to attention at the front of the disabled section of the crowd. I put thoughts of declamation to one side, for now at least. I decided, instead, to walk among my people.

I descended the steps of the stage to adulation bordering on hysteria. I pushed my way past a couple of wheelchairs and approached Blind Cearbhúil. The crowd fell silent. I laid a healing hand on his forehead.

With my free hand I removed his sunglasses and tossed them, with a theatrical flourish into the crowd.

'Let there be light!' I cried.

Cearbhúil's stunned silence resounded in my ears, and I may, I admit, have got slightly carried away at this point. I could do no wrong, it seemed, and when I spotted a small group of youthful merrymakers sipping bottled water, it seemed churlish not to turn it into something a tad more festive. Difficult to know how the Biblical sleight of hand was achieved, or what the local Temperance League had to say on the matter, but no amount of alchemical trickery was going to work with a modern audience. I therefore prised a six-pack of super-strength lager from Possibly-Sighted Cearbhúil's startled grasp and flung it at the water-quaffers.

'Go ye and do likewise,' I intoned enigmatically. 'For so it is written.'

Now the more theologically trained reader will have noted my conscious attempt to emulate the author of best-selling memoir the Bible, and so I continued, dispensing medical and mystical largesse as I went. I may, for instance, have rid the crowd of leprosy at a stroke. Difficult to tell without the statistical data to back it up. What is indisputable, however, is that I overplayed my hand on the Suffer the Little Children question.

In my defence I would say simply this: Christ was hardly required to sign forms in triplicate before he started plonking minors on his knee, and times have possibly changed since those days. Suffice to say that no sooner had I suffered the first child – small; pink dress; probably female – than the mood changed palpably. For thus it ever was with the rabble: fickle; flighty; prone to turning ugly on a whim. And there, in the shape of a Botticelli nightmare, was that whim.

I returned the child forthwith to its alleged parents and took immediate flight. Constabulary whistles. Cries of 'Pervert!' A surfeit of cobbles. I was chased through the chartered streets past many a careering unicyclist till I found myself, at last, panting and exhausted, but thankfully alone; seeking refuge in the darkened doorway of a second-hand clothes shop.

LIII

I entered as if fated to do so. A pleasing mustiness enveloped the racks. I accustomed myself to the half-light and felt curiously at home the further I retreated into its shadowy alcoves. I was drawn – I know not how – to an alcove beyond shadow; to a coat beyond Biblical black. A frisson of excitement enveloped my corporeal frame. I ran my fingertips along the broad shoulders of the coat; felt its essence; almost heard it growl.

I felt impelled to try it on. And so, doffing my own coat, its leather elbow patches holding on by a mere thread to the surrounding fabric, I slipped its replacement on. A perfect fit. As if the tailor had held it up all those years ago and said 'Cometh the hour, cometh MacFiach.'

And come I assuredly had.

I peered round the side of the alcove. A pair of homely women deep in prattle on either side of the ancient till had failed to register my presence. Relaxing into my new greatcoat I appraised myself in a full-length mirror, and was pleased to note that I looked, to the casual observer – myself, in this case – magnificently broody. Curious. I appeared to have a light sprouting of hair on my cheeks. My forehead. My eyeballs. I raised my hands in the gloom. A light covering of down graced both palms. I moved closer to the mirror. A grey, gossamer growth suffused my outer being. I felt a curious sensation which was not un-euphoric. A tingling of the blood. A kind of rapturous glee.

The mirror cracked. I sauntered, no doubt still broody, from the shop, the aforementioned ladies preoccupied, on my exit, with the great affairs of their day.

LIV

The sun had fled. A thick, dank fog rolled in from the sea. As I stepped back into the litter-strewn cobbles of old Edinburgh, it was as if the world outside had suddenly aged. Or retreated to a dark, nightmarish past.

Austere buildings rose up from the gloom like Gothic ships. Metal shutters glistened in the mist. The fretters and strutters were driven like a plague from the land. No sound but the lonesome cry of the harlot. I transferred my quill, my notes, my slim volume from my old coat to my new, shedding my old self like a snake shedding its skin or a black butterfly emerging from the chrysalis of its former existence. I tossed the cocoon of my discarded life in a nearby gutter – for one less fortunate than I – and sauntered on.

Just then a unicylist, separated from his fellows, scurried past, gripping his ridiculous conveyance by its saddle. Seizing my chance, I grabbed the offending vehicle and thrashed him gaily about the head till he sank, chastened and bloodied, to his knees. Curious. He appeared to metamorphose, by so sinking, into an aged man with a walking frame. No one else there, however, so no harm done. I bade him a speedy recovery and moved on.

Ageing spires loomed out of the swirling sea of mist. I negotiated the wynds and closes of this once historic city, my teeming brain aflame. My newly acquired coat enveloped me like a pelt, and gull-streaked hair encrusted my head like an honorary doctorate from the Immortals. I felt magnificent.

The murk of day succumbed to the blackness of night. A reverberant bell tolled one. Two. Three. I pulled my new coat tighter around me and loped back to the graveyard emitting a low growl of contentment. It was then that I remembered my bottle of rice wine. I would raise a toast to my fellow poets, reflect on the past and, no doubt, look to the future with no small degree of equanimity. I entered the main gate and was making my way past my heavily snoring peers towards my own quarters when I spotted, in the tenebrous gloom, the outline of a body laid out in my place. On closer inspection the outline was dressed in my discarded coat. And cradling, like a babe newborn, my undiscarded bottle. Drained of its Eastern brew.

I was about to accost the comatose culprit when I heard a roar that stopped me short.

'Got you at last, you blackguard!'

I ducked, just in time, behind a neighbouring gravestone as my uncle staggered out of the all-encircling darkness and fell, with screams and imprecations, on a startled Hamish Sheaney. For it was undoubtedly he who had appropriated my coat, my resting place, my wine! Sheaney, terrified, grabbed my uncle's wrist. They grappled furiously as the empty bottle slipped from the inebriate poet's grasp and smashed on the grave beneath.

I stole into the shadows and watched as the gravestone, which cradled my life's work, groaned perceptibly. I could only hope the two combatants recognised the necessity of protecting works of Art in a time of conflict. At any rate the preternatural struggle continued. The gravestone, under-mined perhaps by my earlier excavation, creaked like an enormous blackened tooth. It creaked again and, loosened from the binding gums of earth, keeled over in an instant and solved, serendipitously, the mystery of the unfinished inscrip-tion. At the base of the stone, and released fortuitously from the obstruction of the enveloping undergrowth:

And
his wyf

So. Not MacFiach after all. But then, foresight is not the strong suit of the ecclesiastical class.

The stonemason thus exonerated, however, the raw materi-als of his trade crushed both parties in their fight to the – as it turned out – death. Two deaths caused, inadvertently perhaps, by that outstanding pillar of the community, Farquharson Hogg.

And, to a lesser extent, his wyf.

I reflected on the fact that the deeds men do indeed live on as I scooped pens, journals and a recently delivered letter from the redistributed earth. I then bade farewell to the residents of Poets' Corner as a light fall of late August snow fell on all of the living and, with two recent additions in this particular location, all of the dead.

LV

Under a flickering street lamp I paused and peered at the envelope. A child's artless scribble. My pulse raced. The lamp flickered out. Impossible to decipher the writing in the dark, but I had, let us say, an inkling. If correct, it would change everything. I could hardly contain my excitement when I heard voices approaching.

Drunken voices. Lustful voices. Tinkling-with-laughter voices. I pocketed the letter and stood still, hands thrust deep into my hell-black coat, my face caressed by the swirling fog. The voices moved off. I followed on behind. Through the mirk I made out the unmistakable shape of my flaxen-haired brother with his latest floozy. A statuette and a magnum of champagne in one hand, floozy in the other, he staggered along the footpath in several directions at once.

I followed their shrill laughter from a distance as he bombarded the impressionable strumpet with tacky gags.

'To the crags,' he slurred, grabbing the giggling strumpet close. 'To the crags.'

'Oh, Finn,' she shrieked. 'You are so *romantic.*'

Soon I had followed them to the foot of the long slope leading to the mighty rock face of Salisbury Crags. I followed at a discreet distance as my brother, now ribald, now maudlin, entertained the object of his lust with honeyed platitudes.

'Oh, Finn,' she shrilled. 'You have the soul of a poet.'

And still they staggered on through the dark and swirling mist. Onwards and upwards through the dense, damp undergrowth. I may have been only feet away from them. Difficult to say. I passed but one solitary walker on the long upward journey. He appeared looming out of the mist. I recognised him at once as the man who sold me the matt black emulsion. Ebony hair. Scarlet lips. Cloven brogues.

I was about to upbraid him for the inferior quality of his product when a startled raven flapped from the undergrowth.

The sounds of movement ceased up ahead.

'What was that?' said the strumpet.

I froze and peered through the mist.

'What?' slurred my brother. 'What was what?'

'That sound.'

'Twas but the sound of the wynd soughing through the trees. Come,' said my brother.

And with a quick trill of laughter and a 'Finn, you are *so funny*,' they resumed their upward journey.

I turned my attention back to the paint salesman. Gone! Vanished! This, I note in passing, is typical of the merchant class. Ubiquitous at the point of sale. But try to track them down for a refund! I made a brief, if slightly moist, note to that effect and renewed my dogged pursuit.

I heard nothing for a while, just the echo of my solitary trudge, and then – was that the sound of breathing? I edged slowly upwards, as quiet as my mounting excitement would allow, and almost stumbled into them as they grappled in the grass beneath my raised left boot. I stumbled back, heart palpitating, till the swirling mist hid them from view.

And yet I inhaled the fetid stench of their lust. And heard the panting. And the strumpet's disjointed prattle. Her father, it seems, was a man of the cloth. Were he alive today, apparently, my brother would be crucified on the altar of his Presbyterian displeasure.

Not her exact words, but I very much agreed with his post-humous wisdom and couch it, therefore, as I feel he would have wished. The same brother snorted with derision. Just as well he's not here, then, he sniggered, and the strumpet squealed with delight.

I inched forward and was busy planning my next step – I would, perforce, confront my sibling with the magnitude of his own mediocrity – when the fog momentarily cleared. My black coat swirling in a sudden gust, my face set in the obdurate stone of my distaste, I found myself gazing down on the now transfixed form of my accursed twin.

He staggered to his feet and backed away in terror.

'Jesus Christ!' he cried, struggling with his nether garments. 'I thought you said he was . . .'

His final word was lost in an agonising and fast-fading scream as he disappeared, miraculously, from view. The word he was grappling with, I surmised, was 'dead'. His female companion, her face contorted with horror, rushed after him.

'Oh my God!' she shrieked. 'The . . .'

She, too, disappeared dramatically from view, her final word lost, forever, in the swirling mist. The word, and this is pure conjecture on my part, was assuredly 'crags'.

The fog dispersed as her shrieks trailed into the distance. The lights of the city twinkled below my feet and I experienced a curious feeling of elation. I thrust my hands deep into the pockets of my new coat and felt the rustle of the long-forgotten letter. I whipped it out. A sliver of moon bathed the paper in a pale, milky light. The writing was now clear. The letter had indeed been written in a child's awkward hand.

I paused to allow the implications to sink in. I had been right about the Faber dynasty. It had indeed passed on to the next generation – a touch prematurely if truth be told – and here, to prove it, was a letter from Child Faber.

At last!

I tore it open in a state of no small excitement, angled it toward the light of the moon, and began to read:

'Dear Daddy . . .'

What?!

I held the letter slightly closer and tried again.

'Dear Daddy . . .'

No. I had been right the first time. This . . . this was cata-strophic. I, Fiachra MacFiach, had been the victim of a cruel hoax. It was bad enough, surely, to get no letter at all. But the wrong letter! This, surely, was beyond endurance. Still stand-ing at the edge of the precipice, I began to shake visibly. Far below, the lights of the city blurred and swayed. Loose gravel trickled over the edge of the cliff.

Loose gravel, yes, but MacFiach? No.

I steeled myself to my lofty purpose, ripped the offend-ing letter into tiny squares and scattered it, like malevolent confetti, on all that lay beneath.

LVI

Time, I knew, to leave this once historic city. Furiously I strode along for many days. Weeks? Years? Who knows, for who can comprehend the feet of genius? A perambulation, at any rate, which allowed time for reflection and meditation and philo-sophical discourse with myself.

Now there are those who will say 'Whoa, MacFiach. We feel the end of this thrilling tome is in sight. Never mind the inside of your head stuff. How does it all pan out?' Some of these – younger readers, I imagine – will have flicked impa-tiently to the final, beautifully realised scene. Others will be champing at the metaphorical bit so to do. No need. Those not wishing to hear my ruminations will be delighted to know that all ends triumphantly. There. You've just ruined it for everyone else.

Or have you?

Of course not. Narrative thrust, strict chronology and so forth have their place in what might usefully be termed low art. I have mentioned the modern Irish novel in this context. Let us draw a discreet veil over the rest. There are egos present. But the true MacFiachophile will savour each judiciously chosen image, each beautifully polished phrase.

I had gone to Edinburgh as the last bastion of culture only to be snubbed, shunned and thwarted at every turn. Was there one who had suffered as much as I? A rhetorical question – but no. Inference? Edinburgh culture? *Pah!* Oxbridge culture? Double *pah*. And as for Faber!

A suppurating boil on the collective bottom of all three!

I was a man alone. A man with a mission. A man of manifest destiny. I would plough my own furrow, although not, as my father had done in a blameless yet futile existence, literally.

Now my acolytes will be wondering about the *Definitive Anthology*. To my shame I had allowed the appalling egotism of my ex-sibling to distract me from this monumental undertaking. And perhaps the paucity of talent unearthed thus far had jaded the editorial palate. Whatever the reason, I was about to readdress this seminal work with vim, gusto and a fresh infusion of artistic blood. And I was about to do so in the most unlikely setting possible.

I had, as I say, been in transit for some time. No rambling lad of pleasure I, however. My peregrinations were distinctly unmerry. Lo and yon I careered, up hill and down dale, or nearest modern equivalent. Which in most cases meant hugging the crash barrier of yet another motorway. And my eating arrangements were similarly improvised. As witness the following:

In the absence of a pavement trattoria or similar along a particularly desolate stretch of the M Something, I had opted for the dubious delights of a transport cafeteria specialising in that rarefied breed – the long-distance lorry driver. I placed myself at a convenient table which groaned under the combined elbows of three gargantuan truckers, and awaited the inevitable question:

'Are you one of us?' Or, given the overfamiliarity of the proletarian classes, 'Are you one of us, *mate*?'

I most decidedly was not one of them; nor they, for that matter, one of me.

But as I sat amongst them and stared into their broad, vacant faces as they swilled chipped mugs of mouse brown tea and wiped bacon grease from their mountainous chins, I was struck by a serendipitous thought. I had been let down by the world. Oxbridge. Edinburgh. Faber. All had been tried and all had been found wanting. But perhaps, curious thought, I had been aiming too low.

Consider:

I had conversed with the Immortals.

I had picked up the gauntlet.

I had embarked on *The Definitive Anthology of Irish Poetry*.

I had just arrived at Yeats. This towering genius of Irish verse. This gargantuan talent. This veritable long-distance lorry driver of the intellect.

Emboldened by the artistic implications of the above I felt a quickening of my pulse. A twitching of my nib. The weight of history on my slender shoulders. This moment would be dwelt upon, by academic and layman alike, for aeons. On such and such a date, at this particular table, on this particular sheet of paper, MacFiach wrote . . . but what?

A statement of intent!

An article of faith!

A battle cry!

A cri de coeur leading, inexorably, to a cri de guerre!

But paper. I needed paper. My new-found friends were busy masticating and swilling, so I left them to it.

I rooted around on the table, but the closest I got to a sheet of paper was the back of a used tobacco packet. I say used.

More accurate, perhaps, to say open. I had to deposit the contents in a convenient mug. Vague mutterings of discontent in the background.

No matter.

I was lost to the world as I pondered the pithy cri de guerre. The spur to immortality. And as I pondered my mind turned to the cry of dead poets through the ages.

What do we want?

To bask in the everlasting glow of Posterity's approval.

When do we want it?

Posthumously.

This, of course, was all very well for *them*. Luminaries of kinder, gentler, *slower* ages, they could well afford to wait. Not so MacFiach. In the mad dash of the modern world, the future waits for no man.

I raised the pen.

I steadied the packet.

The pen leaped into action.

POSTERITY, it wrote, NOW!

The deed done, the bold clarion call committed to paper, I returned from the ever beckoning future to the ever present present. I appeared to be banging the table with great exhilaration, demanding to see the wine list, and ordering lightly broiled pollack with mung beans although it wasn't, strictly speaking, on the menu.

Best not to dwell too lovingly on the outcome. Let me just say that I received, for my pains, a forthright response. To their credit, the lorry drivers blanched as the proprietor set about me. They also pled my case from the doorway as my head was immersed in the deep fat fryer.

LVII

Memo to peripatetic poets in search of sustenance: Avoid Lil's.

But I was still in a state of high, if literally battered, excitement for some time afterwards. Posterity Now. I liked the sound of that. Onwards I marched. On! On! And I was about to traverse a post-industrial conurbation: deserted factories; rusted rail tracks; a veritable mountain range of rat-infested refuse; how bleak it was, how bleak. I was, as I say, about to traverse this veritable dystopian wasteland when I decided, instead, to point to its very heart.

Wilful lunacy? Not so. Rather, I fancy, an intuitive grasp of what it takes to be truly great. To strip away all extraneosities and pierce, at last, to the very core of genius.

On I continued to march! On again! Further on!

As I passed through a desert of outlying scrubland, my eyes were drawn to a block of proletarian flats of such faded functionalism even the plebeians had fled.

Perfect.

Metal grilles studded the windows like plaques of remembrance with, here and there, a lone pocket of resistance. A door here. A grey net curtain there. It was almost as if the Immortals had whispered, 'Try 167. Sixteenth floor. Just a thought.'

As I prepared to negotiate the interminable steps with a weary spring – for I was bodily weary, mentally sprung – a wizened face peered out from a ground-floor window. I met it stare for fleeting stare and passed on.

Many steps later I reached the relevant sixteenth floor and located the pre-ordained number. 167.

The metal grille fell away with a welcoming clatter.

I entered.

Bare room.

Enough.

I chose a corner farthest from the pigeon-infested balcony, laid out my worldly goods, and set to immediate work. I could now devote my not inconsiderable erudition to my not inconsiderable task. The genius of my people compressed and codified for all time.

And before me towered Yeats.

My poetic instinct, daunted perhaps by the sheer magnitude – some would say effrontery – of the Yeats reputation, was to include everything the man had produced. But such blind idolatry is not the MacFiach way. Moreover, a carefully crafted aside from the Immortals had alerted me to the need for critical vigilance as I began to tackle the self-styled icon's oeuvre.

'We'd watch out for that boy if we were you,' they'd muttered. 'He's after your job.'

Constant vigilance, then, was all my cry. And, although it pains me to begin with the monkey gland implant of his so-called maturity, this self-inflicted defilement begs the serious question: who wrote the later verse? Yeats or the chimpanzee? I suggest co-authorship at the very least. The implication? The poetry of Yeats' pre-eminence was half-simian. And if 'The Great Man' is capable of this level of deceit in his dotage, think what he might have got up to early on.

'The Song of Wandering Aengus', for instance, bears all the hallmarks of the Jewish songsmiths of Tin Pan Alley, while his most celebrated lyric, 'The Lake Isle of Innisfree', hardly bears up under serious scrutiny.

Nine bean rows? A hive for the honey bee? Not much in the way of victuals there for a grown man. Frankly, I'm used to roughing it, but clay and wattles? Leaving aside the impracticality of the materials, you'd never get that past the planning stage, *unless you had access to someone in the relevant depart-ment.* My italics.

That he submitted the poem in question to the *New Yorker* magazine is beyond dispute, but what is perhaps of more interest at this distance is his almost fanatical suppression of the fact checker's report. Here is but a brief sample:

My Dear Yeats,
A solitary N, I rather fancy, in the title. And I haven't been
to that particular quarter, but does peace come dropping? Is
noon purple? And is there honey still for tea? Please advise.

Pretty damning stuff – and he appears to have dropped the honey reference as a sop to that august organ – but we then come to the autobiography: To call one's autobiogra-phy *Autobiographies* suggests nothing less than Multiple Personality Disorder. That was enough for me.

The wrecking ball of my intellect had left no stone unsmashed. Emboldened by my critical acuity I scribbled a quick note to Yeats' estate. It had been a difficult decision I imparted to them, but he had failed, sadly, to merit inclusion in my seminal work. If, however, they had any undiscovered snippets lying about the office, I'd be more than willing to give them the once over.

To be honest, though, I had already seen through the old ham in my very own 'Lines for WB Yeats', a piece of juvenilia I had penned, along with a lesbian schoolgirl novella, before I found my voice.

You wrote a lot of pretty rhymes
They say you were a genius
But I prefer my poetry
A bit more Seamus Heaneyous.

Yeats, then, a minor literary figure now chiefly remembered for his wine lodges, binned.

And as for the monkey. It wasn't actually Irish, so doesn't qualify for the anthology on grounds of nationality. I note, however, that the operation took place in Vienna, and have submitted the Yeatsian poems of this period for possible inclusion in an anthology of Austrian verse. Who knows. Perhaps their standards are less rigorous.

LVIII

On I laboured. My great work of scholarship had just reached the modern era. The years following Yeats had been binned at a single sitting. But what about Kavanagh, I hear you cry. Permit me to reply as follows: I regard myself as a poet who dabbled, as a child, in farming. I have long since rejected this outmoded way of life. Kavanagh, however, tried it the other way round, and a farmer who dabbled in verse has no place here.

I was getting close to the end. Time, perhaps, to alert a few interested parties in the publishing world. Gideon, as previously mentioned, had given the Bible their best shot, but how often does the modern hotel guest toss a heavy suitcase aside and frantically riffle the relevant bedside drawer?

Faber, too, might just benefit from a reminder. Not to mention Faber. And it might even be worthwhile phoning my old agent friend. *Come back in 200 years, MacFiach?* Oh, I think we can knock a couple of centuries off *that*.

And so it was that off I went in search of a public phone. I trudged down the sixteen floors of steps to ground level. It was either that or the lift shaft. No wizened face peered out from the bottom flat as I passed – just an agonised yowling from within. The wizened face, I noted, was on its way to the phone box, located on the scrubland mere yards from the stairwell. An old Irish woman of indeterminate age – who may well have left to escape the worst ravages of the potato famine – she wailed something about her husband, a light-bulb and a makeshift step ladder as she hobbled closer to her goal.

I swerved gracefully to avoid my ancient compatriot. She was obviously intent on some interminable telephonic chat, but my need, at that particular juncture, was, I had no doubt, greater. I beat her, in a word, to it. And I was just about to close the door on *her* yowling – it crossed my mind that I might have stumbled across a family of Gaelic singers down on their luck – when I heard an all too familiar voice.

'Fiachra, me jewel and darlin' boy.'

I recognised the speaker immediately. Father, the cleric I had last seen at the funeral, bore blissfully down on the box. My efforts to slam the door in his face were met with a jovial fist on the handle.

'The thing is' – and he dropped his voice to a conspiratorial chuckle – 'I got wind of your presence shall we say. There's no secrets from the Lord. Anyways, I've brought you a small token from mother church.'

He thrust a bag at me; a bag laden down with his spiritual bribe.

'£432.78,' he said. 'And a button.' His voice rose again. 'A button from a poor old blind woman with one leg, a severe dose of rickets and an address in one of Limerick's less fashionable areas is more pleasing in the eyes of the Lord than a suitcase full of used fivers from a man with a dodgy bank account in the Caymans.'

He leaned over me for dramatic effect.

'Although to be brutally honest about it,' he chortled, 'I'd settle for the cash.'

I thrust the bag back at him.

'Here,' I cried, 'take this. And keep your infernal button.'

He cradled the bag and sighed with pleasure.

'A gift for mother church,' he beamed. 'You're a gentleman and a scholar.'

And with that he waddled happily off.

As for myself, the mental exhaustion of listening to clerical blather at such close range had sapped any remaining energy. I decided to hold off on the calls and, a gentleman to the last, held the door with extreme courtesy for the venerable ancient, desperate, at her last sighting, for the phone.

And where was she? Hobbling off into the distance no less – *in spite of the strangled cries emanating from her flat*. My italics to suggest a beggaring of belief.

But what did this betray? Lack of consideration on her part? Callous indifference? No. I put it down to Attention Span Deficit, a condition which has only recently come to light, but which has afflicted the female third of the population down through the ages. She had no doubt simply forgotten why she was there in the first place, and had merely sauntered off to indulge her passion for mortification/Bingo/drink. Delete as appropriate.

She had no sooner turned the corner on the continued howls of her husband than the phone rang. Not having an obliging Glaswegian to hand, I picked it up myself.

'Hello, son,' said my mother. 'I've just phoned to bring you the sad news of your brother's debt.'

LIX

Excellent. From news of my brother's parlous financial state – and I gently reassured my mother that all debts were cancelled where *he'd* gone – I was able to segue neatly to my own financial needs with a note of my current address. That dealt with to our mutual satisfaction, I left the phone box a happy man.

On the way back to my flat I rapped on the old couple's door, where the husband was still engaged in his interminable yowl. And while I'm all in favour of traditional singing as a means of alerting the emergency services, it patently hadn't worked. Perhaps, I suggested tersely, he should try the phone. I delivered that final salvo curtly through the letterbox and returned to my endeavour.

On I worked. On! On! Which brought me neatly to the present day. Or, to put it another way, Heaney. The same Heaney, however, proved a bit of a stumbling block, which placed me on the horns of an exquisite dilemma. As a matter of courtesy I wrote to him as follows:

> *My Dear Heaney! I am presently compiling an exhaustive but not, I trust, exhausting anthology of Irish verse.* Banter aside, I cut straight to the crux. *Sadly, you hail from that quarter of our tragic isle that is still technically British. You have six months to rectify the situation. MacFiach.*

I am bound to admit that I then resolved to do everything in my power to scupper any hopes of a united Ireland, in *his* lifetime at least. Heaney, as I couldn't bring myself to tell him, had already been excluded on merit.

As a footnote to the above, it might be pointed out that I, too, am of the Northern Irish persuasion. And I would have to concede that, yes, this is true *up to a point.* For my Art transcends boundaries, gender and creeds. Even time itself. *The Faber Book of 16th-Century Verse by Cloistered Women in Persia?*

I might, at a pinch, get in.

But I digress. It had been a long haul. My task was almost complete. I was exhausted but not yet – and I am leavening my prose with humour here – *exhaustive.*

I should have reached the final hurdle a happy man, but I

was reminded of the excitable Thesaura woman and her still present seed of doubt. What if she was right about Rosemary? I was still, in a word, riven.

One final push, then. And what a push.

I decided, in the first instance, to write to Rosemary's estate. Standard practice, of course, but imagine my surprise when I discovered that the letter was addressed to myself. The response, when it came, was trenchant to say the least. The executor replied to the furious effect that others might suffer from the unwarranted attention occasioned by 'the tragic waif's inclusion in this most prestigious of enterprises', including, he need hardly add, the selfless if Byronic figure who had nursed her through her final debilitating illness.

Fair point, but Art is cruel, and I felt I was being bullied into a possible miscarriage of poetic justice. Incorruptible to the last, I decided to ignore the somewhat hectoring note and concentrate solely on the eligibility, or otherwise, of the work. The result? Rosemary's failure to make the final cut, whilst regrettable – and no, I don't discuss individual cases – was hardly surprising given the rigorous editorial stance. No women. As a steadfast and unwavering feminist I fully support the recent phenomenon of female versification, and the breakthrough will assuredly come.

But not yet.

LX

I trembled on the brink of the completion of my task. One poet remaining. But would he make the cut? I chuckled wryly. No one else had. Why, then, he? I hadn't, I freely admit, read his verse for some time, and therein lay the crux of the matter.

Time, passage of. How had his work withstood the inter-vening weeks? But I must admit I felt somewhat sanguine. Genius, I reasoned, will out.

So confident did I feel, in fact, that I penned a quick missive to the Irish Writers' Museum, rejoicing in their decision to move to larger premises, and reassuring them that any initial outlay would be more than offset by the increase in future revenue.

I then hunkered on the floor in search of the relevant masterpiece. Well, I say masterpiece, but that had still to be decided. The work in question had yet to be subjected to the deeply rigorous editorial eye. I quailed before it and gulped internally.

All around me the mountainous out-tray of Irish literature. The dross and the detritus.

But . . . where was the in-tray?

I experienced a dryness of the mouth as if in anticipation of bad news. Crumpled paper everywhere. But where, in a word, was the penmanship of MacFiach?

I scrabbled about on the floor in search of what appeared to be a lost masterpiece. I even checked the pockets of my trousers and coat, ripping open the breast pocket in my increasing consternation. Nothing. The game was up. *Deep Probings*, that slim volume of exquisite poeticity, was nowhere to be seen.

I cried out to the Immortals.

'Succour!' I cried. 'Succour!'

But the Immortals heard me not.

'Why have you forsaken me?' I cried.

But still they heard me not.

Devastated, I sank to the floor, spent.

To sleep perchance . . . but wait!

In need of a pillow, I had just begun to unbutton my coat to rest my weary head. But just as I reached the final button, I heard a far-off tapping sound; as of a tiny fist upon a tiny door in a far and distant land.

And there it was again. Tap tap tap.

I staggered, exhausted, to my feet. The floor was a white sea of paper, and I knew exactly how Moses must have felt faced with all that water. No supernatural help for MacFiach, though, as I was forced to wade through ever higher levels of paper on my own particular journey towards the door.

I was treated, as I worked my way across the room, to an almost nostalgic trudge through Irish poetic development in reverse, and finally located the door behind the rejected later Yeats.

LXI

I approached the spyhole with caution. Looked out. Nothing. A momentary silence. Another tiny tap. Still nothing in the way of a person or persons, known or otherwise.

And then . . .

A tiny figure stepped back. Small and oval in her tiny black coat and clutching a tiny suitcase in her matching tiny fist.

Little Aoifra. So small. So . . . Fiachraesque. I felt a sudden twinge of . . .

As I struggled for the appropriate word she moved forward again. Disappeared. Tapped tinily again. And again stepped back.

Reappeared.

A twinge of . . .

No. The word I sought perched on the tip of my brain, but I simply couldn't forward it to the processing section. I would simply have to refer to a dictionary on the subject. Yes. That was it. A quick flick through the *Oxford English* was exactly what was required. And yet, for reason or reasons unknown, I was unable to drag myself away from the spyhole. And all the while little Aoifra simply stood there in her tiny black coat. Waiting.

And as she waited, something began to well up inside me. A sensation I had never before experienced. I had no idea what it was. A not displeasing form of pink nausea, perhaps, or, if you will, mental blancmange. I forced it back down but still it continued to well. I felt compelled to open the door and behave in a way that ill befitted an ascetic of the first rank. And yet . . .

My hand was drawn to the door handle. There it trembled, unable to detach itself. Unable, by the same seeming paralysis, to turn the handle. It finally steeled itself and was about to perform this simplest of tasks when, simultaneously, little Aoifra gripped her bag tinily and walked, with ever increasing tininess, away.

The moment had passed.

I turned, trembling, from the spyhole.

I trudged back from whence I had come, undid the final button, removed, folded, and laid my coat on the floor. And perhaps it was a trick of the light, or maybe it was just my state of extreme fatigue, but I felt a darkness leave me, almost as if it had been a living, breathing thing. As I lay me down to sleep, as if to reflect the subtle change within, the wallpaper began to glow a blushing pink. And as my eyes grew weary, words in a child's handwriting began to seep through the lustrous glow.

Me. Uv. Oo. Dada.

What could they possibly mean?

Then quietly at first, but growing in volume, a choir. Thousands of little girl voices in shrill unison – you could almost hear the gap in the teeth.

> *You're big and you're tough*
> *And your skin is so rough*
> *But me uv oo Dada . . .*

For copyright reasons I am unable to reproduce the verses in full. But that is not the point. The point is that I began, slowly but inexorably, perplexingly, almost – whisper it softly – *joyously*, to hum along. I began to find the luminous wallpaper not altogether displeasing. To find a not unartless merit in the lyric. Again the pink sensation welled up. And to my astonishment I sat on the floor and began to weep – yes, weep! – tears of redemptive joy.

At last I discovered that which had eluded me for so long. The redemptive power of . . . what was the word?

I had just reached L in the *Concise Oxford* (1932 edition) when the dictionary slipped from my grasp and I fell, instead, into a deep and purgative sleep. And dreamed a deep and purgative dream.

A dream of peace.

A dream of hope.

A dream of normality.

No aunts.

LXII

I awoke a changed man.

How long I had slept I knew not. Nor cared. Nor, I repeat joyously, cared. For I, MacFiach, was a soul newborn.

I prised my way through the crumpled mass of paper – time to clear up later prior to a quick hoover – and opened, as if for the first time, which in fact it was, the balcony door. Wishing to gaze upon the world with fresh eyes I blinked into the grey light of morning. Afternoon? Evening? Difficult to say. I would purchase a wristwatch with my first pay packet. For I, the same MacFiach, was about to look for the day job.

I would take my place in the unsung ranks. I would be a better person. Father. Provider.

I even found my body, almost involuntarily, taking that first tentative step on the road to conformity: the practice golf swing.

My reborn heart bursting with eagerness to begin my new life, I made my way back through the white sea of paper, located and opened the front door, and toppled straight over a bin bag. Having almost ruptured my spleen, I was about to vent the same organ on the d**n f**l who put it there. Just in time, however, I remembered my vow of normality and read, instead, the handwritten note on the bag.

'A second gift from Mother Church. I took the liberty of purchasing the enclosed with the aforementioned cash. The button I tossed in a skip.'

I opened the bag and removed the contents.

A suit of finest blue serge. One. As new.

Shirt. One.

Shaving foam. Razor. Ditto.

Directions to sink.

Shoes for walking thereto.

I wept with rapture at such munificence, such bounty, and resolved to be an even better person than the better person I'd already resolved to be.

Swiftly I divested myself of my garments. The estimable cleric had fallen down somewhat in the underpant department – a perfectly understandable nod to propriety – but soon I was a new man, both outwardly and in the deepest recesses of my psyche. The suit, though lacking several inches in the legs and arms and painfully tight on the crotch, was otherwise a perfect fit. As, with the insertion of the complete early Yeats, were the magnificent leather brogues.

I patted my hair down with spit, an old trick learned from my mother; strode, unimpeded, from the flat; and set off, with a childish song in my blissful, reborn heart, in search of honest toil.

Sliding gaily down the lift shaft, I toyed with the idea of contacting the estimable Heaney and proffering belated congratulations on his piscine award. A truly great day for fish. The old lady with the limp, however, had just opened her front door. From which smoke appeared to be, if not exactly billowing, at least wisping gently.

And whatever it was. The sky-blue sky. That golden orb, the sun. The pink cloud which enveloped my heart. Who knows? But I was in one of those after-you-madam moods which mark me out as, perhaps, a bit of an anomaly. A staunch feminist and a gentleman of the old school in one.

As she shuffled along the footpath chanting a wild Gaelic dirge about her husband, cardiac arrest, and something about a chip pan, I pointed at the public phone box with a selfless-ness bordering on the saintly.

'It's all yours,' I bellowed over the sound of her singing. 'I'll contact Heaney later.'

With that I turned the corner, strode off towards my future, and left her magnanimously to it.

And so the mood continued. The spring in the step, the merry whistle, the gay abandon as I tripped the light fantastic to the bustling heart of town.

Strutting along the High Street I passed the brightly lit charity shops, the bus stops, the public houses and turf accountants, the glorious throng of humanity in all its myriad myriadness.

I patted a callow youth affectionately on the head and escaped, the element of surprise being all, with my life. I peered into an open-top pram and consoled the distraught mother as she waited for the police. I helped an old lady cross the street and chuckled wryly at her loud protestations. Yes, she admitted, she had fully intended to cross the street, no quarrel there, but forty-three hardly constituted old. Under rigorous interrogation she admitted to fifty-four, but only on condition that I respect the imposition of a permanent exclusion zone.

On I strode, nay *gambolled,* my newfound humility a harbinger of joy, which spread out beyond its essential self to embrace the street, the city, the world and, for all I knew, the entire known universe.

I passed an interior decorators – Women on the Wall – sporting cousin Rosemary's scribblings as feminist décor, if you will. Poor dead Rosemary, I thought. So much to offer yet gone, alas, forever, her embryonic typing skills immutably untapped. I passed yet another MacFiach's. *Tonite* (sic) *A Tribute to Finn.* Dear departed Finn:

> *He had so much to give*
> *And yet he gave so little.*

It began to rain. Gently at first, but with promise of greater things to come. I tripped into a doorway. Praise be! A shrine to the Great God Literature. And there, in front of me, I saw a sign: *Shelf Stacker Wanted.*

I would work there in humble anonymity and atone for the sins of my past.

I went in. The bookshop in question was vast, nay, voluminous! A bibliophile's delight.

I approached a gawky adolescent reorganising the cookery section at the front of the shop.

'I wish to speak to the manager,' I intoned with all the humility I could muster.

'I *am* the manager,' he quipped.

Cheeky? Delusional? Difficult to tell. I toyed with the idea of thrashing him to within an inch of his life, but that was the Fiachra of old. *New* Fiachra counted slowly to 432 – his lucky number – and, equilibrium restored, pressed on.

'I'm here about the job,' I murmured, eyes downcast in supplicant mode.

He continued to rearrange.

'I was expecting someone younger,' he said in an unnaturally deep voice, as if trying to convince himself that his voice had broken. 'It's only a shelf stacker job.'

And he looked at me for the first time.

'Do you know anything about books?' he said.

I gave the matter my earnest consideration.

'I know nothing about books,' I replied, 'but I'm always willing to learn.'

'In that case,' he said, 'you can start straight away. Name?'

'MacFiach,' bellowed my inner voice. Impossible, however, to say MacFiach without intimations of grandeur. I cast my gaze lower still, seeming almost to seek out the soles of his shoes.

'The name,' I whispered, 'is Meek.'

LXIII

Odd how a name can change everything.

Confronted with my submissive demeanour the child manager rose in his own estimation. I was taken on for a five-year trial period, after which I would qualify for the minimum wage.

I returned home, eyes downcast, a changed man. Climbing the stairs I resolved to clean all 320 of them. And that wasn't all. On entering the flat and finding the floor was awash with paper, I resolved to pile it together, file it alphabetically, and lay it in neat stacks against the wall. I resolved also to purchase a hoover or similar at the earliest available opportunity. I further resolved to locate the kitchen. Possibly even write to my mother.

I became, in short, a truly good person.

Each morning I sallied forth to embrace the joy of stacking. I stacked Sport. I stacked Cookery. I stacked Poetry, Philosophy, Art. And as I stacked Religion – *Popes and Popery*; *Here's Poping* and, a black mark here against my shelf-stacking predecessor, *Pump It Up with Popeye* – I felt, for the first time in my life, truly humble.

Picture me, gentle reader, as I shuffled my way along the bottom shelf, knelt in prayerful submission. To surrender to the higher power of true humility was sweet release indeed, and I thought of my former life as that of a sinner and transgressor. As a good Christian, however, I forgave myself. I began to look on the world with eyes that were blind but now could see. And lo, I raised mine eyes from my labours and beheld, peering at me from the other side of the bookshelf, a face.

A round and roseate face. Beaming.

'Fiachra,' it said, 'no need to stand.'

I knelt deeper into myself.

'Bless me, Father,' I said meekly. 'It is twenty-seven years, six months and seventeen days since my last confession.'

I began with the tale of Little Father. So small. So vulnerable. So defunct. There but for the grace of God and a double helping of Kerr's Pinks . . .

I choked on the memory of our final meal together. The flowery potatoes. His trembling hands and big saucer eyes. The thwack of his little face as it hit the empty plate. The . . .

'Well never mind about that now,' admonished the gently solicitous cleric. He removed several copies of *Twice a Catholic* from the shelf between us and leaned in closer.

'You were seen going in to Widow Bernelle's,' he winked. 'Is there a story?'

LXIV

Some hours later I had admitted, in graphic detail, to sins of thought, word and deed running into treble figures. I had also, thanks to Sin Regression Therapy, asked for 432 other iniquities to be taken into consideration. All without leaving the libidinous widow's flat. The very reverend father then eased his generous frame from the floor with a satisfied sigh – for he had feasted on a veritable plateful of mortal sins – and left me to my penance.

I closed my eyes and surrendered to my own minute minisculity.

Yea, deep within me I knew, at last, the peace that passeth understanding. And all because of the gentle tapping of a tiny child on a miserable sinner's door.

I had opened my heart, and redemption had entered therein.

LXV

Although I looked for no earthly reward – for goodness is its own reward – I was about to be rewarded nonetheless.

All morning I had worked diligently on. MacFiach – or rather say *Meek* – The Happy Stacker. When lunchtime came, I went for a meditative stroll, fasting as was my habit, and casting out covetous thoughts.

Shelf Stacker of the Month. Covet it not.

Thy neighbour's ass. Covet that not either.

And covet not the coin in thy dead brother's eye.

Possibly metaphorical, that one, but all thoughts of coveting were banished as I arrived back from my break a regulation ten minutes later.

For lo! I beheld, on the door, a sign.

MACFIACH READING IN MEZZANINE – 2.30

It swam before my eyes. Recognition! At last! For *this* sign, surely, was A Sign. Of meekness rewarded. Of righteousness vindicated. I had been cleansed of sin, and here, in the most unexpected way possible, was my earthly reward.

But humility will out. I was being paid to stack shelves, and stack shelves I would until that celestial sphere, the sun, chimed two-thirty.

I returned, therefore, to my work. Children's section. Bottom shelf. Abject. Submissive. And yet. And yet.

Time passed slowly. The sun inched languorously across the heavens. A shadow fell across the *Pop-up Bible* in which I had been engrossed.

The child-manager towered above me on the balls of his feet.

'Well done, Meek,' he rasped squeakily. 'Good lad.'

I glanced at his wrist to check the time. 2.29. This truly smacked of Divine Intervention. As the manager descended from his extremities and moved off, I stacked the book on its appropriate shelf and began to make my way to the mezzanine.

A hubbub of excited voices guided me to my earthly reward. Before me a sea of people, hushed with expectation. And there, at the back of the crowd, Father. As I approached, meek yet righteous, he placed a giant paternal paw on my shoulder.

'This must be a very proud day, my child,' he said.

'Oh, it is, Father,' I gushed humbly, 'it is.'

As I tried to pull my jacket sleeves down below my elbows in readiness for my return, Father leaned towards me.

'A wonderful book,' he gushed. 'Such talent in one so young. Such a firm grasp of what it is to be human. It's . . . what's the bloomin' word . . . transcendent.'

I leave the word bloomin' intact. A borderline case on the school syllabus front, but it *was* uttered by a cleric. Interesting, though.

I was about to thank him for his kind words when I suddenly realised I didn't have a copy of my book. True, I'd obviously written the blessed thing but couldn't be expected to have it committed to memory. For goodness sake, I wasn't even aware of its mass publication. Faber, perhaps? Yes. Doubtless Faber had relented. I stopped tugging on my sleeve and tugged on the padre's instead.

'Father,' I hissed, as the crowd before me hushed in anticipation. 'A book. I must have a book.'

'Sure isn't the table over there full of them,' he whispered. 'Hush now. I think we're about to start.'

I sidled over to the table in question and extracted a copy from the pile. No time to look at it now – although I did note with approval that Faber had, indeed, finally come good – but not to worry. It would all come back to me once I was up there.

Imagine my amazement when I discovered that my erstwhile adversary Thesaura – ah, the wonders of Divine Intervention – had bagged the introductory honours. I felt strangely moved as I braced myself for my humble passage to the stage. Thesaura's honeyed and warm-hearted words about my transcendent childhood washed over me as I moved modestly forward. Curious. She too made great play of my youth. Of how I had overcome great hardship and personal loss by immersing myself in my creative gift. True, but I was pleasantly surprised by her apparent passion at my courage, fortitude and strength of personality in rising above such shocking neglect.

Excusing myself as I brushed past row upon row of the faithful, I finally reached the foothills of the podium. Before me, now, only the volubly gushing Thesaura. The *luminosity* of my writing. Its sheer, exquisite *limpidity*. She also mentioned something about a nine-figure advance, which was pleasant news to me. Her almost hyperbolic onslaught seeming unstoppable, I coughed modestly from the side of the stage.

'So please welcome' – I closed my eyes, gave thanks for the gift I was about to receive, and prepared to face the crowd – 'Aoifra MacFiach.'

What?!! Obviously a verbal typographical error. Whilst awaiting a correction I glanced at the cover of the book.

How to Survive a No Parent Family
by Aoifra MacFiach (aged 6½)
'Highly wrought,' Seamus Heaney

Trembling uncontrollably I opened the front cover.

For Dada
Me still uv oo

Father winked at me. A conspiratorial, two-fathers-together wink. But I, Fiachra MacFiach, was having none of it. My body expanded to incorporate my growing fury. I fully expected the suit to rip asunder, revealing, in the process, the Leviathan of my rage. The suit strained at the leash but stayed intact.

A small gift from Mother Church? I'd give them a small gift from Mother Church. I emitted a roar of righteous ire as I divested myself of every last vestige of charity.

Shoes. I yanked them off and flung them into the astonished crowd.

Jacket. I tugged it off and flung it after the shoes.

Shirt.

Vest.

Trousers.

I was about to finish the job when Father raised a podgy clerical hand.

'Hold it there, Fiachra,' he simpered. 'The underpants are yours.'

With Christ-like fervour I overturned a couple of tables on the way out, tipped a greasy till from its perch and stormed off. Out the door. Along the rain-spattered street. Back to the sanctuary of home.

Saved from redemption, MacFiach was mad as hell.

As I thundered furiously along, the sky grew dark. The clouds burst. I turned the final corner, my hirsute pelt glistening in the deluge. The air was filled with the sight and smell of smoke, not wisping now but in full, majestic flow. The crone, still bawling on about her woes in that self-centred way that is all too prevalent these days – and doubly reprehensible in the geriatric who ought to know better – had just reached the outskirts of the phone box.

As she heard my furious footsteps she seemed, suddenly, to lose heart and turned, with a weary sigh, from the box. No time to explain that I had no further use for the phone – I am nothing if not single-minded – I swerved towards the stairs and stormed upstairs to the flat.

As I reached the sixteenth landing a flash of lightning lit up the lowering sky. Thunder crashed as I burst into the flat. A gale blew the balcony door open and howled through the room like an old woman mourning the loss of her chip pan. Crumpled paper swirled through the balcony door like snowflakes swirling in a cyclone.

But wait! What was this!

The gale subsided. I stood in the empty room. Bare save for three sheets of paper which lay face down on the floor.

Three sheets?

I felt the Immortals' hot breath on my back.

Three thousand years of Irish poetic genius consigned by an act of nature to the dustbin of literary endeavour – and all that remained were three solitary sheets.

Whose could they possibly be?

I knelt down, breathed in, braced myself.

The tension was palpable.

I turned the first one over with trembling hand and gasped with delighted shock.

'Lines for Seamus Heaney'

The first poem from my very own collection, *Deep Probings*. But would it, I heard myself cry, get in? A magnificent bolt of lightning lit up the sky. The Immortals had spoken. That was good enough for me.

Kneeling still, but not now in supplication, I turned the second sheet over.

'Further Lines for Seamus Heaney'

Thunder cracked like a bullwhip. Oh, my good goodness! Two out of three from the crowning glory of my life's work.

I placed my outstretched fingers down for number three.

Wind whistled through the room with renewed intensity and yanked the balcony door off its hinges. The paper was scooped from the floor by the gust, described a double arc, and descended, gently swaying to and fro till it found my waiting palm.

And there rested 'Yet Further Lines for Seamus Heaney'. I began to tremble uncontrollably. Exhaustion? Exhausted I was, but no. Rather Ecstasy! Ecstasy and its hyperactive twin Rapture!

For I, MacFiach alone, had made the final cut.

I leapt to my feet and punched the air, relief commingled with delight. Yes and Yes and Yes Yes Yes! What is it about joy that makes us shout Yes!? I know not, but Yes! I cried as I kissed my anthology and Yes! as I penned a biographical note that ran to 187 pages and Yes! as I raced outside and slalomed down the lift shaft and Yes! as I banged on the grilles of sixteen floors of flats and the burnt-out shell of the old woman's former home as the sirens wailed and the blue lights flashed and water spurted from the unfurled hoses and Yes! as I raced back upstairs to the balcony and Yes! as I leapt on the barrier and watched the swirling rejects – Lo a Yeats! Yon a Joseph 'Mary'! – flurry and flail in the merciless wind and flutter to rank oblivion and Yes! as the front door splintered open and in behind me rushed – who? Faber? Faber? Faber Faber Faber? – too late it was, too late as the sun's magnificent rays burst from behind the storm clouds and bathed me – underpants Yes! hair Yes! outstretched arms – in the golden light of triumph because I! Yes! Am! The Chosen One!

Epilogue

I sit here in Dublin's Writers' Museum, home at last.

All is exactly as I stipulated on arrival. Chair. Desk. Bed. Paper. Pen.

The benefits of permanent exhibition are immense. Queues form to observe me at my work. Scholars. Poets. The Common Herd. A glass screen protects my oeuvre from the vultures. The scavengers. Those who would pilfer my waste basket.

But oh! the infuriating staff.

That infernal prying female with her 'And how is our resident genius today?' And her pillow plumping. And her eternal plastic glasses of syrup-sweet crème de menthe.

Plastic, if you please! I tossed the first one all over the white starch of her coat, but the curators rushed in and foolishly took her side. In a towering fit of rage I threatened to place my prodigious gift elsewhere. New York. Paris. Helsinki. But they eventually managed to cajole me into staying put. And they held me fast as they earnestly pled their case.

I stayed, and is my heart not glad. I have achieved what I set out to achieve: *Posterity Now.*

Picture me if you will, Dear Reader, in quintessential mode.

Dusk falls. Light from a single candle fades. The crowd files reluctantly out. A young girl in a black coat stands, frowning, for a long moment. A small, pale finger gently pressed to the glass. I meet, with a curious ache, her silent gaze.

But the blank page beckons. The quill throbs. My eyes return to my work.

A pause.

The sound of footsteps fades. Tip tap. Tip tap. Tip. Tap.

A door creaks closed. The candle flickers. All that remains is the scrape of nib on vellum.

The rest is . . .

---

1 *Heaney, S* – Fishmonger (deceased).

Acknowledgements

Ian would like to thank Donnie Macpherson for his generosity; Seán Bradley for his tireless work as midwife to Book One; Alison Rae for help and encouragement above and beyond the call of duty; Rob Wringham for his gleeful enthusiasm; Mark Ecob for the excellent cover; the Robert Louis Stevenson Fellowship for six idyllic weeks at Grez-sur-Loing; Magi Gibson for everything – including marriage during the final edit; his daughters Rosie and Maeve for being his daughters; Ireland and the people of Ireland for supplying the raw material of MacFiach's magnificent art; and Rory Bannerman-Coutts of *Gnarled Tree Press* for thinking he could make money out of it.